THE APOCALYPSE MEN

THE APOCALYPSE MEN

JOHN CHENEY

SHURLAND PRESS

ISBN: 978-0692518984
ISBN-10: 0692518983

THE APOCALYPSE MEN

Foreword

Since the initial release of *The Apocalypse Men*, several readers—more than I would like—have asked me, "Do you really think that is what is going to happen? Will the global state of affairs play out that way?" The answer is an unequivocal *no*. *The Apocalypse Men* is fiction. I did not write it to play prophet or prognosticator. For the fiction author, there are only two primary concerns: to tell a compelling story, and to make the telling of it plausible. *The Apocalypse Men* does, however, offer an exploration and commentary on the state of the world, using the one advantage fiction provides that nonfiction cannot afford: to ask *what if?* Sometimes in leaving strict fact, in playing out various scenarios, we can illuminate issues in ways we have not thought to discover. A large segment of literature, the *cautionary tale*, serves this purpose. To some extent, *The Apocalypse Men* is a cautionary tale. But perhaps I can better explain why I wrote the book by explaining its origins.

Several years ago I awoke from a distinctly unusual dream. The bulk of that dream comprises the first chapter of *The Apocalypse Men*. I also awoke in the same manner as Kyle Ferguson, with the high-pitched whine morphing from dream to the reality of a refrigerator motor. It is a surreal moment when you realize that a real external force has influenced your dreams, but even more astounding was the verbatim expression of a character in my dream—*we know the state of the world, we know its history, and most of all, what it will be!*

The dream was the genesis of story that interweaves

two movements—modern terrorism, and eschatology, or belief in the end of the world. Terrorism, one of the most persistent problems on our planet, has strengthened in the last twenty years. Anti-terrorism experts know they will be fighting it for entire careers. In addition to strengthening, terrorism has changed. The political terrorism of the 1970s has given way to the radical Islamic terrorism of the early 21st century.

Terrorism, by definition, causes greater psychological damage than physical damage. As brutal as the actions of Al Qaeda and ISIS have been, the fear they have caused is greater. But as these groups see the West as their enemy, the West also finds their barbarism cloaked in an esoteric ideology. Although Islam is practiced by more than 1.5 billion believers across the world, the religion is largely foreign to the West. These radical groups have warped the tenets of Islam for the purposes of power and killing. In *The Apocalypse Men*, the terrorists seize upon beliefs that more Westerners can readily identify—Christianity and the tenets of the Book of Revelation in particular—to bring their acts a more frightening psychological potency. Fictional or real, the terrorists' ideology is the same—pure tyranny clothed in the caustic mutation of a major religion.

This brings me to the second movement—belief in the end of the world. Ancient and modern cultures have believed in the end of the world, of cataclysms both natural and man-made that would usher in a new and different era. Both Christians and Muslims, comprising roughly half of the world population, believe in a messianic future. As prophesied in Revelation and other scripture, world events will result in a climactic battle where Jesus will return and usher in a new and better world. Though Christianity and

Islam have differing views on Jesus, both religions believe he will return and save his people at the last great battle. As such, many Christians and Muslims look with anticipation toward that day. But belief in the end of the world as we know it reaches beyond religion. This is evidenced by the large 'prepper' movement. 'Preppers' see world events and conditions as harbingers of a coming cataclysm.

In the Cold War, the threat of nuclear annihilation was real. For the first time in history, mankind possessed the means to craft its own doom. But the dissolution of the Soviet Union should have eased such tensions. Still, fears of worldwide catastrophe exist. Y2K, 9/11, and the end of the Mayan calendar in 2012 have all been seized upon as heralds to the end of the world. Fanatics such as ISIS, the Branch Davidians, and Aum Shinrikyo have all acted intentionally to bring about doomsday. Their extreme views and actions have been thoroughly denounced. But because the belief in the end of the world is so deep-seated, at what point does civilization go from preparing for catastrophe, to precipitating it? Since fear of annihilation seems so prevalent in our modern culture, is it in man's DNA to craft his own doom? And when faced with the prospect of mass destruction, what holds mankind together, and what tears it apart? These are questions that *The Apocalypse Men* explores. Answers are not readily apparent. The struggle between mankind's destructive and creative natures dominates not only the novel, but our civilization. Where there is fear, there is also hope; where there is despair, there is also resolve. Society and individuals alike must decide which side will win.

John Cheney
September 2016

1

State of the World

The world was melting. The van had no air conditioning, and with the windows up, it was a furnace like the scorched earth outside. Sitting in the front passenger seat, reporter Adrian Bennett wished she could lower the window just a crack, but driver and cameraman Mark Watkins insisted the pervasive dust would damage their mobile television unit. Watkins had another reason for wanting the windows up: it provided a thin barrier between them and the writhing mass of people crowded around the van. Gripping the steering wheel tightly, Watkins hoped Adrian wouldn't see his apprehension. He felt obligated to appear cool. Panic wouldn't do for a veteran cameraman with twenty years' experience in every international hotspot. Yet in all his professional travels, he had never felt so on edge as now, slowly moving through the crowd toward Kubu Stadium.

Adrian tried to find a bright side to this furnace as the van crawled at a snail's pace through the crowd. She closed her eyes and breathed in the suffocating heat, the stench of sweat, and the particles of dust that still crept into the van. Immediately she was brought back to her childhood. Her first visit to Africa had been a journey much like this one. Her family's Land Rover had no air conditioning, and her delicate mother had insisted they keep the windows up or else the whole family might develop asthma from the dust. Sweltering in the back seat, these first sensations of Africa were forever seared on her memory. Adrian smiled as she thought of her father, a life-long Canadian diplomat. He had sparked her interest in world travel and various cultures that led to her career as a foreign correspondent for British Cable News.

It was obvious why the 29 year-old had risen quickly from mundane assignments to more high-profile locales: Adrian had a combination of natural beauty, ruggedness, intelligence, and bravado that was highly telegenic. She seemed to flourish in the most unique way. Far more comely than her male counterparts, Adrian would often make channel flippers put down the remote, and yet she seemed to naturally fit into the most chaotic surroundings. BCN executives never needed to worry that she appear like an ex-beauty queen recklessly dropped into the middle of a war zone—Adrian was far too focused to ever appear frazzled or image-conscious. More than once, such as when reporting on flooding in China, the brunette had forgone makeup when the story began unfolding too quickly for her to prep for broadcast.

Adrian reminded herself to call her father when she reached her hotel that evening. She felt a constant pang when thinking of him—he had been diagnosed with lung cancer five months ago, and was faring poorly. Adrian's father had expressed concern for her on this assignment. He knew she was heading into what had been considered the most dangerous part of Africa for nearly seven years. The turmoil had begun in this central African country with civil war. That soon spilled over into the neighboring country, and a prolonged and bitter conflict resulted. Only four months ago peace had been declared, but tensions remained high. Now a key World Cup qualifier match between the two nations was seen as a potential step toward mending relations or renewing the conflict. Adrian had reported from many dangerous locales, and her father had experienced his share of chaos in his own diplomatic career; yet this assignment, more than any other of his daughter's, inexplicably made his hair stand on end.

The van finally arrived at the security perimeter outside the stadium. Watkins carefully steered toward the entrance for press vehicles. Despite the main spectator entrances being on the other side of the perimeter, pedestrians still flooded the street. Inside the perimeter, however, at least by the press entrance, it was nearly empty. Four soldiers armed with assault rifles stood watch at the gate. Watkins looked out along the fence and noticed armed soldiers posted every twenty yards or so, as far as he could see. *Am I entering a war zone or sporting event?*

Two soldiers manning the gate approached both sides of the van, gesturing for Watkins and Adrian to roll down their windows.

"Identification," the one on Watkins' side coldly ordered.

Watkins and Adrian handed the soldiers their press credentials. After examining the IDs and comparing them to their faces, the soldier at Watkins' door gestured toward the back of the van. "Open please." This time the edge was gone, replaced with a relaxed sort of formality.

Watkins turned to step out of the van, but Adrian beat him. "I'll get it," she said, her door already halfway open. The sliding door was on her side of the van, but she was just grateful to step out and stretch her legs. Even with the dust and hot wind, it was better outside than in the oven-like heat of the van.

The soldier took his time scanning over all of their equipment, even unzipping their camera bag to look inside. Since he didn't actually disturb anything, Adrian remained silent. But as the examination dragged on, she began to wonder why Watkins didn't protest. He had been adamant about keeping the windows up to avoid dust, yet the sliding door had been kept wide open for several minutes now. Finally the soldier stepped back and ushered them on with a simple wave of his hand. The two other guards opened the gate and let the van through. Watkins drove to the small parking lot at the north end of the stadium where several other television trucks and press vehicles were gathered in a staging area.

Adrian hopped out and glanced at her watch. "We're late." She didn't bother to hide her disappointment. "I'll go find a place to set up in the stadium. Go ahead and get the uplink."

Adrian grabbed their camera tripod and headed toward the nearest portal as Watkins began to extend the large antenna on top of their van that would give them a live satellite feed to BCN Studios in London. As he worked, Watkins' thoughts turned to his family, especially his nine year-old daughter, Emma. He wished he hadn't taken this assignment; he had missed too much of her life working in foreign lands. He had promised to stick with domestic work from now on, but then corporate had called and told him Adrian's regular cameraman, Sam Rogers, had been stricken with malaria. They needed him to step in. They knew it was a dangerous assignment. BCN didn't even bother to send in a producer, leaving Watkins and Bennett to handle the logistics of the shoot alone. But it had to be covered. *I'll skype Emma tonight*, he thought. He hurried to finish the uplink and prep the camera equipment.

Adrian stepped into the interior of the stadium and was greeted by a sight similar to an agitated bee swarm. The stands were writhing as fans danced, jumped up and down, sang, and waved banners. Amidst the colorful pageantry was a more sobering sight—armed soldiers standing throughout the stadium as sentinels, an ever-present reminder that this event was as much a powder keg as a sports match. Security had to be tight for the presence of the two presidents, Mutu and Nisra. Adrian scanned over the stadium for the best place to get camera angles.

Kubu Stadium was erected in the 1970s with two large Brutalist concrete grandstands. Within a decade, a curved concrete stand was added to the south end to create a horseshoe stadium. All of the stands were covered with a large concrete overhang to block out the harsh African sun. Like many older soccer stadiums across the world, the spectators were divided from each other with large barriers. A running track also kept fans farther away from the action. The stadium had a capacity of 24,000, but today over 30,000 fans and dignitaries were crammed into the facility.

Despite the palpable tension throughout the gathering, Adrian still took a moment to drink in the atmosphere. For some people, the best place to bask in pageantry is a parade. For Adrian, it was a sporting event. She liked the sight of the stadium, the roar of the crowd, the interplay of sun and shadow from the overhang on the grass field. She breathed it all in, then set her mind to task.

At the north end of the stadium stood an elevated concrete apron. Here a dais was set up for ceremonies preceding and following the game. Adrian's assignment was to cover the social and political significance of the event, not the match itself. She decided it would be best to set up just below the apron. They could easily shoot towards the dais, then swivel around to focus on the dignitaries section of the grandstand where the two presidents would watch the game.

Adrian had to show her press credentials to three different security guards before she finally arrived at the field level just below the apron. By the time she had set up the tripod, Watkins came in, sweating and breathless, the large camera bag slung over his shoulder.

"Let's get going," Adrian said, not giving Watkins a chance to catch his breath. Despite being winded, he had the camera out of the bag and mounted on the tripod within thirty seconds. Watkins was adjusting the white balance when an excited murmur rippled through the crowd.

"They're here." Adrian grabbed Watkins' shoulder and turned him around. He quickly swiveled the camera on the tripod and adjusted his aperture and focus on the grandstand. There, in the middle of the dignitary seating, presidents Mutu and Nisra approached from separate entrances with their respective security details. Much like their countries' differing policies, the men appeared as polar opposites. Mutu looked stout in a green military uniform with red and gold collar tabs, while Nisra appeared thin in a demure black suit. Watkins hurriedly focused in just as the men took their seats in the middle of the grandstand. There was still a distance of some ten meters between the two men—magnified significantly by the optics of the camera's lens.

Knowing he hadn't time to set up the microphones to record sound, Watkins clucked at the sight. "That will play well for reconciliation."

Adrian waited until Watkins had shot enough b-roll of the two presidents, then grabbed her microphone. "C'mon, let's get sound and transmission going."

Taskmaster, Watkins thought. He knew Bennett had a reputation for being a consummate professional, but he didn't know it included an impatient streak. *Well, it's probably because we were late getting here with the traffic,* Watkins thought, trying to give her the benefit of the doubt. It took him several minutes to get their wireless signal to connect with the receiver in their van. The security and other media around the stadium caused a lot of radio interference, but eventually Watkins was able to establish a live feed to London. Adrian prepped herself for camera and put in her earpiece. Within moments, a producer in London was cueing her that they'd be going on-air in two minutes.

Adrian acknowledged her producer just as a commotion broke out on the dignitary stand. She and Watkins turned to see half the security details for each president dogpiling on each other. At the epicenter of the melee was a guard in a plain black suit, waving a handgun above his head. The swarm of guards rapidly crushed him to the ground. Adrian and Watkins couldn't tell whose security team the man belonged to, but both sides were adamant about quashing the threat. Now Mutu and Nisra were standing, shouting at one another in accusation. The scene had turned into a bizarre circus, and judging from the unrest within the crowd, could easily escalate into a riot. Watkins kept rolling, focusing on the grandstand, but his unease had grown. Somewhere deep within his nerves a primal instinct was shouting at him to get out of here. Still, Watkins' professional training took control. Adrian also stayed calm, but she immediately determined from the noise and chaos that going live would be a bad idea. She told Watkins to keep rolling—this was definitely something worth capturing for television—then yelled to the studio they couldn't go live. The crowd had erupted in so much noise that she had to repeat herself several times, but eventually the message got through.

Within a minute, the security guard at the center of the fray was dragged off, and after several more seconds of loud shouts and gestures, the two presidents sat back down. It appeared tensions were calming, if only by degrees, and the game might indeed go on. A stadium announcer came through the loudspeakers with a message to calm the crowd. But just as the voice instructed the spectators to remain seated and enjoy the game, another voice broke in over the stadium's PA system. It was a strange, edgy voice, and the crowd, including Watkins and Bennett, immediately sought its source.

"We know the state of the world," the voice said.

Adrian turned and faced the concrete apron at the north of the stadium. There, at the microphone at the center of the dais was a man in a tan trench coat. She immediately recognized he was not from sub-Saharan Africa. Watkins turned the camera toward the man. As they watched him, Watkins felt his inner terror had found a focal point. Clenching his jaw tightly, he could only utter a strained, scared grunt. For the first time, Adrian was also gripped with a sudden fear.

"We know its history," the man continued.

"No...no..." was all she could muster as instinctive dread seized her.

The man's voice escalated to a frenzied euphoria as he stretched out his hands. "And most of all—what it will be!"

Adrian didn't have time to recognize the gigantic explosion. The last sensation her brain registered was a high-pitched whine, just before she and the entire stadium were enveloped in a blinding flash of white.

2

The Messenger

Kyle Ferguson awoke with a start. A strange high-pitch whine permeated his brain, the remnant of something he had experienced in a horrific dream. Only when he began to slowly push away the cobwebs of sleep did he realize that this sound had an external, real-world source: the motor on the mini fridge in his hotel room was whirring away, the ball bearings in its compressor probably loose. Kyle couldn't remember the dream he just had, but he was still filled with the panic it had caused. It took a moment to calm his racing heartbeat before he could reorient himself to his surroundings.

Once his body was under control, Kyle threw back the bed covers and stepped out onto the rug. The feel of the springy plush carpet under his feet was the first tangible sensation that brought him back to life. Kyle padded over to the window and pulled the long drapes aside, filling the room with bright afternoon sun. Looking across the lush greenery of Berlin's Tiergarten park, Kyle could see the sun glint off of the golden wings of the *Siegessäule* statue. Circling its base was a steady flow of traffic. Cars scurried like ants along main arteries that branched outward through the park into the city. The bright whitish haze above the greenery was too much for Kyle's eyes, and he quickly let the red drapes fall back into place, throwing the room into a maroon semi-darkness.

Kyle groggily made his way to the wet bar next to the mini fridge. For a moment, he considered kicking the whining steel box, but thought better of it. He knew it wouldn't stop the high-pitched noise, but it would bruise his bare foot. He didn't reach for any of the miniature alcoholic beverage bottles either; he needed to wake up, not dull his senses again. Kyle ran the tap on the small sink, cupped his hands under the faucet, and splashed water on his face. The water was lukewarm, and didn't give him the wake up he expected, but it would have to do.

Turning to a nearby mirror, Kyle examined the low-hanging bags under his eyes. He wasn't exactly sure what time it was, but guessing by the strong afternoon light he had seen out the window, he knew it had only been a few hours since he had fallen asleep. It wasn't enough. Six hours' time shift and a sleepless overnight flight had caused too great a sleep debt to recover in just a few hours' sleep. His whole body could have told him that, but the bags under his eyes were enough. Kyle had never been able to sleep on an airplane; perhaps it was his lanky frame that never quite fit into those inadequately reclining seats, or maybe it was just the anticipation of his destination. He only knew sleep evaded him when flying.

Kyle now took in the full reflection of his appearance. His disheveled reddish-brown mane and scraggly day-long beard growth were enough for him to consider cleaning up, but the general malaise in his limbs countered with an argument for settling back in bed. He never had a chance to decide. The phone rang with a sharpness that pierced the relative lull of the room. Offended by this aural intruder, Kyle made his way over to the bedside table and picked up the phone.

"Yeah," he said, noticing for the first time that his vocal chords had tightened with sleep and his mouth felt cottony.

The voice on the other end of the line came clear and vibrant. "Were you asleep?"

"It's called jet lag," Kyle replied. "Besides, I don't have to present at the conference until this evening." A smile crept into the corner of Kyle's mouth. Colonel Nate Knox would never let him get away with any excuse. But instead of hearing an expected comeback, Knox's tone was abrupt.

"Forget the conference, Ferguson. Get to the embassy now."

Alarmed by the urgency, Kyle felt a sudden surge of adrenaline. "What's wrong?"

"Get down here. Terrorism just went nuclear."

Kyle was dressed in three minutes. He didn't bother to shave and only gave his hair a cursory combing to remove the bedhead, but while he frantically pulled on a suit and tie, he switched on the television and searched for a news channel. Finding only a German-speaking station with a reporter against a non-descript backdrop, Kyle threw down the remote in frustration. "Don't they have CNN International?"

He tied his shoes and remembered to grab his ID before heading out the door. Just as the door slammed behind him in the hallway, Ferguson recalled he'd forgotten to grab his room key. No matter; the front desk could let him in. He hurried down the corridor, thinking to himself. *Calm down. Get control. No one's going to listen to you if you don't sound calm and collected.* But Kyle's hands were still shaking moments later as he gripped the bar at the back of the elevator. *You always knew this was going to happen. It was inevitable.* Then, delayed by initial shock at the news, an incredulous thought hit him: *the first act of nuclear terrorism hits while I'm at an international counter-terrorism conference. What are the chances of that?* As Kyle watched the floor numbers tick down too slowly on the display, another thought dawned. *At least it didn't happen here.* It wasn't selfishness that guided Kyle's thoughts so much as the fear that taking out many of the world's top minds on counter-terrorism would be catastrophic.

As an analyst for the CIA, Kyle had learned if the problem of terrorism was to ever be solved, it would have to be through close international cooperation. That job was already getting harder. The massive U.S. intelligence apparatus was alienating allies. In 2013, the German government became livid when they learned Chancellor Angela Merkel's cell phone had been tapped by the NSA. This was a devastating blow to U.S.-German relations. Merkel revitalized ties that had been strained under her predecessor Gerhard Schröder, a vigorous opponent of the Iraq War. It was alarming that Merkel, who had grown up in the invasive police and surveillance state of East Germany, would be targeted for U.S. surveillance. Further disclosures of widespread U.S. spying in Germany led to the expulsion of the CIA's Berlin station chief in 2014. Trust was eroding. Kyle and other U.S. officials had hoped to rebuild it at the conference.

The U.S. Embassy stood only yards from the historic Brandenburg Gate and one door down from the hotel. Still, the additional three minutes Kyle took to reach the embassy's security checkpoint seemed like the longest of his life. By the time he had cleared security, there was a flurry of activity. Most of the staff were turning to television sets. Kyle didn't stop to listen. He knew he would get answers soon enough.

The CIA offices in the embassy were a fortress. The U.S. learned through major Cold War fiascoes that securing sensitive information had to be top priority in every embassy. This facility was finished in 2008 and built for the Age of Terrorism. In a central hub was an Operations Center with an array of computers and video equipment. The room had a secured video link with Langley and had other encrypted communications abilities. Colonel Knox greeted Kyle at the door. Knox was by all appearances unreal—the most handsome and capable man in any room. He had been an all-Big Ten quarterback, married his college sweetheart, and rose quickly in Naval Intelligence. He served nine years with SEALs, transitioning within the last year to become a liaison between the Defense Intelligence Agency and CIA.

Knox turned to introduce three other people in the room. "Kyle, this is Wesley Connors, station chief here in Berlin." Kyle shook hands with the thin, balding man in his forties. Connors had a phone to his ear, apparently waiting on hold. Knox gestured to a thirty-something woman who was working the nearest computer. "Olivia Parks, on loan from NSA." Knox finally turned to a weakly-built man with a vitamin D deficiency. "T.J. Bentley, NSA." Kyle could see from first glance that Bentley oozed ego. There were two others in the room manning computers, but Colonel Knox didn't bother to introduce them. Kyle figured Knox didn't want to interrupt them. He already knew one of them, but followed Knox's lead and didn't bother him at his work.

Kyle turned with the others to the screens covering one wall of the room. In the center screen, a television broadcast showed a huge pillar of smoke rising from an epicenter that must have been a quarter of a mile wide. The shot was taken by a telephoto lens, probably a few miles away. Kyle could see bits of flame dancing here and there in the huge column of smoke and touches of an arid landscape, but little else to define the location. "Where did it happen?"

"Africa."

"Against our interests?"

Knox shook his head. "A soccer match."

"Soccer match?" Kyle was caught off guard.

"Yeah. World Cup qualifier. Presidents Mutu and Nisra were there."

"That makes no sense. Anyone who would want to take either of them out wouldn't be able to afford a nuclear weapon."

"Not to mention the overkill," Parks jumped in. "All you would need is a truck with ammonium nitrate fertilizer parked outside the stadium, or if you're really lucky, just get close enough to either of them with a suicide bomb. That would cost just a few thousand dollars, not hundreds of millions."

"It doesn't make sense," Connors agreed, hanging up the phone. "Langley doesn't have anything for us yet."

"Maybe the objective was to cut off the heads of both governments at once," Parks said. "Cause anarchy."

"Clearly that will be the result," Bentley stated, "but the objective?"

"Doesn't fit the modus operandi of any known terrorist group," Connors answered.

Knox broke in. "The larger question remains—how did they get an atomic bomb?"

Bentley leaned forward, watching the news coverage. "Well, at least they used it in Africa. We might have dodged a bullet."

Nobody dignified Bentley's statement with a response, but Kyle wondered if they were thinking the same thing as he: *what a jerk.* He turned his attention to the center screen.

"What's this we're watching?"

"CNN," Knox said. "Police set up a ten-mile security radius around the stadium and are trying to keep the media upwind."

They now watched a screen to the left that showed a cellphone video. It was taken moments after the blast from within the city, looking toward the outskirts where the stadium lay. A massive mushroom cloud now rose from the location. Although Kyle had long braced himself against this day, it was startling to see the column of fire rise up from a city. He was familiar with the old footage of test detonations in Nevada and the Pacific. He had even seen the black and white film of one of the a-bombs dropped over Japan. That one, taken by one of the bomber crew, showed the mushroom cloud rising in a grainy black and white image that largely obscured the city. Here he could clearly see the detonation had devastated a civilized area where people had been, and it was chilling.

"As far as response units…" Knox continued, "…well, they don't have anybody to answer this kind of situation. We've got very little information."

"What about broadcasts from the stadium? Anything show the moment of detonation?"

"We've been scouring the broadcasts, but nothing yet,"

Connors said. "Most were focused on the field or the stands. There was a fight that broke out between both presidents' security forces just prior to the explosion."

Kyle raised his eyebrows.

Parks shook her head and played the incident back for them on the center screen. "Doesn't look like the kind of urgency a bomb will create," she said.

"Chaos, yes; fear, no," Bentley assessed in a cold, dispassionate tone. Kyle almost drew the conclusion that the situation bored him.

One of the men at the other computers turned to the group. He was a man of Middle Eastern descent in his late twenties, and wore a pinstriped shirt. The man's name was Yousif Kaddouri, although Kyle and everyone else at CIA knew him as Sadiq. Sadiq's family had emigrated from Jordan before he was born, and though he was born in America, he was fluent in Arabic, Farsi, and Urdu.

"How about this?" He punched a few keystrokes and another news feed filled the center screen. The view was of the end of the same melee they had seen, although from a different angle. The camera then panned away to a young woman, a reporter that Kyle had never seen before. It was Adrian Bennett. "Friend of mine in MI6 just sent this over." The group watched the video and immediately noticed some rough edges. The camera was continually adjusting the frame and focus, and the voice of a news producer communicating from the studio could be heard on the soundtrack.

"Was this broadcast?" Connors asked.

Sadiq shook his head. "Live feed from BCN, but it didn't air. Watch this."

The camera racked focus from Adrian to the elevated

podium behind her. Adrian turned as well, and both she and the camera focused on the figure on the dais. Something deep within Kyle's subconscious told him he had seen this image before, but he couldn't see how that was possible. The news producer's voice could be heard in transmission: "Adrian, what's going on?" The man in the trench coat appeared Middle Eastern. He had a powerful, almost prophetic presence on the platform. This time, though the man seemed to speak for the same duration, it was in a strange, foreign tongue.

Adrian's voice, seized with fear, sounded. "No...no..."

"Adrian, if there's a problem," the news producer said, concern growing, "You should..." But he got no further.

The man in the trench coat reached his hands out and shouted. Kyle thought the man strangely appeared like Moses, beckoning the waves of the Red Sea to part. A bright flash of white blew out the image, accompanied by a sharp electronic hiss. It only took a fraction of a second—barely a frame of video—but with that, the transmission went dead.

A pall fell over the room. After a moment, Connors quietly asked the technician to play the video again. Everyone watched in silence, scouring the images. When it was finished, Parks was the first to speak. "What did he say?" The words sounded Semitic to her, but beyond that, she could not recognize the language.

"We know the state of the world, we know its history...and most of all, what it will be," Kyle said, nearly in a whisper.

"You know Aramaic," Sadiq said, impressed. Aramaic is a dead language. It was spoken in Jerusalem in the time of Jesus, but is only well-known by scholars today. Sadiq had learned the language in college.

"No," Kyle shook his head, his answer haunting him. It was truly bewildering to know the words but not the language. Seeing the video for the second time, they came to him as if from a half-remembered dream. "This is a message," Kyle said.

"But for whom?" Parks wondered.

Knox had Sadiq rewind to a point where they could best see the man clearly, then had him freeze on the image. "Get facial recognition on him," Knox ordered.

"Already running."

On another computer, Parks was scouring the news for any other information. "There's been a dozen claims of responsibility in the past twenty minutes."

"Plenty of terrorists want the world to believe they have nukes," Connors said. "But what they gain in status disappears when they don't check out."

"Who's gonna believe any of them when a dozen organizations claim responsibility all at once?" Bentley snorted.

"Here." Sadiq brought another video onto the center screen. "I just got this from a contact at Voice of the World. Says they got this on a thumb drive about forty minutes before the bombing." Voice of the World was an Arabic news network. The screen showed a stark image—a silhouetted figure against a blood-red backdrop. Light appeared to come from somewhere behind and below the subject. The silhouette had few features; the head appeared clothed in a hood or wrap so that no hair was visible, and the shoulders appeared masculine but unremarkable. The figure began to speak, his voice slightly raspy.

"By now you will all be wondering at what has happened in Africa," the man said in accented English. "Indeed, the hour is coming—I almost conceal it. But those who know the beginning shall also know the end. In Africa were the earliest beginnings of man; listen to this herald now. He that hath ears let him hear, for the time is at hand." The man continued briefly in a foreign language, then the video ended.

Kyle looked to Knox and the others, who all seemed baffled by the statement.

"What was the last part?" Kyle asked.

Sadiq frowned at him. "You don't know? That's also Aramaic. 'Come and see, for they who go forth are the Horsemen.'"

"Sounds familiar," Parks said.

"Sounds like maniacal prophecy," Connors retorted.

"It's a quote from the Book of Revelation," Sadiq explained. The group looked blankly at him. "Didn't any of you go to Sunday School?"

"Wasn't taught in Aramaic," Kyle said under his breath, wondering how he could understand one statement in the language and not another.

Sadiq shrugged and rewound the video back to the beginning.

"Well, they certainly have a flair for the dramatic," Connors concluded. "That's no Al Qaeda video. If Voice of the World hadn't gotten it beforehand, I'd have dismissed it as fake."

"Who are the 'Horsemen'?" Parks put the question out there, but everyone was perplexed. "I mean, other than the Sunday School version."

"Never heard of such an organization," Kyle said. "But if the video is legitimate, and they're responsible for the attack—it could be a pseudonym. Or they could be an entirely new organization."

Sadiq looked up from a text message on his phone. "The contact confirmed the video was delivered in a plain manila envelope by courier. They screened it for security, found it safe, but nothing really identified the source. The metadata's useless."

"See if you can enhance the image," Bentley said, pointing to the silhouette.

Sadiq typed a few keystrokes and tried to lighten the image. He fiddled with several adjustments, then leaned back. "Nothing."

The man's still-blank face revealed no features.

Bentley soured. "Nothing?"

"He could be wearing a sheer black mask. There's no further detail in the pixels."

"If this is evidence, we need more time," Knox said. "How long can we keep it off the air and the net?"

"With Voice of the World, not long," Connors frowned. "They're not going to hold it for us."

The secure phone on the back wall started blinking. Connors picked it up and spoke briefly. Kyle was transfixed by the image on the screen, trying to study the black abyss where the man's face should have been.

"We've got orders," Connors broke in. "Ferguson, Parks, and Kaddouri—they want you back in Washington ASAP."

"Cancel the speech?" Kyle asked. He was looking more for direction on handling the conference staff than challenging his orders.

Connors gave a curt nod. "Yup. Knox and I will liaise with other agencies here at the conference to see if we can dig up any other leads." Kyle noted Connors didn't say anything to Bentley. That figured. He was NSA, and even if Connors had orders for him, he'd just as likely go his own way.

"Looks like I'm off again," Kyle said to Knox.

"Don't sleep on the job—that's what the plane ride's for."

"Easy for you to say. I'll be sitting on my thumbs for the next seven hours while you're working this mess." Kyle wanted to say it was good to see Knox again, but given the circumstances, thought better of it. He took one last look at the silhouetted image on the screen and left.

CIA Director Leslie Farrell watched the news from her office in Langley, Virginia. The bombing had taken her, like the rest of the intelligence community, by surprise—and that was unacceptable. The first woman to head CIA, Farrell was tenacious when she needed to be and tactful when called for. She'd only cut people off at the knees when they deserved it, but she expected professionalism, and she expected results. Her agency should have seen something this big coming.

The Director of CIA's National Clandestine Service is the head of CIA's covert operations, and works under the aegis of the Director of the Central Intelligence Agency. Director of NCS Neil Ruston hurried into Farrell's office. "It's worse than we thought. *ORACLE* was at the scene—and hasn't checked back in."

ORACLE was the codename for one of CIA's top agents.

"What was *ORACLE* doing there?"

"Meeting a contact," Ruston explained. "Last report

was that the contact was going to reveal information on something big."

Farrell shook her head. She didn't believe in coincidences. That left only two possibilities. First, the contact had lured *ORACLE* into a trap, resulting in the agent's death. Farrell knew *ORACLE* couldn't have been the main target of the attack—a nuclear bomb was by far overkill for one agent—but what if the agent had been lured there to stop *ORACLE* from finding out something worse? The second possibility was truly unthinkable—that *ORACLE* had turned on them, and used the bombing as a smokescreen to get away. *ORACLE* had been hand-picked by Ruston, and both he and Farrell doubted the agent would ever go rogue. But if it had happened, was *ORACLE* now working against them? The thought was almost as frightening as the knowledge that CIA did not know who had set off the bomb, or if the perpetrators had more.

3

Death Rides a Pale Horse

The black Mercedes-Maybach seemed out of place on the barren road. The exterior of the car was covered in a patina of dust—an inadequate camouflage for an elegant sedan. Nothing so expensive ever ventured into the countryside an hour outside of Peshawar. Those inside the Mercedes had little to fear; the car was nearly as armored as the U.S. presidential limousine.

More improbable than the Mercedes-Maybach's presence was the identity of the passenger sitting comfortably in the back seat. He was one of the wealthiest men in the world. Barely noticing the bumps in the road, he sat with his eyes closed and listened to the soothing 2nd Movement of Beethoven's Piano Concerto No. 5. In the cooled, comfortable leather interior of the sedan, the man might have easily imagined himself on his yacht.

The Mercedes slowly decelerated to a stop. Only then did the passenger in the back seat notice the police roadblock ahead.

"Sir," the driver said with some concern.

The sexagenarian passenger picked up his satellite phone and dialed a number. His fingers moved rapidly over the buttons, unhurried but knowing the number exactly by memory. He raised the phone to his ear. "I'm going to be late."

A constable approached the Mercedes and tapped the driver's window. Resigned, the driver lowered the glass.

"You're lost," the constable said, smiling wide. He looked toward the back seat. "No one with any *respectable* business comes out here."

It was a shakedown. Brandishing weapons, the policemen ordered the driver and passenger out of the Mercedes and into the back of a police van. Within minutes, they were dragged into a police station that was little more than a filthy shack. The constable rubbed his mustache as he smiled at his captives. "What are you doing here?" Silence didn't deter him. "I have nothing but time."

The driver and passenger sat in handcuffs at a small table, the constable across from them. The room was stifling. The single light bulb at the top of the windowless room only served to add to the heat. The single rotating fan was angled away from the prisoners. Still, the wealthy man retained an extraordinary measure of dignity. Despite the beads of sweat on his face, he only unbuttoned the collar of his pressed shirt. It remained an immaculate white, even in this grimy room. He placed his suit coat across his lap. The driver had less nerve, but he tried to follow his boss's lead and remained silent. Still, he was sweating profusely, and his throat was parched with a terrible thirst. He didn't know how long he could hold out.

"I don't know who you are," the constable continued, "but I know you don't belong here. You will only cause trouble, and we don't like troublemakers." The constable lit a cigarette and breathed the smoke into his prisoners' faces. The driver couldn't help but let out a small cough. His boss remained still. He knew his suit cost more than the salary of any of these cops, and sooner or later, the issue would turn to money.

"None of your friends know you're here," the constable pressed, "so if you want to make things easier for yourselves, you'd better start talking."

The driver shifted his eyes toward his boss, but catching the gaze of one of the armed policeman toward the back of the room, the driver looked back down.

"No? Well, just wait until the inspector gets here." The constable stood and walked over to a small table by the front wall. He pulled open a drawer and drew out an object covered in canvas. The constable unwrapped it, revealing a machete. Dramatically slamming the blade into the surface of the table, the constable let it reverberate for effect. "You'll wish that you had spoken to me then."

The constable headed out the door, taking one of the policemen with him. Another policeman, armed with an MP5, remained to guard the prisoners. The two men could hear the constables talking just outside the doorway. It was clear they were haggling over how much they would demand for ransom. Only when they had agreed on a substantially large price would they allow the prisoners to make a call and transfer the funds. *Bail, bribe, blackmail,* the driver thought ruefully—in the rougher corners of the world, they were synonyms.

The debate was interrupted by the sound of an approaching vehicle. The car drew closer until the crunch of gravel under its tires was heard just outside the front entrance. The car door slammed and the driver heard an excited exchange between the constables. The inspector had arrived. A hulk of a man soon filled the doorway.

Though afraid, the driver's first impression was strangely comic—*if Pakistan ever took up Sumo wrestling, he'd be a champion.* Then the driver looked at the inspector's massive fists. His knuckles were scarred from countless blows of inflicted brutality. Behind the brute, the constable grinned in anticipation. The driver reared back. His boss locked eyes with the inspector—and then something strange happened. Without a word, the inspector came over and removed the billionaire's handcuffs. The constables stood open-mouthed in shock. The driver was so surprised when the inspector removed his manacles that the policeman had to pull him up. The two freed men proceeded to the doorway, the driver following his boss and still trying to fathom what had just happened.

The billionaire paused next to the inspector. A question appeared on the policeman's face, but he said nothing. The billionaire gave a small, almost imperceptible nod. In one swift action, the inspector drew his Beretta from its holster and fired at the chief constable's hand. Hit with a sudden, excruciating pain, the constable screamed as he raised the pulverized stumps of two fingers. Before the other two constables knew how to react, the inspector turned and fired, killing both of them. The inspector then grasped the wounded constable by the scalp and seized the machete. In a second, the constable's wild screams were silenced with a killing blow.

The inspector turned to the billionaire. "I'm sorry."

The billionaire looked coldly at the slaughter surrounding him, then back at the inspector. "No one is to know I'm here."

The inspector nodded, a gesture the driver noticed was nearly a bow. "Yes, Mister Mashiri."

Mashiri turned to his driver. "Abdul."

Shaking from what he had just witnessed, the driver stumbled out of the station toward the Mercedes-Maybach, now parked on the side of the building. Mashiri strode coolly towards the car, not bothering to wait for Abdul to open the door for him. Abdul climbed into the driver's seat and took off. His hands were still trembling as he gripped the steering wheel and looked back in the rear-view mirror. His mind would not be able to shake the surreal scene long after the station had left their view.

A noise behind Abdul startled him. It was the soft strains of Beethoven's Piano Concerto No. 5. Mashiri had turned it back on, and was now laid back, absorbed in its soothing tones. Abdul felt goosebumps on his arms and the back of his neck. He had driven twenty-two years for Mashiri and never witnessed anything like this. Never in all those years of service had he desperately wanted to be somewhere else. Two chilling thoughts seized him simultaneously—one, that his own life was as extinguishable as any of the policemen, and two—his long-time employer, one of the world's most powerful and secretive men, was now unmasked to him. *Sheitan.*

The house stood just below the cusp of a ravine, hidden from view of anyone who did not take the small winding path to it. The area was already considerably remote. Aaban Assad Zahir Al-Mashiri had instructed Abdul to exit the dirt road a hundred yards before reaching the ravine, and they parked the Mercedes within a thick grove of trees fifty yards away. Dusk was falling, and as the two men approached the rustic house, they saw the gleam of a yellow light fall onto the path just outside the door. Abdul hesitated, fearing another confrontation, but Mashiri put a reassuring hand on his shoulder. Again, the silver-haired sexagenarian led the way.

Mashiri entered the house, his dark eyes shining in the light of the lantern in the center of the room. A young man, about thirty, rose from the table. His straight back displayed a military bearing. He stood stone-faced in greeting. Mashiri smiled warmly and gestured for him to sit. Mashiri sat across from him.

"Despite having arranged this meeting, I'm surprised you're here," Mashiri began.

"That makes two of us."

The flame in the lantern began to flicker, causing shadows to dance across their faces. "It must not have been easy to get here, but I had to see how far you would go. I don't make half-hearted commitments."

"Nor I."

"Tell me, why are you doing this?"

"I'm sure your people told you," the young man said.

"Yes, they did. But I want to hear it from you. It's not for money?"

The soldier shook his head. "The money's fine, although I don't think I'll live long enough to use it."

A realist, Mashiri thought. He was beginning to like the young man.

"This is personal," the soldier said, leaving it at that. He was not a man of many words, but Mashiri saw the rage that seethed beneath his surface.

Let's put all the cards on the table, Mashiri thought. "There are not many native sons of your country who will betray it. They might not have invented patriotism, but they've taken it to new...'heights'. I also heard you were once a man of peace."

"What does it matter what I was? I am here now."

"Don't you believe in beating swords into plowshares?" Mashiri examined the young man's face. "No, of course you don't."

"Earth has but one use—for burying. I have done my share. Now they will do theirs."

Mashiri smiled. "I see...you are still a man of principle. Your principles are just not those of your countrymen."

"When I say I will do this, I *will*. Can you do it?"

"What we'll give your people will frighten them enough. They'll act on it."

The young man smirked, not sure he believed him. He knew Mashiri was one of the wealthiest men in the world, with nearly unlimited resources, but he found it hard to believe he could feed his nation's intelligence sources enough bait to provoke a mission.

"Only question is," Mashiri said, "how long will it take?"

"The '81 mission took months of training. This recent threat we've anticipated for some time. To do it right—maybe a month, month and a half. But if you frighten them too much, they could send us in tomorrow. That would be bad. We couldn't guarantee success."

"We can attenuate the data for that window," Mashiri said.

Still, the young man wondered—just how far could this really go? Doubt flickered in the back of his mind like a trapped moth. But he was here now. He had come too far to back out. He was committed, and one way or another, he was going to fulfill his mission. He had already bet on Mashiri giving him the means of achieving it. He still believed Mashiri could take him all the way. There was one question he had to ask, just to make sure.

"How do you know I'll be tapped for the mission?"

"That doesn't matter, really," Mashiri said. "Just as long as it's done."

Busting my chops, the young man thought with a smile. He knew he would be assigned—he was the best pilot and squadron commander for this mission. The look Mashiri gave in return showed he knew it too.

Mashiri stood, his long shadow falling across the room like a dark cloak. "You'll have word within three days. Plan for the operation in six weeks."

"Done."

The men shook hands.

"You should know," Mashiri said, "My colleagues and I never fail. Neither can you."

The young man's eyes narrowed. "You chose me because I can't fail."

He extinguished the lantern, and the two men slipped out into the night.

4

Leg Work

Kyle tried to lean his seat back as far as it would go. It wasn't enough. This was his second transatlantic flight in 24 hours, and he didn't know how much his body would take. Sleep, as always, was out. Unfortunately so was leg room. The agency never paid for him to fly anything other than coach—"they pay you for your mind, not your body," an agent who handled travel arrangements once joked. Kyle turned to the window and watched the vast dark blue of the North Atlantic far below. From this distance, he could barely make out several white caps that speckled the glazed surface of the ocean. A few wisps of clouds, the water, and the reflection of the afternoon sun made quite a view.

Kyle's thoughts inevitably turned back to Africa. Given the heightened security presence around Kubu Stadium, how had anyone gotten a nuclear device close enough to the premises? Kyle figured the answer to that was probably collusion with some security forces. And though he couldn't be sure, the device was most likely loaded on a vehicle that was parked just outside the stadium. Buses, TV trucks, and even police and army vehicles could be used to transport a small nuclear bomb, but to pass security inspection, someone had to let it in. It was possible they would never identify the conspirators, since any witnesses were most likely dead, and any transport vehicle would have been completely destroyed. There would eventually be an on-site investigation, but Kyle wouldn't be holding his breath for answers.

Kyle turned his thoughts to the video delivered to Voice of the World. The fact that the video had been created and received before the incident was key to its credibility. Kyle had to consider that it did not guarantee, however, that the author was the same as the bomber. It was possible, though unlikely, that the person who made the video had caught wind of the plan and decided to capitalize on the opportunity for world attention it provided. But as strange as the video seemed in its aesthetics, the tone and message were in keeping with the trigger man's speech at the stadium. *Both spoke prophetically*, Kyle thought. *The only difference is the Voice of the World video quoted written prophecy.* But why had both men spoken in a dead language? Was it to obscure their intent, or, at least in the case of the second video, a strange attempt to connect with the author of Revelation by speaking in his original tongue? The skeptic in Kyle said the whole thing seemed too weird, too out of the methods and language of any known terrorist agency in the world. Someone was jerking the entire intelligence community's chain. And yet Kyle could not refute the evidence, made horrifyingly clear in the last broadcast from Kubu Stadium.

The most urgent questions lay in combining fact and what the speeches could portend. Since someone had been able to successfully detonate a nuclear weapon in a terrorist attack, would there be similar incidents? Where had the weapon come from? Why had no intelligence agency—American or otherwise, to his knowledge—detected a single shred of evidence that such a weapon was in the hands of a rogue organization? Tracking nuclear weapons had been a top priority of every intelligence agency since the breakup of the Soviet Union. The War on Terror had made this task even more urgent. And what of the choice of target? The CIA had long conducted counter-terrorism operations in Africa, the Middle East, and Asia. These operations had been covered in the Worldwide Attack Matrix, a document presented to the president just days after 9/11 that became the blueprint for the War on Terror. Yet the failure to even detect—let alone prevent—a terrorist nuclear detonation showed something was lacking in the current approach to counter-terrorism. The CIA would have to find out exactly what that was and remedy it before another strike.

By now, most of the other passengers on the half-full plane had closed their shades and drifted off to sleep, but the questions kept Kyle awake. He tried laying his head back and closing his eyes, but nothing worked. Kyle finally opened his laptop and brought up the browser. His screen was now the only light in the cabin. Kyle typed in the keyword search *African Atomic Bomb Videos* and immediately found the cell phone footage he had seen on the news earlier. There were a few other videos, mostly from the news. There were also a few crackpot videos on YouTube; one theorized the bombing was the work of the Illuminati, while another predicted it was a sign of the end of the world.

Kyle found the silhouetted man video had been posted on the Voice of the World website. *That didn't take long*, he thought. Connors was right. Kyle watched the video again, looking to glean any new clues. Then he did another keyword search for *Horsemen+Revelation*. Kyle clicked on one of the first results and found a page with a chilling rendering of *Death on a Pale Horse* by William Blake. The accompanying text read:

The Four Horsemen of the Apocalypse
The Four Horsemen are symbolic figures detailed in the Book of Revelation in the Bible. They are red, black, white, and pale (often interpreted as greenish) in color and represent war, famine, conquest, and death. Biblical scholars disagree on the timing of these misfortunes; some claim they represent past epochs, while others see them as harbingers of future calamities.

Kyle closed his laptop and looked around the cabin. As far as he could tell, most of the passengers were still asleep. A boy in an aisle seat a few rows ahead of him caught his eye. The boy had a mop of brown hair just like his son Adam, and seemed to be about the same age. Kyle laid his head back and closed his eyes.

His mind drifted back to the day of Adam's last field trip. He had helped Adam get out the door that day. Usually, his wife Krissy saw Adam off, but on that day, Kyle had the pleasure of sending him to school. "Looking forward to your field trip?" he had asked.

"Yeah, we're going to see the monuments," Adam said as he pulled on his backpack.

"Which monuments?"

"The ones for the presidents."

"Yeah? Lincoln, Washington, Jefferson?"

Kyle knelt down to help Adam straighten one of the straps on his backpack.

"Yup," Adam said.

"Do you know what they did? What did Washington do?"

"Founded the country," Adam said matter-of-factly.

"And Lincoln?"

"Freed the slaves and won the Civil War."

"Good. And Jefferson? He wrote something. What did he write?"

"The Declaration of Independence." Adam suddenly looked at his father with an expression of disdain only a child can deliver. "Gee, Dad, you sure didn't learn a lot in school."

Kyle tousled his son's hair. *Kids. They bust your chops without knowing it.* "Yeah, but you will." He gave his son a hug and smiled. "Now get outta here."

Kyle's mind suddenly flashed to other images—these were disjointed and horrific. He saw glimpses of white marble pillars, a flock of birds rising black like a cloud of locusts, a sharp scream, and the distorted, resonant boom of an explosion.

Kyle's eyes shot open as he sat up in his seat. Shaking these images from his mind, he looked around to ensure no one noticed his distress. He lifted his shade and gazed out the window. The last rays of the sunset tinted the ocean waves red. Many people would find such a sight to be beautiful, but Kyle's reaction was different. Something about the view gave him a distinct feeling of unease.

By the time the plane landed, Kyle had been awake for twenty hours. He had only slept four in the last forty-eight. Kyle made his way to the baggage claim in a daze. He feared people would look at him like he was some kind of walking zombie. As he stood waiting for his bags to come down the conveyor, he noticed a man and woman kiss and embrace each other in greeting.

Kyle's thoughts went back to the morning of Adam's last field trip, but this time, he thought of Krissy. She had stood at the bathroom mirror, fixing her hair.

"What time is the ultrasound?" Kyle asked.

"Four o'clock."

"I'll make it."

Kyle wrapped his arms around Krissy, noticing how her pregnant belly shortened his reach.

"From across the river?" she asked, shaking off Kyle's arms so she could finish fixing her hair. "Fat chance."

Kyle playfully put his hands on Krissy's waist and mimicked a lumbering dance move. "I won't be waddling in there."

Krissy knew it was a joke, but it went too far. She kicked his shin, hard. Kyle held to the counter, bent over and grimacing in pain. Krissy smiled in satisfaction, then turned and left.

Kyle grit his teeth. "Shouldn't have married a soccer player."

An absent-minded man dropped his suitcase on Kyle's foot as he reached for another bag, stirring Kyle out of his memory.

"Hey."

The man turned back to Kyle and saw the suitcase. "Sorry." He quickly lifted the case and moved back to the conveyer for his other luggage. Kyle's foot smarted, but strangely, a phantom pain in his shin remained. Looking across the baggage claim, he watched the happy couple walk off, then collected his own bags.

Deputy Director of the Central Intelligence Agency Andrew Everton knew when to go with his instincts. He had spent the first fifteen years of his career in the field, and more than once a gut reaction had saved his life. Training and good problem solving were essential, but DD/CIA Everton had a knack for also being right when he had to take a chance.

Everton was en route to the conference in Berlin when he learned of the bombing. He immediately had his private flight diverted to central Africa. Five hours later, the local CIA Station Chief greeted him on the tarmac. The Chief's report was just as Everton expected; chaos was brewing. The governments of both the country and capital city, as well as the police force, had all been decapitated in the attack. Now a severely undermanned and junior police staff was trying to keep order. An hour after the bombing, the winds shifted toward the city, bringing nuclear fallout over the population. The police tried to enforce an orderly evacuation, but the streets were immediately clogged with panicked civilians. Other neighborhoods were left without police protection, inviting looters and rioters. Ninety minutes after the attack rumors began circulating that a TV truck had caused the explosion. Adamant supporters of President Mutu took their rage out on foreign journalists. No journalists were killed, but many were severely beaten. It wasn't the kind of publicity the country needed, especially on the worst day in its history. To top it off, roughly four hours after the blast, a General Kawambe from the neighboring country claimed the bombing was orchestrated to assassinate President Nisra. Illogically, he claimed the host country carried out the deed, deeming Mutu as acceptable collateral damage. The world, or at least this part of it, had gone crazy.

"It's like Mad Max," the Station Chief summed up.

Everton quickly assessed the situation. "Where's General Nigabe?" Nigabe was the highest-ranking government official still alive in the country.

"In the jungle hinterlands, hunting down rebels."

"Okay. Let's get going."

"Going…where?"

Within half an hour, Everton set out with the Station Chief and a small security force in a Huey toward the rainforest. They canvassed the area where Nigabe was thought to have been operating, then set down at dusk. Everton wasn't about to waste time. Leading his security detail into the thick jungle, the group hiked until they reached Nigabe's field headquarters just after dawn. Although he had worked a desk for nearly two decades, Everton never lost the fitness he had maintained as an operations officer. Two of the security agents couldn't believe they were panting to keep up with a man at least fifteen years' their senior. Everton welcomed the rare chance to be back in the field again.

When the party arrived at Nigabe's field headquarters, the sentries were almost as surprised to hear CIA agents wanted to meet with the general as they were to have any visitors at all. The location was extremely remote. Nigabe had chosen the spot for its seclusion as much for its ideal staging point to contain the rebels. The sentries demanded that only Everton and his assistant, Marcus Jefferson, could proceed to the general's field tent. They also patted down the two men and ordered them to surrender any weapons. Everton came unarmed, but Jefferson reluctantly surrendered his sidearm.

Jefferson looked up at the sky. "You know there's an armed drone up there. If anything happens to us, this camp goes up in thirty seconds."

The sentries squinted as their eyes scoured the cloudless sky.

"I don't see anything," one said.

"You never do...until it's too late." Jefferson smirked as the sentries led them to Nigabe's tent. There was, of course, no drone, but Jefferson didn't like feeling vulnerable, and he didn't mind playing head games.

General Nigabe was hunched over a map when the sentries ushered Everton and Jefferson into his tent. Nigabe stood to greet his guests. He was taller and more athletic than Mutu, and several years younger than the late president.

"What does the CIA want with me?" Nigabe was blunt, but directness was a virtue for a soldier. This was a man oriented on results. Diplomacy was for politicians.

"Are you aware of what's happening in your capital?" Everton began.

"I do not need the CIA to tell me my president is dead." Nigabe, looking suddenly disinterested, went back to the map.

Everton was undeterred. He circled around the table to face Nigabe again. "I mean what has happened since the attack. Things are falling apart."

Nigabe set his jaw. "My president ordered me to root out the rebels that are a cancer to our country. I am honoring his last wishes. This is what I do."

"Things have changed. Your president and most of his government are gone. The police—what's left of them—are completely overwhelmed. Riots have begun in the capital. Of those who are left, you're the leader with the most experience. If you stay out here…there will be nothing to fight for."

Nigabe lashed out. "Who are you to give me orders? We are not the province of an empire." He tried to let the last bit hang, convinced the CIA was America's most insidious empire-builder. In the last fifty years, U.S. troops had fought in southeast Asia and the Middle East, but the list of countries and regions where the CIA had interfered was much longer. Nigabe had entertained his guests out of mere interest. Now he was convinced they wanted him as their puppet.

Everton shook his head. "I'm not here to give you orders. I'm telling you how it is. I'm asking you to do everyone—your countrymen, mine, and many others—a favor."

"Favor?"

"You don't have the means of conducting a full investigation into the bombing. We do. We can trace the compositional footprint of the bomb back to the source where the materiel was processed. It can help us determine the origin of the bomb—who built it, and who set it off. But we can't conduct an investigation unless you stabilize the situation in your capital."

"If I take control of the capital, everyone will think I have done this thing. They will believe I have betrayed my president to gain control."

Everton saw the fear behind Nigabe's words. "I'm sure the results of our investigation will exonerate you from any culpability. We're willing to declassify as much information as necessary to prove that to the world." This was the concession Everton was least willing to give. He knew it would give the culprits an advantage and could increase international tension. Everton was sure the bomb had originated from some government stockpile. The implication that any nuclear state was either not in control of their weapons or had sanctioned an act of terror by providing the bomb was sure to fan the flames. It also had to be the truth. And without this concession to Nigabe, Everton reckoned he'd have no chance to conduct an investigation at all.

Everton saw the wheels turning in Nigabe's brain. "Kawambe is saying I did this to assassinate his president. If I take control of the capital, he will see why this bomb killed my president too. It doesn't matter that I could never get my hands on a nuclear bomb. He will see it as a coup. And while you conduct your investigation, I will be fighting another war."

It was surprising to see the general be so honest, and yet Everton was also concerned that Nigabe's fears were being laid bare. He had not calculated that the general would be so afraid, but he attributed Nigabe's state to the sudden loss of a friend and mentor. Nigabe had always been able to rely on Mutu for his leadership and guidance. Now Nigabe was thrust into greater responsibilities than he had ever borne.

"We know you didn't do it," Everton said. The assurance gave Nigabe courage, though Jefferson's eyes widened at Everton's declaration. "I'd be happy to speak with Kawambe," Everton offered. "His country is as much invested in the results of our investigation as yours. The international community has no interest in seeing another war between your two countries. I'm sure we can prevail upon him to wait out the results of our investigation."

Nigabe nodded, absorbing Everton's pitch. It made sense.

Everton now aimed to allay Nigabe's fears about political control. "All we need is for you to restore order to your country, beginning with the capital. If you stabilize the situation and establish the kind of order that the police cannot, we can proceed with our investigation. At the same time, we can work to organize councils—possibly with the help of the UN—to re-establish the political structure of your government. You have my word that the CIA will not be involved beyond the scope of the investigation into the bombing, and the U.S. government will only be involved to the extent that any international effort to re-establish your government is pursued. We don't want to colonize your country, General Nigabe, and we don't want to set you up as a dictator. We just want you to be the protector your country needs now." In addition to his innate ability to size up any situation, Everton had a gift for diplomacy that he could call upon when necessary. He had no interest in diplomatic work, but it was one of his gifts that helped him rise to the position of DD/CIA. The Deputy Director watched as Nigabe processed his argument. Naturally, Everton expected Nigabe to be wary—Everton was CIA, and cynics throughout the world believed spooks did nothing but lie. Yet there was a logic in Everton's argument that Nigabe couldn't deny.

"I don't want to see any of your people when I take control," Nigabe ordered. "It is my country, not yours."

Everton wanted to smile, at least inwardly. "You'll only see us if we need help facilitating our investigation. Any political organizing to re-establish your government will be transparent, done through official diplomatic channels, and an international effort. We need to find who is a nuclear terrorist. You need to get your country back on its feet. We're willing to help you achieve your goals insomuch they can help us achieve ours."

Nigabe agreed and the two men discussed how the general would lead troops into the capital by late that afternoon. An armored battalion would be called up to give further support. Nigabe hated to abandon his efforts to root out the guerrillas in the jungle, but Everton prevailed on him that once the core of the country was stabilized, the rebels would remain a manageable threat. An investigative team was now on standby and would be ready to arrive at the capital airport as soon as the city was secure.

Everton and Jefferson left the general's tent, their escorts walking several paces ahead and behind them. Seeing an opportunity to speak discreetly with his boss, Jefferson leaned over and whispered, "How did you know he wasn't involved in the bombing?" Jefferson knew it was unlikely for Nigabe to find access to a nuclear weapon, but he still was surprised by Everton's assurance in speaking to the general.

"I didn't," Everton admitted. "It was worth a gamble. I reckoned he wasn't involved, and I needed him to facilitate our investigation."

Collecting his sidearm at the security checkpoint, Jefferson shook his head and smiled. "Sir, how 'bout we go to Monte Carlo?"

"You wish."

The Deputy Director walked ahead, reaching for a satellite phone to communicate the news of his agreement to Langley.

Jefferson looked at the jungle surrounding him. It was still going to take most of the day to hike out of here. Quietly, he muttered to himself. "Yeah, I wish."

5

Chasing Shadows

Kyle spent the next day and a half trying to make sense of what they had on the African bombing. The entire U.S. intelligence community brought all of its considerable resources to bear. The NSA was running a voice-recognition search on both the video from the stadium and the Voice of the World video, trying to determine if either of the men were any figures of note in the terrorist world. The CIA was poring over everything they had and comparing it to any known terrorist groups, trying to determine if one terrorist organization had suddenly increased its capabilities, or even morphed into another. All were searching out the financial footprint of the act. Despite plenty of black market dealers who would be happy to deal in uranium, purchasing a full nuclear bomb would be out of reach of most terrorists. Someone had a boatload of money, and try as they might, the traces of it couldn't be hidden forever. Then there was the origin of the bomb itself. Ferguson learned of Deputy Director Everton's deal with General Nigabe and that the investigative team would be in country shortly.

Kyle's part was to compare this act with the modus operandi of any other terrorist organization, but just as he suspected when he first saw footage in Berlin, this was something new. The world now knew that terrorists had successfully seized and used a nuclear weapon, and this game-changer had given everyone in intelligence a new sense of urgency. Kyle didn't want to admit it, but something deep in his gut told him this was familiar territory. Kyle started working as an analyst at CIA only eight months before the nation was rocked by 9/11. The attack brutally ripped away the notion that the country was insulated from the worldwide phenomenon of terror, but it also exposed the inefficiencies of the nation's defenses. Up to the morning of 9/11, American defenses were still focused on fighting the last war. A NORAD exercise, simulating a Cold War-type air attack from a foreign nation, was interrupted when the military was alerted of the hijacked civilian airliners. The military scrambled to respond to this new threat, but could only put unarmed fighters in the air. By that time, the nation watched helplessly as terrorists flew the planes into the World Trade Center and Pentagon. Something told Kyle that now, just as on that day, the nation's defenses and intelligence community had not caught up with the reality of the threat.

There had been real progress since 9/11—bureaucratic walls between CIA, the FBI, and other government agencies had been torn away so that information could be shared as freely as necessary. The U.S. had also been considerably successful in the fight against Al Qaeda. Funding for the terrorist group had been located, frozen, and seized. Al Qaeda leadership had been decimated by U.S. operations that either captured or killed its top men. But new problems had emerged. Terrorism had grown into a global grass-roots problem. Fanatics were coming out of the woodwork. The power of hatred and belief ensured terrorism would not end with the destruction of any one organization.

There were practical and ethical considerations for the U.S. intelligence community as well. Unlike an enemy from a foreign nation, terrorists were extremely hard to locate, but easier to kill. Human intelligence, which had been a basis of gathering information throughout the life of CIA, was a practical impossibility in the age of terrorism. Terrorist organizations notoriously operated in cells that compartmentalized information and recruited solely from among those they could trust. Penetrating any of these cells with U.S. operatives was extremely rare. The level of fanaticism within terrorist organizations also made the likelihood of turning any member into a double agent nearly impossible. When terrorists were captured alive, agents had been able to withdraw information from interrogations. However, those took time. Worse, some methods—waterboarding and renditions to black op sites in foreign countries, for instance—were extremely controversial with the public. When revealed, they served to damage the image of the United States across the world.

Most information gathering was done by signals intelligence. The NSA and CIA raked in most of their information on terrorist organizations through digital means. This provided its own challenges. The main problem with intelligence has always been discerning the real threat from the mountain of data that is collected. A good analyst must learn to decipher the pertinent data and dismiss the unimportant or intentionally misleading details. Yet with the ubiquitous nature of modern technology, the mountain of data had grown exponentially. While metadata and keyword searches could sift through much of the digital morass, humans still had to examine and determine the importance or irrelevance of each piece of information.

The methods of mining this digital information had also presented the biggest ethical dilemma. Since 9/11, the most gnawing question was how could a free society successfully fight against an insidious and hidden enemy and not change its character for the worst. Clearly America had changed. While most Americans debated about the invasive nature of the TSA's airport screening procedures, the NSA quietly went about implementing a massive digital collection program. PRISM was a massive data mining program that monitored practically all internet and phone communications worldwide. As this included access to the communications of American citizens without a warrant, the program was highly controversial and even deemed unconstitutional in the Foreign Intelligence Surveillance Court, which oversees intelligence activities. Yet the covert nature of the program sealed that decision, and the data mining continued until whistleblower Edward Snowden revealed PRISM in 2013. Public outrage could not end the program, and the government continued to insist the necessity of PRISM for U.S. defense even as Americans' freedom shrank under these intelligence programs.

Kyle knew the search for these terrorists was in its early stages, but he couldn't escape the feeling that this opponent was more formidable than anyone anticipated. It wasn't so much that setting off a nuclear bomb in Africa was irrational. What really disturbed Kyle was that he was chasing ghosts. Other than the bombing itself and the video, there was no other evidence to go on. Kyle knew that "chatter" often preceded a major terrorist strike anywhere in the world. Sometimes the information would be considerably vague, but good intelligence agencies could piece together tracks that led to the perpetrators before or after the attack. Kyle saw no tracks emerge. There was no solid information that could identify this group. As much as intelligence analysis could be trying to find a needle in a stack of needles, this assignment was harder than ever. Even the financial track seemed bare. How could hundreds of millions of dollars, the amount needed to purchase a nuclear weapon, be untraceable? Kyle had no logical answers, but his gut was telling him this group wasn't leaving traces now. That was extremely important—there had to be an urgency to find this group, because when they acted again, it could be even more devastating. So Kyle had pored through every ounce of data that might possibly build a better picture of this new group. His boss, Casey Larsen, had his entire team put in a thirty-hour day. Finally, thoroughly exhausted, Kyle slept four hours at his desk. Six hours' sleep in the last fifty-six hours. Not nearly enough.

Everton's agreement with Nigabe paid off handsomely. Within forty-eight hours of the bombing, the nuclear investigative team was on the ground, scrounging through the ruins outside Kubu stadium. Eighteen hours later, they had an answer. The team immediately sent the data to Langley. Everton forwarded it to Connors and Knox in Berlin. Knox welcomed the news. Despite having gathered two hundred of the best minds in counter-terrorism, the conference hadn't produced any real information leading to the identity or motive of the bombers.

Knox entered the large atrium in the Westin Grand Hotel and spotted Boris Petrusiv on a balcony three floors above.

Petrusiv was a senior officer in Ukraine's Foreign Intelligence Service and one of the craftiest spies around. Knox made his way up to Petrusiv, knowing the Ukrainian would have a hard time believing the news.

"We know," Knox whispered to Petrusiv when they were alone. "Our team in Africa just confirmed."

"How do they know?" Petrusiv asked. Was Knox playing him, and if so, why?

"Radioactive fingerprint from the uranium. Wait 'til you hear where the bomb was manufactured."

Petrusiv raised his eyebrows as he waited for the answer. *Here it comes*, he thought.

"Ukraine."

"Impossible. We gave up nuclear weapons with independence."

"…Soviet era," Knox added in explanation. "But that means someone nurtured it for decades, then sold it on the black market."

"Are you sure?"

Knox leaned in. "Come on, Boris…you know where to look, and who to look at."

"Then so do you." Petrusiv wasn't giving an inch of ground. The idea that the bomb was from Soviet-era Ukrainian stock seemed incredible.

"Not as well as you," Knox said without guile. "You were there at the revolution. You know where things went, and who went with them. You know where something could have slipped through the cracks."

The gears in Petrusiv's head worked quickly. "If we help you, you'll help us." He paused long enough for Knox to wonder what arrangement he had in mind. "During the

Cold War, you listened to the conversations of Politburo members on their car phones."

Knox shook his head. "A myth, Boris. But an effective one."

"And you have no such capabilities today? We must know what is going on in the Kremlin."

"Why should we exchange information that only benefits your country for information that benefits everyone?"

Petrusiv set his jaw. "If your country was being devoured limb by limb, tell me you'd do differently."

He has a point, Knox thought. He ran the ramifications of the deal through his mind. "Under no circumstances can we be linked. That might restrict how you'd use the information."

"We're willing to accept that." Petrusiv was sounding magnanimous.

"I'll see what we can do."

From across the atrium, a set of piercing blue eyes locked onto the two men.

Knox had just entered the conference room when the same set of eyes found him. The man strode across the room toward him. *Oh great*, Knox thought. Yuri Kolnikov—from Russia's FSB—wanted to talk with him.

"Yuri," Knox said as Kolnikov approached. He hoped greeting him first would throw Kolnikov off balance. It did, if only for the fraction of a second.

"I have a proposal for you, Colonel Knox," Kolnikov said in a conspiratorially low tone.

"Two minutes," Knox said, conceding. He knew what was coming, and thought it'd be a waste, but in the interest of diplomatic relations, he owed hearing Kolnikov out.

The two men retreated to a quiet corner. "I have heard about your team in Africa…and where they think the bomb originated. But you do not know what we know," Kolnikov said. Knox saw what was coming. The fact the bomb was Russian, even if it was Soviet-era manufacture, left egg on their faces. The Russians would have to work hard to ensure the bedrock established by several START treaties dating back 40 years would not be shaken. If the Russians had not controlled their nuclear stockpile, the U.S. could easily argue that they had also maliciously hidden several of their weapons from official counts. The trust that had slowly been built over decades of arms reductions could be wiped out in an instant. Knox listened and tried not to smile. This had to be good.

"What do you know?" Knox asked, playing along.

"You want to know who used the bomb, and how they got it. We can help, if you help us."

"Careful, Yuri. You might just make us think your people were in on this."

"Preposterous."

Knox lowered his head, trying to hide his amusement. This was too much fun, but he could tell he was angering the Russian.

"What's your proposal?" Knox said, stifling his smile.

"We can give you the names of four arms dealers—men your intelligence services are not aware of—but are most likely to have provided the bomb. We know you can track them better than us." This was a lie. The U.S. surveillance apparatus, including the NSA's PRISM program, reached far enough to make its allies extremely unsettled. But the Russians had much more experience in invasive surveillance. To Knox, the FSB was only marginally better than its notorious predecessor, the KGB.

"And what do you want?" Knox asked.

"All of the data you collect on the four men."

"And?"

"And when the correct dealer is detained, you let us take custody."

Knox saw this coming. It would be a major coup for the Russians if they snagged the arms dealer. They might just convince the world—the intelligence community, at least—that they took the use of their nuclear stockpile for terrorist acts seriously, and thereby exonerate themselves from culpability for the bombing.

Knox shook his head. "Sorry, Yuri, but you're late."

Kolnikov's mouth dropped open in furious shock.

"We've got a better deal," Knox explained as he stepped away.

The Russian caught his arm. "Don't be a fool." Kolnikov's tone was pleading as much as it was threatening. "You'll need our help."

Knox looked down at Kolnikov's hand on his arm. It was enough for the Russian to let go. Knox turned again to leave.

"You may think you know your friends," Kolnikov said louder, "but do you?"

Knox turned back. What did this mean? He searched the Russian's eyes for an answer, but they would reveal no secrets. Maybe he was just playing him. "I hope so."

6

The First Vials

Kyle was working at his desk when Sadiq came in. "My contact at Voice of the World sent another video." Sadiq handed Kyle a flash drive.

Kyle cued up the video on his computer. It featured the same shrouded figure against the blood-red backdrop. The figure began to speak. *"For the great day of his wrath has come; who shall be able to stand?"*

"Revelation, again," Sadiq said.

"Looks familiar."

"But one main difference." Sadiq moved the cursor on the video and fast forwarded. When he stopped, the figure was speaking in a different foreign language.

"I don't understand it," Sadiq said.

Kyle listened. Instinctively, almost as if someone else answered for him, he spoke. "It's ancient Greek."

Sadiq ran a hand through his hair and scratched the back of his head. "You study that in college?"

"Maybe I slept through a class. I don't know." Kyle was as disturbed as Sadiq.

"I speak six languages, but I don't pick them up as fast as you."

"Don't worry about it. Probably I'm some kind of savant," Kyle shrugged.

"Yeah, right." Sadiq frowned at the screen. "I figured it was Greek."

"Don't say it."

"I won't. What does it mean?"

Kyle closed his eyes and inhaled, then opened his eyes and began to translate. "*And the first angel poured his vial out upon the earth; and there fell a grievous sore upon the men that bore the mark of the beast.*"

"Another attack?"

Kyle furrowed his brow. "Could be. Grievous sore?"

"Radiation? Or possibly chemical or biological attack."

"But which of the three?"

Sadiq shook his head, unsure. "Better report this to Larsen."

Dusk was settling on the Chesapeake Bay as the captain of the oil tanker looked out. In the distance, he could see city lights. He turned his gaze farther north, where the black form of another tanker stood on the horizon. The captain watched as the other tanker's signal light began to blink a message in Morse code. Moving along the rail, the captain approached the crewman at his ship's signal light. He gave a short nod for the crewman to respond, and the man began to send a reply.

The captain moved along a gangway and slid down a set of stairs. He passed through a doorway and down another passage until he reached the pump room. There, he nodded to another crew member at a control panel. The crewman pulled a lever on the panel, and a deep rushing noise began to sound from within the ship's tank. The crewman moved to a small observation window, where he watched as reddish water—not oil—rushed from the tank through a specially-made drain into the ocean.

The five-star restaurant sat along Marbella's waterfront, where diners could look out and watch the boats coming and going. Dr. Miroslav Slobodin wiped his glasses with a handkerchief and put them back on his balding head. Dressed in a cheap tweed suit, he looked terribly out of place among the swank clientele. Slobodin had only flown in this morning, and though he was sweating profusely, he didn't remove his suit coat. His sweat wasn't just from the Mediterranean sun.

Slobodin scanned the tables until he spotted a tan middle-aged man in a loose white shirt. The man's blonde hair was cropped short, and his shirt was only buttoned halfway, revealing a tan, broad and hairless chest. Slobodin recognized the man immediately as Anton Bondarenko. Bondarenko might have looked like a wealthy sailor but for his oily edge. He was sitting at the table with two other people—a beautiful woman in a tight white dress, and a man in a suit who looked like a heavy operator. The table was filled with a fabulous spread, and the three were relaxed. Bondarenko looked at ease, smiling and laughing.

Slobodin stopped a passing waiter. He whispered something into his ear as he pressed a note into the waiter's hand. Slobodin stood back and watched as the waiter approached Bondarenko's table. The waiter placed a fresh bottle of wine on the table, took back an empty one, and discreetly slipped Slobodin's note in front of Bondarenko. Slobodin admired the waiter's ease of delivery. *Five-star service.* As Bondarenko read the note, his demeanor changed instantly.

He looked back toward the waiter, then excused himself from the table.

Across the room, a man watched over his wine glass as Bondarenko headed toward a back corridor where the restrooms were located. Bondarenko met Slobodin in an alcove by the restroom doors. He smirked at Slobodin's sweaty appearance.

"I didn't expect to hear from you," Bondarenko said.

"Nor I. I mean…I didn't plan to come here."

Bondarenko almost laughed. He couldn't picture Slobodin in a more unsuitable place than Marbella. The Russian scientist would never learn how to unwind.

"It's been twenty years, Slobodin. You should have waited another twenty."

"Zyuganov contacted me. Have you seen him?"

Bondarenko smiled, but his eyes remained cold. "That's not your concern."

"I haven't been involved in years," Slobodin said. "Now he wants to meet."

"You're scared of him?" Bondarenko shrugged. "Well, you should be."

"What should I do?"

"I won't tell you what you should do. That's up to you. But I know what you want to do."

Slobodin loosened his tie. His collar was wet and suffocating him. "What's that?"

"Run."

"Where should I run to? There's nowhere safe from him."

"Then you have your answer. You should meet. If it's inevitable, running would be worse."

"I didn't do anything," Slobodin insisted. "I kept my promises."

"Then you have nothing to fear." Bondarenko turned to leave.

"Are you two planning something?" Slobodin asked, raising his voice enough to stop Bondarenko. "I want to make clear—I don't want any part of it. I'm retired."

Bondarenko didn't like being lectured. "Address it with him," he said sternly.

"Can you protect me?"

Bondarenko's expression changed quickly. He walked back to Slobodin with a warm smile. "If Zyuganov wants something from you, he'd rather use your gifts than destroy them. That's your safeguard." Bondarenko patted Slobodin's arm, then left.

Slobodin inhaled sharply, trying to relax. He hoped Bondarenko was right.

Across the room, the same man watched over his wine glass as Bondarenko and Slobodin left.

In the marina across the street, two men sat in the cabin of a sailboat. One watched the front of the restaurant with binoculars, while the other, Boris Petrusiv, watched a small monitor. The screen showed the view from a mini-cam, hidden on the watchful diner in the restaurant. The screen focused on Slobodin as he walked out.

"Do you recognize him?" Petrusiv asked the other man.

The man set his binoculars down.

"That's Miroslav Slobodin."

Petrusiv nodded. "Former head of the Soviet biological weapons program. So Bondarenko's not just dealing in arms anymore."

The soft ripple of water could be heard just above the summer crickets, and beneath it all, the electric hum of the filtration plant. It was after midnight, and had the location not been so isolated and the plant unmanned, the tanker truck backing up the service road would certainly have been noticed. Both men in the cab wore balaclavas. The passenger looked out his side and saw the thickly wooded slope that ran down to the Hudson. There, moonlight sparkled off of the water. One false move and the truck could be headed into it. But the driver was good, and he gauged the road well.

The truck reached the security gate and both men hopped out. One man spray painted the security camera lenses black while the other used a blowtorch to destroy the lock. Within thirty seconds, the gate was open. The driver backed the truck through the gate toward the treatment basins. Then both men attached six-inch wide hoses to the truck and ran them into the basins. Then they began to dump water from the tank. In fifteen minutes, the tanker was empty. The men packed up the hoses and drove off, closing the gate behind them.

Anton Bondarenko lined up his shot, pulled back, and swung. Perfect. The ball threaded the needle between two high bunkers and landed just a few feet from the pin. Bondarenko's partner nodded in admiration while one of Bondarenko's two bodyguards applauded. Bondarenko strolled down the fairway with his 2 Iron and breathed in the air. Today was beautiful. The green hills surrounding the golf course sloped down toward the deep blue of the Mediterranean Sea, and above all was a clear sky. Living four months a year in Marbella had its rewards.

As Bondarenko approached the green, he saw a man appear from behind a bunker. Bondarenko was furious with this breach of etiquette.

"Get off the course! You're interrupting the game!"

The man smiled. "Anton Bondarenko."

Bondarenko approached and recognized the man. "Oh no. Not today, Boris."

Petrusiv grinned.

"Usually I'd have my men crack your skull." He brandished his 2 Iron, pointing it at Pertrusiv. "Today I'm setting a course record. For that, I'll kill you."

Petrusiv stepped back and Bondarenko exchanged the club with his caddy. Petrusiv put his hands in his pockets, patient, as Bondarenko lined up his putt.

"Like it or not, you're coming with me," Petrusiv said.

Bondarenko's partner wanted to shush him. This certainly was a breach of course etiquette. But despite Petrusiv's relaxed demeanor, he could see the man meant business. One of the bodyguards strode over to Petrusiv and reached for his arm.

"Ah, I wouldn't do that," Petrusiv said calmly, but in a tone forceful enough for the bodyguard to restrain himself.

"Shove off," Bondarenko scoffed at Petrusiv, his head down and focused on the putt. He tapped the ball gently, sending it in a perfect line toward the hole. Six inches from the pin, Petrusiv stepped on the ball and trapped it underfoot.

"Bastard!" Bondarenko exploded, raising his club to swing at Petrusiv. Like insidious insects, a dozen red dots moved swiftly across the green, up Bondarenko's legs, and converged in a glowing point in the middle of his chest. The bodyguards and Bondarenko's partner froze when they looked at each other—all of them had glowing red dots in the center of their foreheads. Petrusiv's commandos, hidden around the course, had their guns sighted in on Bondarenko's party.

"Call it a mulligan," Petrusiv said, smiling.

Bondarenko dropped his club, surrendering. "It will take more than that to get me to talk."

Petrusiv took hold of Bondarenko's arm and led him off the green. "I know."

The Director of National Intelligence is a position created after 9/11 to head the seventeen different intelligence agencies in the U.S. government and provide a more coordinated intelligence community. The DNI reports directly to the President, providing him with key information to make national security decisions. The current Director of National Intelligence, General Maxwell 'Bump' Foley, was pressing hard on the African bombing. That was his nature. Foley's nickname was a result of his tenacity. He had gotten it when he was ten years old, when he accused two other boys of cheating at a schoolyard game of baseball. One of them mocked him for not letting the issue go. "Did you get bumped on your head as a baby?" the kid asked. Foley didn't like the insult. He promptly slugged the boy and his companion, knocking both of them out cold. The 'Bump' nickname stuck—not for stupidity, but because if you got in Maxwell Foley's way, he'd likely bump you off.

Foley had called a progress meeting, and Kyle and the rest of Larsen's team were there. There were representatives from each of the other agencies, including NSA.

"What have we got so far?" Foley asked.

T.J. Bentley was too eager to speak up. "Safe to say the

bomb was black market." Some murmurs erupted through the room, but Bentley held up his hand, asking to be heard out. "The Russians are scrambling. They know that the bomb was from their stock, and it might wipe out the progress from the SALT and START treaties." The Strategic Arms Limitation and Reduction Treaties began in the height of the Cold War, when the U.S. and the Soviet Union possessed the means to destroy the world several times over. Pulling their fingers from the button, the SALT and START treaties had reduced nuclear stockpiles and eased tensions. They represented forty years of scaling down the nuclear threat, with the most recent treaty being signed by Presidents Obama and Medvedev in 2010. "That's not a problem they were willing to create," Bentley said, "which also precludes a sale to a foreign nation."

Foley had already figured all this, but if a hotshot wanted to speak up, he'd put him on the spot. "Okay then, so who did this?"

"Well, when you look at it, it's pretty clear. Muslim radicals."

"In that part of Africa? How can you be sure?" Foley asked. He was looking directly at Bentley, and he wanted to see if he'd squirm.

"It's a slam—" Bentley caught himself. He almost said 'slam dunk'—fateful words in the intelligence community. Former CIA Director George Tenet had used them to describe the evidence of weapons of mass destruction in Iraq. It became one of the key points in making the fateful decision to invade the country. "I guarantee you," Bentley said. He wouldn't correct himself—he was too assured of his position—but he wouldn't jinx himself, either. "Boko Haram has been gaining strength beyond Nigeria—"

"No way Boko Haram could afford a nuclear bomb," Sadiq interjected.

"And ISIS has essentially become a nation of terrorists in the Middle East," Bentley said, undeterred. "It's built on claiming territory. Either Boko Haram or their confederates—ISIS, Al Qaeda, maybe others—saw an opportunity to create a vacuum and build their own power base in Africa. The blast took out the leaders of two nations."

"But no jihadist group has the capability to purchase and use a nuclear weapon," Sadiq said.

Bentley wasn't about to give up. "Six jihadist groups, including those mentioned, claimed responsibility within an hour of the attacks. We're filtering through the claims, but it's one of them." He glared at Sadiq. "Don't forget the word 'Islam' means 'submission.' There's thousands of Muslim radicals who would love to bring that by the sword."

Bentley had crossed the line. "And yet there's another one and a half billion Muslims for whom submission means prostrating themselves five times a day in prayer to Allah. They've never been involved in violence. Don't slander an entire religion by characterizing it by the actions of radicals," Sadiq said, burning with indignation.

Foley felt it was time to put the argument to rest. "Separate the wheat from the tares," he said, looking at the two men. "That's our job."

"I don't think this is Islamic terrorism," Kyle interjected. "It doesn't bear the same marks. And there's this." Kyle cued up the first video of the silhouetted man on a large wall screen. "You remember this video, sir? It was turned in to Voice of the World *before* the attack." Kyle let his eyes wander over to Bentley. "We've received another."

"Uh, actually two more," Sadiq said, correcting him.

Kyle blinked. He hadn't heard this.

"I just found one online this morning," Sadiq explained. He played the new video on the wall screen.

"It wasn't turned in to Voice of the World?" Foley asked.

"No sir, uploaded directly," Sadiq said. "We've liaised with the NSA on this," he looked over to Parks. "All we know is it's a new user account, and uploaded in Africa."

The room watched the silhouetted figure speak. "Who is this?" Foley asked.

"We're not sure," Kyle answered. "The videos seem to feature the same figure, but he speaks lines in English, Aramaic, and ancient Greek. He identifies a group name at the end of the first video by saying, 'those who come forth are the Horsemen.'"

"Horsemen?"

"Of the Apocalypse. From the Book of Revelation."

"Then it *is* ISIS," Bentley protested. "Their avowed goal, after building a caliphate, is provoking an Armageddon—a great last battle where they will conquer the infidels of the West. They've just chosen to communicate that message in a way the West can understand."

"Have you seen ISIS videos?" Sadiq countered. "They look like car commercials. Soaring aerial shots and all. Doesn't matter if it's stock footage, their propaganda makes this look like Community Access in comparison."

"I wouldn't characterize it as that," Kyle said, "though the videos are rather simplified. The point is, no Islamic group has ever made videos like this. It's not their m.o. to quote Revelation."

"That's not the only quote," Sadiq added. "These next

two videos speak of angels pouring out vials. The first, causing a sore upon men—"

"Radiation, biological, or chemical threat, we believe—we're not sure which one yet," Kyle added.

"And the latest, poisoning the sea and rivers," Sadiq explained, "turning them to blood."

The words hung in the room, leaving a feeling of unease. Still, Foley wasn't convinced. "Dig up more."

7

Whispers

Kyle was still hunched over his computer at 4 A.M. His office was mostly dark, lit only by his desk lamp and computer screen, but he was too absorbed in his research to bother turning the main lights on. Kyle's research had turned to Revelation—a subject he realized he knew little about. He found a dozen articles all authored by the same academic, Dr. Richard Hightower. Moments later, he found a book Hightower had written, *Armageddon and the Modern World*. Kyle read the professor's biography:

Dr. Richard Hightower is one of the foremost scholars in Biblical exegesis. He is the author of 31 books and over 100 academic papers on the Bible and ancient scripture. Dr. Hightower is a Professor of Religion at Princeton University.

Kyle found the professor's profile on Princeton's website and wrote down his information. He'd call Dr. Hightower in the morning. Kyle propped his head up with his hand. He was exhausted from hours of research, and slowly, against his will, his eyes closed and sleep came.

Kyle had a horrific dream. He was sitting on a cushioned bench across from another man. There was nothing special about the man's features, and when he awakened, Kyle would not remember them at all. It was what the man did that stuck with him. The man seemed to twitch just under the corner of his left eye. He lifted his left hand to scratch at his face, but instead of alleviating the itch, a bulge started to appear from underneath his cheek. Soon another appeared, and another. In seconds the whole left side of the man's face began to grow with welts. Kyle watched as the man's hands also grew with lesions, and within seconds, his entire face and hands were covered. Just as the man began to shriek in pain, an overpowering stench of disease and death filled Kyle's nostrils. Kyle turned away, then found himself suddenly transported to an outdoor plaza.

Schoolchildren moved along in a disorganized line as their teacher tried to corral them. Tourists wandered aimlessly about the plaza. Kyle turned around and discovered he was in front of the Jefferson Memorial. It was a lovely day to be out, and yet something filled him with a sharp sense of foreboding. Kyle looked around and found his son Adam among the schoolchildren. As he moved toward Adam, Kyle scanned the crowd, looking for a source of his fear. His eyes fell on a Middle Eastern man wearing a backpack. Kyle was struck with an immediate impression of evil.

The man began to shout in Arabic. "There is no god but Allah, and Mohammed is his messenger!"

Kyle rushed to Adam and tried to shield him with his body. The man with the backpack exploded, sending out a huge fireball that consumed everything in its path. Kyle held his son tight, but shrapnel pierced through his body and thrust into the boy. Adam whimpered in pain. Unable to protect his son, Kyle roared in agony, just before the fireball closed around them.

Kyle awoke with an urge to retch. He tried to bend forward and suppress his heaving diaphragm, but it was no good. He turned his head and threw up in the wastebasket. It took some time to calm his nerves and remember his surroundings. When the unpleasant contractions of his stomach muscles subsided, Kyle breathed out in relief. Reaching into the bottom drawer of his desk, he moved several files that covered a child's baseball cap. Kyle drew his hand back, hesitant to pick it up, but the urge to hold it won out. Kyle held the cap to his nose, hoping to breathe in his son's smell, but there was nothing. Still, he clutched it tightly and closed his eyes. It calmed him. Suddenly, images of the explosion returned to him. His nose was filled with a burning smell. Kyle bent over the wastebasket and threw up again.

"Go home."

Kyle turned and saw his boss, Casey Larsen, standing in the doorway.

"Sir, I—"

"Get some sleep," Larsen said. "You've been working this thing hard. We all have. But you're no good to anyone now."

"It's just—"

"You're going to argue with me? It's six o'clock in the morning and you're throwing up in the garbage. Take the day off. I'll see you tomorrow." Larsen left, leaving the aroma of gourmet coffee wafting through the door. The smell roused Kyle enough to stretch his sore limbs and gather his things. He considered placing the baseball cap back in his desk, but took it with him.

Bentley watched from a window over the parking lot as

Kyle headed for his car. Larsen stood next to him. "What's with Ferguson?" Bentley asked.

"He needed a break. He wasn't going to take it, so I made him."

Bentley looked at the child's baseball cap in Kyle's hand. "I don't think it was a good idea to keep him on."

"He's a terrific analyst. We're lucky to have him."

"Still, it's not good policy to keep the victim of a—"

"He understands. He's been working this thing as hard as anybody." Larsen turned to Bentley. "Harder, even."

As soon as Kyle hit fresh air, he knew he was too tired to drive, so he reclined the front passenger seat of his Prius as far as it could go and laid out. It was only marginally more comfortable than an airplane seat, but he was too exhausted to mind. When he closed his eyes, a terrible thought came to him—perhaps sleep deprivation had caused his nightmare. This presented a dilemma: he needed sleep, but if he slept again, he risked another nightmare. His mind was completely frazzled, but he tried to chase the dream away and stay awake. Before long, his body decided for him, and he drifted off to sleep.

Unlike the last two times he had slept, he had no fitful dreams, and though he didn't sleep long, this gave Kyle the most restful sleep. When he awoke just before nine, he thought of his family. He hadn't time to get them anything in Berlin, but he wanted to pick up something before he saw them again. He'd head over to the Smithsonian.

The drive down the Parkway was uneventful, but Kyle had to keep himself from wandering into a listless daze. For his own health he had to keep his mind off work and leave it at the office, but nothing else kept his attention. Morning radio was inane, he couldn't absorb any kind of music, and even the pleasant weather couldn't keep him in the here and now. The best he could do was watch for brake lights ahead of him so he didn't drift into the back of the preceding car. Kyle passed over the Roosevelt Bridge and continued along Constitution Avenue past the Mall.

Early bird tourists were taking in the monuments while morning walkers and joggers stretched their legs. Kyle made a mental note to get some sleep this afternoon and then work out. After two transatlantic plane rides and thirty hours at his desk, his legs felt like lead. A good run would sort him out. Kyle turned right on 14th Street, passed the Washington Memorial, and waited to turn left onto Independence Avenue.

Although he couldn't see it from the intersection, Kyle knew the Tidal Pool Basin and Jefferson Memorial were just ahead. Something compelled him to pull out of the left-turn lane and head straight for the Memorial. Cars honked behind him, and he barely dodged being rear-ended by a Volvo, but Kyle didn't care. It took some time to find a parking place, but Kyle was soon standing before the neoclassical building dedicated to the man who wrote the Declaration of Independence. In the plaza before the front steps was a large and uneven configuration of new paving stones. Efforts had been made to blend them into the existing stones, but the edge of the stones hinted at the reason for this replacement: a faint residue of scorching remained.

More noticeable was the makeshift memorial that covered nearly all the new stones—withered flowers, weathered teddy bears, faded messages of condolence and remembrance. It had been five years since the event, and there weren't many new items at the memorial, but Park

Police wouldn't touch the shrine. They had tried, once, to move the most weathered items, but when the action was covered on TV news, the American people went ballistic. There had been plans for a more permanent memorial, but the proposal had fallen victim to bureaucratic red tape.

Kyle knelt in front of the shrine next to a fresh pile of roses and fading daisies. He held the baseball cap in his hand. Slowly, he placed it among the other items. Kyle hesitated, wondering if he wanted to leave the cap. Finally, he relented and stood. As he turned from the Memorial and headed back to his car, Kyle vowed he would never return.

8

The First Angel

President James Wallace stepped down from the podium to great applause. The enthusiasm was unfounded—it hadn't been a terrific speech. He hadn't received applause like this in over a year, but he was among supporters. It was good to know he still had them.

Wallace made his way through the well-heeled crowd, shaking hands as he went. One woman, who was something north of forty, was bouncing on her toes like a schoolgirl. Wallace would have preferred to avoid her, but this was a fundraiser after all. He could tell by the woman's expensive clothes, makeup, and surgery-stretched face that she had deluded herself into thinking she was much younger. *Have some dignity, woman.* Wallace extended his hand.

"It's such a pleasure to meet you, Mr. President," the woman gushed.

"Thank you for your support." Wallace turned to an official photographer, and a picture was quickly taken.

"We all hope to see you carry out your agenda in the next four years," the woman said loudly so she could be heard over the din of the room, but Wallace had moved on to the next VIP with the photographer. The woman, still starstruck, didn't mind.

Minutes later, Wallace climbed into the presidential

limo and slathered his hands with sanitizer. *One of the hazards of the job, I guess.* Having seen a study on the amount of bacteria the average door handle carried, he didn't want to guess what germs all those people had on their hands. The motorcade started up and passed out of the underground garage into daylight. Wallace looked out at the streets of Washington and thought how he'd hate to leave here. He needed another four years. It wouldn't be easy. Not as easy as last time, at least.

Wallace's rise to the presidency had been meteoric. He first became a national figure as an attorney in a heated police brutality case in California. Wallace's stances on police restriction and minority rights resonated with libertarians on the right and civil rights activists on the left. In the wake of the case, he made many appearances on national television. His ease with public speaking and his understanding of television made him a household name. Wallace saw where fame could take him, and knew he needed a public service record. He wanted to run for senator, but would have had to face a three-term veteran who was a key member of the Senate Oversight Committee. Wallace opted instead for representative, and won easily. Within two years, he made the monumental jump to presidential candidate. To the pundits, winning the White House as a member of the House of Representatives seemed all but impossible. But Wallace knew from his media experience how to win people over. His public image had been carefully crafted, and he tapped into something that made the American people impose their hopes and beliefs upon him without learning who the man really was.

Few Americans have paused to think about it, but possibly since the days of John F. Kennedy, and certainly since the days of Ronald Reagan, the skills required to win the presidency have had nothing to do with the day-to-day work of the job itself. Campaign teams are vital, but a candidate must project a certain image to win the American people over. A certain joie de vivre and hipness—whether telegenic handsomeness, quick wit, musical talent, or posturing to win the job in a historic moment—have all proven successful. That's not to say America has always filled the presidency with vapid showmen—many of those who have won the office in the era of television have had significant records of achievement, and many demonstrated substantive reasons why they were preferable to the other candidate. But heaven help those who enter the highest office in the land with only skill in campaigning. A president must constantly make monumental decisions that will affect the lives of millions. It takes the greatest skill to finesse negotiations with other nations and political opponents to move forward an agenda. Those who sit in such boiler rooms are not swayed by the public persona of a president; they must see a person who genuinely knows how to lead.

Wallace quickly learned how unprepared he was for the task before him in his first months as president. Though a gifted speaker and formidable debater, he had no administrative experience. He had never led anything, and now he was in charge of one of the most powerful nations on earth. As he fumbled his way through his first role as a leader, the team that had been so effective in campaigning for Wallace now had to politically spin his failures into something more palatable. The media allowed his team's spin to go unchallenged. Knowing the popularity Wallace had amassed in his run for the presidency, they figured the public would react in one of three ways. First, they would

ignore Wallace's foibles with a willing suspension of disbelief; second, the jarring distinction between the President's
image and reality might lead to a crisis of American faith;
or third—and worst of all—the public might vilify the press
for attacking a man they so revered. Despite the media's
silence, the results spoke for themselves. Not everyone
in America was thriving under Wallace's administration.
Whether the American people were consciously willing to
admit it or not, a malaise had set in from Wallace's failure
to make good on the vision he had promised.

Not all of the President's failures lay with the man himself. Some of his biggest challenges came as he tried to
implement his agenda in Congress. Driven alternately by
public opinion and a hard-line wing of their party, the President's opponents wavered between lily-livered cowering
and outright intransigence. It didn't help that he demonized
them in the press, for while Wallace truly loathed his opponents, such characterizations only made them less willing
to give one inch of ground.

Wallace had few allies in his own party in Congress;
most of them knew him differently than the American public—they remembered him as an inconsequential colleague
who abstained from a record number of votes. To Wallace,
his short-lived tenure in Congress was merely a stepping
stone to a larger prize, but to many of his peers, he was
seen as a man who couldn't be bothered with the day-to-
day business of government. He was too busy polishing his
own star.

Wallace's only major achievement as president was the
policy he ran on to win the office. He had promised to
end the massive NSA surveillance dragnet that collected
the internet records of Americans. Congress had ended tele-

phone surveillance on Americans in 2015, but Wallace wanted a complete drawback of the NSA programs. He had won bipartisan support with the electorate on the issue. This, coupled with his rising star, won Wallace the election handily.

But Wallace's great achievement also hid a more problematic issue. In signing the National Defense Authorization Act that defunded the NSA dragnet, Wallace had also written in broad language which gave which gave him the power to curtail other defense funding. Within six months of signing the presidential order Wallace began to siphon off these funds and redirect them toward social programs. The press didn't see any of it, but there was plenty of grumbling within the Department of Homeland Security and other agencies. Meanwhile, Wallace's social programs, though noble in concept, fell flat with the American public. Within three years it was apparent the political capital he'd won with election was quickly eroding.

"Mr. President?" A voice called Wallace's attention from the window. It was Pete Standish, his National Security Advisor, who sat across from him. "Look at this." Standish handed Wallace a tablet.

The screen showed a video of Secretary of State Marsh Adamson speaking at a news conference. "The perpetrators of this bombing represent the height of 20th century thinking," Adamson said. "It's time they joined the rest of the world in the present."

The President winced at the video. As much as Adamson wanted to promote progressive thinking, his statement smacked of sanctimony.

"It's a total disaster," Standish fumed. He and Wallace had known each other for a long time, and Wallace usually appreciated his unvarnished opinion. Somehow, Wallace wasn't taking it well today. Maybe the fundraiser didn't go well. Still, Standish pressed on. "He's the chief diplomat of the United States, not the fashion police. Worse still, half the world's countries from China to Zimbabwe are calling us hypocrites, because we're the only country to have used the Bomb in anger." It didn't matter that President Truman and his advisers assessed the human toll of invading Japan and considered it much higher than bombing Hiroshima and Nagasaki. History is more about the interpretation of facts than facts alone. And to many, the only country to use nuclear weapons—twice—had no place lecturing the rest of the world about their use. "You should have let me speak on this."

"The National Security Advisor? And let people think they have something to fear?"

"They might."

Standish's answer irritated Wallace. "Do we? Then why don't you figure that out?"

"Just want to impress upon you there's more to handle than just the campaign," Standish said, backing down.

"I'm on top of it," Wallace said as he picked up the phone. "Are you?"

Kyle pulled up to the two-story Brick Colonial house in Chevy Chase, Maryland where his parents lived. Kyle did not grow up here, but it was a good reward for his dad's hard work. Jack Ferguson had a long career as a corporate lawyer in northern Virginia before moving to Maryland, and, at the urging of friends, running for a state judgeship. His tenure was successful enough to lead to an appointment to a federal bench, where he had spent the last seven years.

But in the last few months, Judge Jack Ferguson had cut back his schedule and planned to retire.

Kyle parked in the center of the large curved driveway. Making his way to the front door, he passed the well-manicured flower garden his mother tended daily. He breathed in when he saw none of the flowers had been molested. The last time his son had stayed at his grandparents' house, he'd wandered through the flower garden, stomping on the fledgling azaleas as if he were a giant crushing the landscape. Kyle's mother was nearly apoplectic when she saw the damage. No such disasters this time, at least outside.

Kyle also breathed in relief when his mother answered the door with a smile. It must have been a good couple of days for them. Lyla Ferguson's face, however, quickly turned to surprise.

"Back so soon? What about the conference?"

"I was called back," Kyle answered, unable to hide his exhaustion.

Kyle made his way to a bedroom toward the back of the first floor. There, a boy with a mop of hair slept soundly. He looked like Adam, but was only four years old. "Joshua missed you," Lyla whispered. "He had a rough night."

"Yeah? Me too."

"You can wake him if you want."

"No, let him sleep longer." Kyle tucked the box he had for his son under his arm and closed the door quietly. He and his mother moved down the hallway, still whispering.

"Krissy called," Lyla said. "You should talk to her."

"She wants to be a mother now? It's a little late."

"Joshua's still young," Lyla protested. "And you're not here half the time."

These last words were true, but depressed Kyle. He slumped against the wall. "I'm doing the best I can."

"He needs a mother."

"He's got you."

"A grandmother is not the same."

"She left," Kyle said, baring his teeth. Maybe he was being too harsh on his mother. He leaned back against the wall. Softer, now. "She left."

Kyle and Lyla entered the sunlit kitchen, where his father sat reading the paper. Physically, Kyle had inherited far more genetic traits from his mother than his father. He had her slender bones and reddish hair. Lyla Ferguson was not short, but her frame was nearly pixieish. Her husband on the other hand was a barrel-chested man with large features and brown hair. Kyle had inherited his father's keen mind, but he had always put it to different use. Instead of going into law, Kyle had majored in International Studies at the University of Maryland. He applied to CIA right after graduation and never looked back. Jack Ferguson's shadow was something Kyle didn't want to inhabit. It was easier to find his own path in a different field.

Jack put down the paper. "So, they've got you working on this thing in Africa, huh?"

Jack didn't expect an answer. He knew his son couldn't discuss his work in any sort of detail, so he took Kyle's silence in the affirmative. They frequently resorted to these clipped exchanges about Kyle's work; more often than not, their conversations were filled with silence. "You want some coffee?" Jack got up and moved toward the pot.

"They gave me the day off," Kyle explained.

"Oh?" Lyla said.

"I wanted to spend the day with Josh."

"Why don't you get some sleep?" his mother said, rubbing his shoulder. "He won't even know you're back."

"No, we should go home."

"Up to Mayo?" Lyla frowned. "Why don't you sleep here?"

"And have you tuck me in? No thanks. You can stick with Josh."

"I'm still your mother."

Jack, knowing this could become an endless argument, cut in. "Let's have lunch together, shall we?"

A bouncing ball of energy raced into the kitchen, stomping loudly on the tile as he ran. "Daddy!"

Joshua would have thrown his arms around his father's legs, but Kyle intercepted him and scooped him up in his arms. It was good to see his son. The welcome swept all of his work away, and for the first time in days, Kyle lived in the present. No thought or concern could intrude on this moment.

"Guess what I got for you, Joshy?" Kyle said, pulling a toy space shuttle out of the box.

"A plane," Josh squealed in delight.

"It's a space ship," Kyle explained, imitating its flight. "It's launched with big rockets into space, and then it comes back down to earth like an airplane."

Josh smiled as he flew the space shuttle in his hands, making sound effects of roaring engines.

"Want to see a big one of these, the real one?" Kyle asked.

"Yeah. Where is it?"

"It's at a museum. We can go tomorrow."

"Yeah," Josh smiled.

"And what do you want to do today?" Kyle asked.

"Today? Ummm…"

"Want to see the boats? We can have lunch by the water."

"Yeah!" Josh said enthusiastically.

Kyle looked to his parents. That settled it.

The 7 Express subway train was arriving at New York's Grand Central Terminal. On board the middle car stood an Asian tourist wearing an N100 respirator mask. The N100 respirator was capable of filtering out over 99% of airborne particles. The man barely registered any attention from the crowd of commuters. They were used to seeing anything in a world city. The man had a manual SLR camera slung around his neck. He lifted the camera above the crowd and clicked the shutter. Next to him, a couple of high school boys frowned.

One boy leaned over to the other. "Don't they have rush hour on Japanese subways?"

"Tourists will take a picture of anything," his friend shrugged.

Little did they realize that depressing the shutter button had opened a hole the size of a pencil lead in the camera face, silently releasing an invisible aerosol into the train.

Uptown, a young man in a beanie and dreadlocks wandered through a gallery of modern art paintings at the Guggenheim Museum. He nervously shook an asthma inhaler in his hand, causing a rattle that made more highbrow patrons look at him with disdain. But he walked on, oblivious to their glances. The young man wandered over to the guardrail above the open-spiral atrium and looked out. Standing at the top of the building, he could see the entire height of the museum and across to the other galleries. Holding his breath, the young man pressed the inhaler discreetly and sent the aerosol out into the atrium. As he wandered down the spiral walkway, he repeated the gesture, each time avoiding notice. Just as it had been dispersed on the train, the aerosolized agent would not be detected for hours. By that time, thousands of New Yorkers would be exposed.

Joshua stood and looked over the back of his chair toward the bay. He was fascinated by the boats motoring past the restaurant's large windows.

"Hun, please sit down in your chair," Lyla instructed, reaching out to him.

Joshua sat on his knees and set his chin on the back of his chair, too entranced to turn around.

"No dear," Lyla sighed. She had hoped he'd stay seated and well-mannered. The restaurant's pirate and nautical-themed decor first grabbed Joshua's interest, but now the view of the bay was a stronger siren.

Kyle's interest was directed toward the flat screen TVs around the restaurant. Some were playing sports highlights; the closest was showing the Baltimore noon news with the sound on. Kyle didn't notice the waitress who had approached their table and taken his father's order.

"And for you, sir?"

Kyle turned toward the waitress. "I'll have the oysters."

The waitress turned to Lyla, who was having trouble getting Joshua to tell his preference.

Kyle turned back to the news, where the image was an aerial shot of the Chesapeake Bay. He could see Galesville harbor, where they now sat.

"This morning, VIMS oceanographers confirmed the presence of red tide in Chesapeake Bay," the anchor said. "Algal blooms now stretch from Maine to the Gulf of Mexico, making it the largest outbreak of red tide in the U.S. in over forty years."

Kyle caught the waitress as she headed toward the kitchen. "Uh, I changed my mind. I'll have a steak."

Mary Ellen Rogers closed her eyes and moaned. Today her life had swung like a pendulum from one extreme to the other. This morning she had experienced one of her greatest moments. Now she felt sicker than she ever had before. As she rolled listlessly in her bed, she wondered how she could have gone from such a height to the lowest depths in one day.

Mary Ellen was a social climber. Born and bred a Texas bluebell, she had been as much a modern debutante as you can get in America. A cheerleader and prom queen in high school, she craved a higher status and bigger social circle than suburban life could offer her. She soon realized that political connections gave her the best option for advancement. After graduating from SMU, she moved to New Orleans, where she met her future husband, George. An up-and-coming lawyer, George had his sights on more than just the South. After several watershed cases, George moved himself into the national spotlight, and Mary Ellen came with him.

For a short while, they lived in San Francisco. The cosmopolitan crowd was good for George, but Mary Ellen felt out of water. He was involved in cases across the nation, and soon began lobbying with international groups as well. Spending months at a time on the road, George considered his home base relatively unimportant. But Mary Ellen was unhappy. George's constant travel put a strain on their marriage, although no more than Mary Ellen's inability to adapt and advance in the San Francisco social scene. By now George was a multimillionaire, and though it gave Mary Ellen every creature comfort she'd ever wanted, she was often left to fend for herself socially. In every place she had lived previously, her slight Texas accent was charming and Southern-genteel. Here she was often mistaken for a hick. Worse, her climb up the ranks of the politically connected was stunted. This disturbed her so greatly that she paid little mind to the way the constant travel changed her husband by degrees. Distraught, she pleaded for her husband to find his way to the East Coast. Washington had always been in her sights, but it wasn't until the spring she turned forty that they finally made the move.

Now, after three years of living in the Beltway, Mary Ellen had reached a new summit—a face-to-face meeting with President James Wallace. Since their move, Mary Ellen had been involved in a number of social and political organizations, working her way up the D.C. food chain. But until today, she had not penetrated the inner circle of the Washington elite. As much as President James Wallace loved the spotlight, he also craved a certain exclusivity. To some, it appeared imperial, but Wallace was savvy enough to recognize keeping select company in Washington would elevate his status to further heights. So when Mary Ellen shook hands with the President at the fundraiser breakfast this morning, she knew she had entered an elite club. Better still, she had her ultimate trophy—a personal photograph of her and the President she could put as a centerpiece in her home. It would provoke conversation, and most of all, it was proof she had schmoozed and rubbed elbows with the most powerful political leader in the world.

Mary Ellen first felt ill when she woke that morning. She thought it was jitters, but soon she realized she had a high fever. That wasn't going to stop her from meeting the President. She had waited three years for this chance…when was another going to come? Besides, she was sure it would pass quickly. She made sure to do her makeup well and put on her most gracious face. She would fight through the fever, and no one would ever know she had it. But by the time she returned from the breakfast, she couldn't lie to herself anymore. The symptoms—sore throat, fever, and general body ache—were similar to the flu, but this sickness hit her with a magnitude she had never experienced before. The sudden and strong effect of this illness frightened her. In her complete misery, she didn't hear her husband return home.

"You enjoy your breakfast with the President, hon?" George called as he climbed the stairs. "You shake his hand?" He now stood in the bedroom doorway.

"George," she called, her voice scratchy. "Please call a doctor."

"What's the matter?"

Something was wrong. It wasn't how Mary Ellen had taken a turn for the worse; it was how George stood in place and looked at her with a strange detachment.

"Please, George," Mary Ellen begged, struggling at every word.

After a moment, George walked over to Mary Ellen's side. He grabbed her purse from the bedside table and pulled out her cell phone. But instead of dialing, he turned the phone over and took out the battery and SIM card.

"George…what are you…" Mary Ellen could only watch in disbelief as George walked to the other side of the room and removed the cordless phone from its cradle. Confused, Mary Ellen looked at her husband. What she saw frightened her. George's eyes were cold. There was an expression she had never seen before, something that made her feel as if she were nothing to him. Without a word, George moved to the door.

Confused and unwilling to believe he would be so uncaring, Mary Ellen pleaded with her husband. "George…help me!"

He turned back and looked at his wife with hatred. He smirked as if somehow he was getting payback for every wrong she had done against him. Yet Mary Ellen couldn't fathom what evil she had done to deserve this. As George left, Mary Ellen heard the door click. She looked at the doorknob and noticed for the first time George had replaced it with a double-locking mechanism. With horror, Mary Ellen realized she was a prisoner in her own home.

George shot his hands in his pockets and sauntered downstairs. A man—the same man who wore a respirator mask on the New York subway—was seated at the dining room table. "It's blooming," George said.

"Good. And she got close to him?" the man asked, his voice muffled under the respirator mask.

"Oh yeah. They emailed the pictures this morning. Couldn't wait to show me." George held up a picture on his cell phone. The President was shaking hands with Mary Ellen. She was standing shoulder-to-shoulder with him.

"Very good."

George rolled up his sleeve. "Now, I need that second vaccination."

"Of course." The man pulled out a syringe and injected it into George's bare arm.

George looked down at his arm and shook it. He stepped back. "Hey, wait…"

George stumbled forward, catching himself on the table. He looked up at the masked man in disbelief. Then he slid slowly to the floor. George's breathing was already shaky, but the masked man pulled a plastic bag over his head and pulled it tight. George gasped, sucking the plastic into his mouth. His limbs were too heavy to resist the masked man. Before long, George slipped into a sleep from which he'd never awaken.

9

Red Horse

The Aral Sea in central Asia is one of the biggest ecological disasters in the world. Once it was one of the four largest lakes on Earth, but Soviet-era irrigation projects steadily diverted water and the Aral shrank, leaving huge plains of salt laced with toxic chemicals. Mirsolav Slobodin stood and looked in wonder at the crumbling remains of the once-bustling port city. Now its fishery stood empty and the rusting hulks of fishing trawlers lay in blowing sand over a hundred miles from water.

A Land Rover cruised over the desert and stopped in front of Slobodin. The man who climbed out of the back seat was over sixty, but he was still fit and held a stiff military bearing. Slobodin swallowed. It had been decades since he had last seen Viktor Zyuganov, and yet Zyuganov's specter chilled him. A long-time general in the GRU, the Soviet military equivalent of the KGB, Zyuganov often evoked such a fear.

Zyuganov, however, seemed at ease. He looked around the ghost town and grinned as he stretched his legs. "Things have changed, huh?"

"Was it necessary to come back here?" Slobodin wanted to get this over with as soon as possible.

"I have questions about that night."

"That was over twenty-five years ago. I told you every-thing then."

Zyuganov placed a hand on Slobodin's shoulder and escorted him to the Land Rover. "Questions that can only be answered here."

Zyuganov was being gentle, yet Slobodin felt coerced. But there was no point in resisting. If he was being marched to the gallows, this was as good a place as any.

Slobodin held to the shred of hope Bondarenko had given him—that Zyuganov's intentions did not include harming him.

"You have to show me."

"Where?" Slobodin asked, almost breathing again.

"On Voz Island."

"It's not an island anymore."

Slobodin climbed into the back seat of the Land Rover and slid over as Zyuganov sat next to him. Zyuganov reached forward and patted his driver on the shoulder, cue-ing him to drive on. The Land Rover hurtled over the barren desert. Before long, the ghost town was obscured in a plume of dust.

Contrary to its name, Vozrozhdeniya, or 'Rebirth' Island, is only a place of death. The secret Soviet bio-weapons program began there in 1948 and continued for the next forty-four years. During that time, Soviet scientists engineered strains of anthrax, smallpox, bubonic plague, and tularemia for military use.

The site was isolated and off-limits to the public, so few knew what happened there—until an incident in 1971. A research ship violated the 40 kilometer quarantine around Voz Island, coming within 15 kilometers of the shore. A lab technician on the ship took plankton samples from the top deck, where she was inadvertently exposed to an airborne field test of smallpox from the island. Given the incubation time for the disease, the technician returned home to the port city of Aralsk and infected nine others before a smallpox diagnosis was made. The patient had been vaccinated against smallpox, but this strain still provoked an infection.

Once the smallpox diagnosis was determined, a massive quarantine program went into effect. All traffic to and from Aralsk was stopped, 50,000 residents were vaccinated, and massive amounts of goods and living space were decontaminated by health officials. The program worked. The outbreak ended with only thirty percent patient mortality and total containment, but the lethality of the bio-agents on Voz Island was confirmed.

In 1992, Slobodin personally supervised the shutdown of the facility following the collapse of the Soviet Union. But the scientists' retreat had been hasty. Several anthrax burial sites remained dangerous. In 2002, fearing the anthrax might fall into the hands of terrorists, the U.S. helped the Uzbekistan government make a thorough decontamination of these burial sites. Still, Voz Island remained a place of mystery and danger.

They had been driving for over two hours when Zyuganov tapped the front seat. "All right, that's the perimeter."

The driver stopped as Zyuganov reached into the cargo area behind him and lifted a large duffel bag. Slobodin watched as Zyuganov pulled out three NBC suits and gas masks with chemical face shields. Standard military protective clothing, these suits shielded the wearer from nuclear, biological, and chemical agents. Slobodin handed a suit and gas mask to each man.

"I thought the site was totally cleaned up; everything's inert," Slobodin said, trying to hide the fear in his voice.

"Just a precaution," Zyuganov said as he robotically pulled on the suit. Slobodin and the driver followed. It wasn't very comfortable dressing in the back seat of the Land Rover, but Slobodin feared climbing out of the car would risk exposure. After banging his elbows and knees several times against the seats, he was finally dressed. The driver had the added discomfort of the steering wheel in front of him, but unlike Slobodin, seemed less bothered by the confines.

Before long, the ruins of Voz Island were visible on the horizon. Slobodin hadn't returned since 1992, and it seemed surreal that the site he had always seen surrounded by water was now in the middle of a desert. The facility itself had also changed. Now the buildings were empty husks. Metal piping around the exteriors was rusting away. In the tattered remnants of a greenhouse, the broken glass of beakers and vials littered the ground. The driver parked the Land Rover by some weathered dock pilings, now half-covered in windswept sand.

As the three men got out, the driver held a metering device in the air. Seeing the readout, he turned to Slobodin and Zyuganov. "We should keep them on, to be safe."

That was fine with Slobodin. He had no intention of removing his mask.

Zyuganov gestured to the ruins of the dock. "You remember the night we transported everything?"

"Like yesterday." Slobodin inferred he didn't have to come here to have his memory jogged.

"How did you do it? Show me."

Slobodin pointed to the pilings, realizing with some

strangeness that he was now standing where there was once at least eight feet of water. "The main load was taken by boat at 2 A.M."

"And the crate I requested?"

"Transported it personally, as you ordered," Slobodin shrugged. He realized his face was sweating, causing his glasses to slip on his nose and bead with perspiration. He wished he could adjust them, but with his gas mask on, there was no hope of that now.

"How?" Zyuganov asked.

Slobodin wondered if he was playing dumb. He knew all these answers.

"I brought it to the docks at midnight, when I met the two escorts you sent. They were in a small boat—they didn't use their motor coming in the last kilometer to keep silent. Everything just as you ordered."

"Who else knew about it?"

Slobodin could feel Zyuganov's eyes boring through him, even from behind the chemical face shield on the mask.

"No one. No scientists, no staff. It was completely secret."

Zyuganov nodded and looked down as he started to pace. It appeared like an innocuous movement, but to Slobodin, something felt predatory in Zyuganov's paces. "And after?"

Slobodin swallowed as sweat ran down his cheek. He summoned up his best tone of conviction. "You know I would never tell."

Zyuganov stopped pacing and looked up at him. "Good." With that perfunctory answer, Zyuganov headed for the Land Rover.

Slobodin was so taken aback by the release of tension that he didn't think to censor himself. "Wait..." he said, striding toward Zyuganov, "that's all you needed to ask me? You didn't need to bring me out here for that."

Zyuganov opened the car door and looked back, smiling beneath his mask. "I wanted to make sure."

Suddenly the pieces started to fit in Slobodin's mind. His relief turned to sudden horror. "The only reason you would ask is if there were a release. Has there been?"

Zyuganov now squared his shoulders toward Slobodin. "Can any trace be linked back to here?"

Slobodin was now raving, words flying from his mouth as his mind raced to consider the consequences. "You saw what happened when that research ship got within thirty miles of here! It caused thirty percent mortality! But that was in the 1970s...the strain you requested is much more lethal!" Slobodin was suddenly hyperventilating and tearing at his suit, trying to pull it off.

"Calm yourself, comrade."

"Don't you understand? You released weaponized smallpox into a worldwide population with no immunity! With this strain, vaccines might not be able to control it!" Slobodin threw open the driver's side door and reached for the wheel. He had to tell someone—anyone—as fast as he could.

Zyuganov looked to the driver, who pulled a Makarov from a shoulder bag and fired it at Slobodin's back. Slobodin's arms flung out as he slid to his knees. Stunned, he looked up at Zyuganov.

"That's not your concern any more, doctor." Zyuganov grasped Slobodin's head and snapped it. The gas mask flopped forward and Slobodin's body sank to the ground.

Zyuganov looked in the Land Rover and saw the blood spatter from the driver's gunshot. "Clean that up." Zyuganov climbed into the back seat and slammed the door shut.

Agent Steve Chase leaned back in his chair and stretched his legs. His duties as the head of the President's Secret Service Protective detail were mostly administrative, but every now and then, the President requested him for duty. Tonight, Wallace had asked him to stick around while he watched the ballgame in his White House living quarters. Secret Service usually made themselves scarce in that portion of the White House, maintaining a perimeter and protecting the First Family's privacy. Chase figured Wallace considered it a magnanimous gesture to watch a ballgame with him, though Chase was still on duty. That made for a slightly awkward arrangement. Chase couldn't sit on the couch with the President, drink a beer with him, or engage in a fully involved discussion. Wallace probably liked it that way—the perfect company for watching a ballgame.

It wasn't always this way. During his first year in office, Wallace had invited several friends to the comfortable White House Theater to watch the Super Bowl. Things nearly got out of hand when Wallace drank too much and got into a heated argument with a friend's brother. Chase and other Secret Service agents had stepped in to defuse the situation, but rumors began to surface that Wallace was an angry drunk, or at least, a bad host. Following the advice of his Chief of Staff and other political advisers, Wallace canceled any further watch parties. It was just as well—Wallace had a talent for public charisma, but privately, he tired of the constant charade. He needed time when he wasn't always on. Ballgames gave him the perfect chance to unwind, and the Secret Service were the perfect company. Besides their restrained participation, Wallace knew he didn't have to censor himself with his detail. Privacy, next to protection, was sacrosanct for the Secret Service.

Wallace began watching a baseball game but quickly found it boring. He'd thrown out first pitches and taken in several games at Nationals Park and Camden Yards, but on TV the game was as interesting as watching paint dry. He flipped over to a preseason NFL game. Preseason wasn't great, but it was football, at least.

"Hope you don't mind watching football, Chase," Wallace said without looking behind him.

"It's your television, Mr. President," Chase smiled.

Wallace found himself in a fouler mood than usual. Washington was too hot and muggy this time of year, but affairs of state wouldn't let him take a vacation yet. He was also facing tremendous pressure with the upcoming election. His opponent, Anne Huntington, was running a strong campaign, and Wallace hadn't much of a record to run on. He was desperate for a new achievement to tout in his campaign, and the day-to-day stresses of the job were getting to him. Every president takes office thinking of what they can do for the country, and beyond that, the prestige and power of the job. They don't consider the toll it takes—evident in the gray hair and weathered faces that mark every president leaving office.

Wallace found himself in a combative mood. He could go for a verbal spar. As president, he was confident his rhetorical abilities would always prevail.

The game was Chargers versus Falcons. It was still in

the first quarter, and the score was tied at seven. "Hope you're not a Chargers fan," Wallace said, pointing at the television with the remote. Chase smiled, though the President couldn't see him sitting behind him. Before joining the Secret Service, he'd served ten years in the Navy and been stationed for three of them in San Diego. He rather liked the Chargers. Wallace knew of his service record and guessed as much.

"At least they aren't wearing those light blue uniforms." Wallace took a sip of beer. "Makes them look like big babies."

"Best uniforms in all of sports," Chase said, still smiling. His cheeriness was his best defense. Wallace was swinging, but Chase was slipping the punches.

Wallace bit into a large potato chip just as a pass squirted through a Falcon receiver's hands, off his knee, and into the waiting arms of a Chargers defensive back. The President scoffed in disgust, lodging the chip in his throat. Choking, Wallace leaned forward and began hacking as he tried to cough the chip out.

Chase reached him in a flash. "Mr. President!" Wallace waved him off as he continued to cough, trying to dislodge the chip. The President turned red, then slumped to the ground as he began to pass out. Chase slapped his hand hard against the President's back. The blow worked. Wallace spit out the remnants of the chip and looked to Chase in relieved thanks. But what Chase saw in the President's mouth alarmed him. It was covered with a growing rash of red lesions.

Chase called into his radio. "Get the President's doctor. *Now.*"

10

Opening Revelation

Kyle made his way across Princeton University's Collegiate Gothic campus. Walking across the sun-drenched quads toward 1879 Hall, he took in the Ivy League atmosphere. Here was knowledge, prestige, and tradition, but also a world decidedly different than his own. Kyle was initially reluctant to consult with an academic. He hadn't much use for one since his own college days. One of his college buddies had gone into academia, and he'd seen how inter-departmental politics played with one's head. Worse, to Kyle, most universities were now populated with like-minded professors. They created an atmosphere where the same thought and speech patterns must be parroted. Kyle felt universities no longer pursued the ostensible goal of intellectual honesty in an open debate of ideas—for all intents and purposes, they were now an echo chamber. But Kyle also conceded if you really wanted to know about a subject, you consulted an expert—and Dr. Richard Hightower was, by all accounts, *the* expert on Revelation.

The door to Dr. Hightower's office was open. Kyle figured the professor must have stepped out for a moment, so he stood inside and waited. Hightower's office was distinctly unlike most college professors' cluttered quarters—it was clean and ordered. The desk had no piles of papers. The books on the shelves were no motley collection of colors, but each had a customized dust jacket that made the rows uniform. The large iron-latticed windows let plenty of light into the room, completing the near-monastic effect.

"Mr. Ferguson?"

Kyle turned to see Dr. Hightower in the doorway. Just like the office, Hightower didn't look at all like he expected. Hightower wore a mock turtleneck and blazer like many professors, but instead of brown tweed, the blazer was dark wool. The turtleneck was also black. Together, the image reminded Kyle more of a Catholic priest than a professor. Hightower's soft-spoken nature also exuded humble scholarship—not the intellectual preening and arrogance he was used to seeing from accomplished academics.

Hightower had a pile of books and student papers under his arm. He shifted the pile to the other arm and offered his hand.

"Dr. Hightower. Thank you for the meeting," Kyle said as he shook hands.

"Not at all." Hightower set the pile of papers on his desk and reordered them. He opened a cupboard door behind his desk and placed the papers and books inside. Kyle watched the ritual with some fascination. Everything in Dr. Hightower's surroundings was neat and ordered. "Although this is the first time I've had a request from the CIA for a meeting. I hope you haven't misread anything in my emails." It had been two and a half years since President Wallace ended the NSA's dragnet, but the psychological effects were still prevalent among the public, even if Hightower was being somewhat facetious.

"No, that would be NSA," Kyle said as he sat across from the professor. "And I'm sure they've misread plenty in mine." Kyle straightened. "Before we begin, I need to tell you that while this consultation is research-based, any sensitive information we discuss would fall under the purview of national security, and you would be required to keep it confidential. Understood?"

"I understand. So what can I do for you?"

"I have some questions about Revelation, such as the seven vials. What do they mean?"

"To answer that, it'd help if I knew your point of reference. Not to pry, but have you ever had a religion class? College? Sunday School?"

"Sunday School as a kid. I've forgotten everything."

"Okay, first, you have to understand the basics regarding the Book of Revelation. There are several main schools of thought regarding its interpretation: some believe it refers to the fall of the Roman empire or other past events. Others see it as purely symbolic. Then there's the popular line of thought that these are future events. If that's true, then we have to remember they were seen in vision over two millennia before they will happen. The language, though evocative, is also open to various interpretations."

Kyle shook his head. Only one question and he was already overwhelmed. "Got an aspirin?"

"That's just the beginning. You mentioned the seven vials? There's also sequences of seven seals and seven trumpets."

Kyle paused, considering what to do next. After a moment, he opened his shoulder bag and pulled out a tablet. He cued up the second Horsemen video and played it for Hightower. "Let's start with this."

Hightower had no trouble understanding the ancient Greek; as a professor of ancient scripture, he read it regularly and recited it on occasion. He watched the video to the end before commenting. "This is an apocalyptic group you're tracking?"

Kyle nodded, then played the first Horsemen video. "This video was received by Voice of the World just before the bombing in Africa." When the video was finished, Kyle cued up the video of the bomber at the stadium. "Given the information we have, we think these are all connected."

Hightower's eyes focused sharply on the video. "This group might be made up of syncretic believers."

"Syncretic?"

"The synthesis of opposing religious beliefs. *'The hour is coming, I almost conceal it'*—that's from the Quran, Verse 15, Sura 20. But the rest of the quotes are from Revelation. And he mentions man's origins are in Africa—that's not Biblical."

"If they incorporate Muslim beliefs, why would they emphasize Revelation?"

"Not surprising for a syncretic group with an emphasis on apocalyptic prophecies. But you should know, according to the Hadith, Muslims believe Jesus is the messiah who will return and defeat the Great Deceiver in the last great battle."

"So they've synthesized various beliefs in an effort to bring about the End Times."

"It's a typical objective for these groups. The Branch Davidians in Waco, Aum in Japan. You'll recall Aum was responsible for the 1995 Sarin gas attack on the Tokyo subway."

"Subway?" Kyle's mind flashed back to his dream, to

the image of the man on the cushioned bench. He now realized it was on a train.

"The question is, who is the intended audience?" Hightower leaned forward. "If you know who they're speaking to, you may know their next target."

Kyle had barely stepped out of 1879 Hall when his cell phone began ringing. "Ferguson."

It was Sadiq. "Where are you?"

From the helicopter, Kyle could see they were rapidly approaching the New York skyline. Sadiq sat across from him, reviewing data on a tablet. "By midnight last night, over three hundred people checked into New York City hospitals, all suffering from flu-like symptoms. By morning it was more than a thousand. The first patients are confirmed smallpox cases."

Kyle felt a pit in his stomach. His nightmare was literally happening. "Any indication of the source?"

"Not yet. There's a smaller group in Washington suffering the same aggressive symptoms."

"Don't they have air sensors throughout New York and Washington?"

"Yeah, installed after 9/11. Outdoors and in large public places like Madison Square Garden. But not in every restaurant, gallery, and small theater. By the time the sensors detected anything, the hospitals were already filling up," Sadiq said.

"Who's in charge of the investigation?"

"FBI. But CDC has flown doctors up to treat and also track the virus. We'll take our cues from them."

Flying over Manhattan, the city looked emptier than

Kyle had ever seen it: no pedestrian traffic, no cars on the streets. New York hadn't been this dead since a major storm.

"The mayor issued a quarantine," Sadiq explained. "All residents have been told to remain home. All public transportation is stopped; airports and train stations are closed. No stock market today. Just as if there had been a storm," he said, confirming Kyle's thought.

"Is it working?"

"So far, so good. The mayor used press conferences to educate the public on smallpox symptoms. We were afraid a lot of hypochondriacs would flood the hospitals, but it hasn't happened so far."

How do you shut down a city of 8 million people, Kyle thought. This wasn't like a major storm. The threat of infection could spread panic. There were stores of smallpox vaccine on hand for cases such as this, but would they take hold when an aggressive virus was spread through a major population?

Kyle hadn't bothered to ask about the reaction beyond New York; after all, the outbreak was here. But while New Yorkers had been very business-like and thorough in their response to the threat, the rest of the nation was taken by surprise. The confirmation that the outbreak was smallpox—a disease known to have been eradicated over a generation ago—showed this was no typical epidemic. This wasn't Ebola, Bird or Swine Flu, or SARS—it was terrorism. Average Americans now knew they were facing a new phase of terrorism that they weren't prepared to encounter.

In a sense, this unpreparedness resulted from success. Nearly twenty years of relative peace on America's shores had lulled the population into a feeling of security. There had been various attacks—such as the Boston Marathon bombing—and numerous near-misses, but there hadn't been a terrorist blow this far-reaching since 9/11. In the meantime, domestic concerns such as the economy and social issues came to the forefront. The wars in the Middle East had exhausted the American people, but there had also been a measure of success in the fight. Osama bin Laden had been killed, Al Qaeda had been pushed back, and the military and intelligence agencies had successfully prevented any further large terrorist attacks on American soil. The terror threat hadn't gone away, but American citizens were happy to see it pushed far into their rearview mirror. Now it was right in their faces.

The helicopter navigated to a pad on the roof of a hospital. A policeman escorted Kyle and Sadiq to an anteroom just outside the isolation unit. From the anteroom, they could see through a large window to the isolation ward. Normally only two or three patients would lie here under clear plastic tents, but now there were dozens. The doctor on duty introduced himself as Philip Reyes and briefed them on the overall timeline of the outbreak.

Kyle looked through the window at the patients. "I want to talk with them."

"It's not very safe," Reyes began to protest.

Kyle walked over to a wall where several hazmat suits hung from hooks. He lifted one and gestured toward Reyes.

"Well, yeah," Reyes stammered.

Kyle and Sadiq began to put the suits on. They had only gotten up to their waists when a middle-aged doctor entered the room. Reyes tried to introduce her. "Uh, this is Dr. Carol Klaussen from the CDC, she's—"

Klaussen cut him off. "Sorry fellas, but you're not

going in there." There was an air of finality in her voice. She was the head of the CDC's investigation and had taken control of the isolation ward.

"We need to ask them questions," Kyle said.

"No way. Not unless you've had a year of pathogenic hazard training." She motioned to the window. "You can watch behind the glass."

Kyle threw down his suit. "Fine. You got an intercom? Two-way radio? A phone?"

Reyes shook his head. "Sorry. We're not set up for that."

Ferguson turned to the police escort. "Don't you have a two-way radio?"

"Can't let you use it," the policeman said. "Besides, I wouldn't get it back."

Kyle was about to protest when Klaussen cut in. "He's right. It'd have to go through decontamination. When dealing with a contagion as dangerous as this, the process would basically destroy the electronics."

"Are you going in there?" Kyle asked Dr. Klaussen.

"I can. Dr. Reyes will."

Kyle turned to Sadiq. "Give him your phone."

"Mine?" Sadiq hesitated.

"Yeah, come on, come on." Kyle's patience was about gone.

"Why can't you use your phone?"

Kyle glared in response.

"Look," Sadiq protested, holding out his phone. "I've got pictures of my puppy on there."

"Back them up." Kyle looked at the screen and saw a picture of a Boston Terrier in a sombrero. He turned to the policeman. "Think you can make a case for animal cruelty?"

The policeman leaned in to look at the picture. "Oh yeah."

"See?" Kyle turned to Sadiq. "You won't need it anyway."

Dr. Reyes made his rounds in the isolation ward, checking on each of the patients as Kyle and Sadiq watched from the window outside. One patient, a high school boy, caught Kyle's eye. The boy's condition was more advanced than many of the other patients—all visible parts of his body were covered in telltale whitish bumps. His breathing was labored, and from the number of machines and tubes connected to his body, it was apparent he was not long for this world. Kyle tapped the glass to get Reyes' attention.

"That one," he said, pointing to the boy. "We want to ask him questions."

Dr. Reyes checked the placard above the boy's bed, then held the phone, set on speaker, close to his mask. "His name's Jaxon." His voice was muffled through the suit, but still understandable. Reyes sat down next to the boy and laid Sadiq's phone on the bedside table.

"Hi Jaxon. We need to ask you some questions. I know this may be difficult, but it's important."

The boy nodded.

"When did the symptoms start?"

Jaxon strained to speak. "Around 8 o'clock yesterday night."

Dr. Klaussen stood next to Kyle and Sadiq in the anteroom, listening on Kyle's phone. "Around the same time for most patients in the first wave. They're all progressing rapidly."

"Doesn't smallpox usually take two weeks to incubate?" Kyle asked.

"Yes," Klaussen confirmed. "And the course of the infection several days." She stepped toward the glass. "That boy has hours to live."

"Sounds like a weaponized form of smallpox."

"Without a doubt."

Sadiq stared at the boy in grim fascination. "Engineered in a lab. But where?"

Dr. Reyes continued his questioning. "What else did you do yesterday?"

"Just went to school."

Kyle tried to ask Reyes a question, but it was clear the doctor couldn't hear him through his hazmat suit. Kyle quickly jotted down a note and held it up to the glass, tapping again to get Reyes' attention. Kyle pressed the note against the glass: *Ride subway?*

"How do you get to school?" Reyes asked.

"I—" Jaxon coughed painfully. "I take the Number 7 Express."

"Subway?"

"Yeah."

"Did you notice anything unusual on the train yesterday?"

Kyle leaned into the glass, his breath leaving a slight fog as he waited in anticipation.

"No."

Kyle's shoulders slumped at the answer. He laid a hand on the glass and looked down.

Jaxon turned his head and groaned. "Wait."

Kyle jerked up his head in anticipation.

"There was a tourist…from Japan I think," Jaxon said,

struggling at every word. "He had on a mask. He was taking pictures." Jaxon paused to catch his breath. "Who takes pictures on the subway?"

"No selfies?" Reyes asked.

"No. Just like of the car. It was weird."

"And he had on a mask?"

"Yeah, sorta like one doctors wear…like he didn't want to get sick."

Outside, Kyle and Sadiq were writing notes furiously.

"Tell us more."

Reyes questioned several other patients before going through a decontamination chamber and returning to the anteroom. "Well, it looks like we may have an established timeline," he said. "Over half the patients in the first wave were on that Number 7 Express yesterday morning."

Sadiq looked to Kyle. "You were right."

"What about the rest?"

"They contracted it someplace else, maybe a museum. We're trying to track that down," Reyes said.

"Which one?"

"The Guggenheim," Klaussen said flatly.

Kyle shook his head. This wasn't good news. If it were true, the virus could have been spread to thousands.

"Keep it quiet until we confirm, okay?" Klaussen added with some trepidation.

Kyle wasn't listening. He was looking through the window into the isolation room, where a seven year-old boy lay convulsing. Like Jaxon, he was dying. Kyle was disturbed by the sight. It was too close to one he had seen before.

It was five years earlier when Kyle's son Adam lay in a Washington, D.C. hospital. Kyle maintained a constant vigil at Adam's bedside, but the boy's body was shattered. Covered in bandages and tubes, Adam's body was largely kept alive by machines. The sucking and wheezing of the respirator and the beeping rhythm of the heart monitor were not comforting noises, but Kyle willed them to stay steady and strong. Most of all, he prayed. He had always been able to address his boy's needs and fix any problem, from scraped knees to fears of monsters under the bed. But Kyle found this challenge was beyond him. This he couldn't fix. He could only turn to a higher power. "Please…please," he whispered. "I will give anything." Kyle's words were more earnest than anything he had ever said. "Bring him back to me. Please let him live. I would give anything." He held Adam's hand. "I will give *everything.*"

Kyle got his answer almost immediately. The rhythmic beeping of the heart monitor shifted into a solid flatline tone.

"No!" Kyle cried.

Medical staff swarmed around Adam. A large male nurse began to pull Kyle away from the bed. "We need space to work now," he said, his tone much more comforting than his strong grip.

"No!" Kyle shouted again in disbelief. The room was now abuzz with urgent chatter as the doctors and nurses tended to Adam. Above all was the insistent tone of the flat-lined heart monitor.

"Let us help him," the nurse said as he forcefully pulled Kyle into the hall.

Kyle's arms flailed as he wrestled against the nurse's grip. Everything was happening too fast.

"We're going to do our best for your boy," the nurse said, now shoving him against the far wall in the hallway.

He stretched out his arm and held the palm forward, like a policeman barring Kyle from the scene. "Just give us some room!"

Kyle raised his hands to his head and gave a haunting cry. "Adam!"

Half an hour later, Kyle was back in Adam's room. This time, it was silent. Adam lay still in the bed. The tubes were disconnected, the machines were off. Daylight streamed through white drapes, but Kyle sat in darkness. He had reached out to God—had prayed more ardently than he ever had in his life—and he had gotten no answer.

Kyle had never questioned God's existence—for him there was too much evidence of a creator. The organization of all living cells is too intricate. The blue and green planet Earth, with its perfect mix of breathable air and sustainable water and soil, a rotating ball of life in the vast emptiness of space is too perfect. In that galactic Petri dish where creation occurs, you could throw together biological putty an infinite number of times and not be able to guarantee the life that exists on Earth. Even with prime conditions for life, organics do not grow without seeds. Advanced life does not exist without structure and organization. To assert the order of life occurs by random chance seemed illogical to Kyle. Someone had carefully and deliberately given life its organization. It is noteworthy that skeptics often point to science as proof that God does not exist, for while science can explain the methods of nature, it does nothing to explain or disprove the author of them. Kyle concluded that despite the numerous interpretations of various religions—with that many, someone has to be wrong—there had to be a Creator.

But sitting by the bed that held the lifeless shell of his

son's body, the cold, hard truth hit him: God existed—but in his own life, what did it matter? For all the magnificence of creation, if God did not answer the desperate cries of a father for his son, then what did it matter?

It seemed strange that God would put so much effort into creation and then leave it to its own devices. If God was dead was a matter of rumination far beyond his intellectual depth. All he knew was when he needed God, when he cried out to him, he was left cold, alone, and with the broken remains of his son.

Kyle hadn't been to church in years, but the pastor from his church appeared in the doorway. Kyle didn't turn, so the pastor approached respectfully and sat down next to him. After a long silence, the pastor comfortingly placed his hand on Kyle's shoulder.

Why?" Kyle said hoarsely. The question came from deep within him.

"God's ways are not always ours," the pastor said slowly, measuring his response with restrained sympathy. "Just as his timing is not always—"

"Why are you here?" Kyle asked, correcting him.

"Christ commanded his disciples to 'mourn with those that mourn, and comfort those in need of comforting'."

"That means nothing to me."

The answer threw the pastor off, and his jaw dropped in shock before he could collect himself. "Don't let your grief swallow—"

Kyle turned to the pastor, his eyes hot with tears. Still, his gaze bored through the man. "If God doesn't listen to his children, what good is he?"

Before the pastor could respond, Kyle cut him off. "Never," he said bitterly. "Never again."

11

Contagion

Sadiq watched as the skyscrapers of Manhattan receded into the distance. When they had vanished beyond the horizon, he turned to Kyle. "I can't believe you made me give up my phone."

"Spilled milk." Kyle didn't look up from his own phone. Sadiq thought he was rubbing it in, but Kyle was looking at breaking news. "Looks like we're not the only targets. There's a smallpox outbreak in Brazil, El Salvador, and Kenya."

"Same strain?"

"Looks that way."

"Why those countries?"

Kyle shook his head. "Don't know."

"What's the word on Washington?"

Kyle checked his phone. "Forty-three confirmed cases."

"Much lower than New York."

"Must be person-to-person contact, not airborne dispersal."

"Right."

Kyle continued to read, then stopped and looked up.

"What?"

"Every victim in Washington attended a presidential fundraiser yesterday morning."

As soon as Kyle and Sadiq reached CIA headquarters in Langley, they reported to a buzzing Operations Center. Olivia Parks was hunched over a computer station with two men.

"What's the hope for containment?" Kyle asked Parks.

"We don't know. The CDC and the World Health Organization are liaising with the Kenyan, Brazilian, and Salvadoran governments. Here, they're hoping quarantines will work, but we'll know in a few hours."

"How many are dead so far?" Sadiq asked.

"We're still working on figures for that," one of the men said.

"This is Dr. Sidney Kross, CDC," Parks introduced the man. "And Special Agent Ben Sherman, FBI," she pointed to the other man. "They're working with us."

"We just saw the patients in New York," Kyle said. "Do you think this will spread?"

"We'll know in a few hours," Kross repeated.

"We do have a break, though. We've identified Patient Zero." Sherman pointed to a television screen, where EMTs in hazmat suits were wheeling a gurney with a BioSealed body bag to an ambulance. "Mary Ellen Rogers. D.C. Police recovered her body this morning from her home in Georgetown. A friend went by after she hadn't answered her phone for a day. Just wish we could have kept it out of the media."

"CDC's already conducted an autopsy," Dr. Kross explained. "She was the most advanced of these cases, including New York. Probably succumbed around three in the morning."

Kyle frowned. "Why didn't she seek treatment?"

"We don't know," Kross said.

"She might have been kept from it," Sherman interjected. "Her bedroom door was locked from the outside. The phone was removed."

"Who did that?" Parks asked.

"Probably the husband. He's dead too; suicide by suffocation."

"Who are they?" Kyle asked.

Sherman opened a report and summarized it. "George and Mary Ellen Rogers. He was an attorney, quite successful, international clients. She was a Washington socialite, politically connected. Quite a fan of the President."

Parks was working on another screen. "Oh no."

"What?" the question came in unison.

Parks brought the image on her computer up on the wall screen. "This was taken yesterday."

It was a picture of the President and Mary Ellen Rogers shaking hands.

The James S. Brady Press Briefing Room is known by millions around the world for televising daily presidential briefings and other press conferences. Less known is the room's original purpose: an indoor pool that was specifically installed for FDR's polio therapy. President Nixon covered the pool in 1969 to build the briefing room and expanded press offices next door. When Wallace, an avid swimmer, took office, he considered reverting the room to its original state and holding press briefings in the White House Theater. But Wallace's advisors convinced him that forcing the press corps out and making them traipse over to the East Wing would seem imperial. Additionally, the room had been renamed in honor of the press secretary who had been paralyzed in the assassination attempt on Reagan, so changing the space for the President's private use would have been in bad taste. Still, Wallace privately joked that he should have installed a trap door in the briefing room. Then he could end a particularly confrontational briefing by dunking the whole press corps. Fitting, Wallace said, since in his opinion the press were all wet. Press Secretary Maya McManus sorely wished for that trap door now. The press corps was clamoring for information, and she had little to give.

McManus stood at the podium and tried to quell the rising tide of frustration. She was failing.

"Why hasn't the President made a statement?" a reporter on the first row shouted over the tumult.

"I'm about to deliver his statement, if you'll let me," McManus said.

"Why isn't he making it?" came the retort.

"We've heard the President is in seclusion," another reporter shouted. "Why is he hiding when the American people are in danger?"

"Was the President infected?" a third reporter asked. "What's his condition?"

McManus ignored the questions and went ahead with her statement, hoping the reporters would quiet down as she spoke. "The President recognizes the magnitude of this situation, and he's meeting with his top advisors right now to take action."

A new flurry of questions erupted, sending the room into chaos.

The Presidential Emergency Operations Center lies in a bunker six stories under the White House's East Wing. It was built during World War II and designed to withstand a nuclear bomb. The PEOC features an Executive Briefing Room much like the White House Situation Room under the West Wing, but this facility is much deeper underground. Vice President Cheney was escorted there during the 9/11 attacks. The PEOC is part of a larger bunker which serves as both an emergency shelter and evacuation point for the President. In addition to the Executive Briefing Room, there is a small living quarters with bunker furnishings and an infirmary. Now Vice President Earl Townsend, Attorney General Winston Hodge, and Pete Standish headed down an underground corridor to the bunker. Their Secret Service escort swiped a keycard on a secure door and led them into an anteroom where two other Secret Service agents stood guard. A nurse handed each of the men surgical masks and gave brief instructions not to touch anything. The Secret Service escort swiped his keycard on a second door, and the men were led into the infirmary.

President Wallace lay in the single hospital bed, covered with a clear plastic tent. An IV bag and heart monitor stood next to his bed. The President's doctor sat in a chair next to him, keeping vigil. Secret Service Agent Steve Chase stood at the far end of the room. Wallace looked clearly weak and scarred; the smallpox sores covered his face and arms. His eyes were half shut.

"Mr. President," Standish spoke first, trying to remain upbeat.

"Pete," the President opened his eyes slowly and weakly acknowledged.

"We heard the CDC got a doctor here right away." None of the visitors had enough medical knowledge to know the sores were receding, but they had been briefed by the medical staff that the President was improving.

"And the outlook is good," Townsend said.

"Is that what all of you came to tell me? I've got doctors for that," Wallace sneered.

Well, his temperament hasn't changed, Standish thought.

Attorney General Hodge cleared his throat. "Mr. President, we think it's time to invoke the 25th Amendment."

Wallace shook his head emphatically.

"It was written for this kind of situation," Hodge pressed. "It takes care of the country and lets you focus on your recovery."

Townsend stood to the back of the group and shifted nervously. Since he'd be the one to temporarily receive the President's powers, he knew he'd be the target of Wallace's wrath.

"It's only temporary," Standish said, backing Hodge up.

"No," Wallace growled, his voice growing stronger.

Hodge was insistent. "If you slip into a coma—"

"Winny, as long as I'm awake, I'm in charge." Wallace's eyes were wide with fury.

Hodge was especially irritated when Wallace called him Winny. "And if you lose your ability to talk?"

"Then you get me one of those Stephen Hawking machines."

Townsend shook his head. This wasn't going well at all, and Standish and Hodge weren't getting through to the President.

"They came after me. *Me!*" Wallace nearly shouted.

The doctor shot up and reached over to the President. This was too much exertion.

"You get them. That's your first order. *Get them!*" Wallace was taking a national security matter far too personally. True, the attack had targeted him, but he was now operating on emotion—a dangerous point of reference for a president's decision-making.

Standish determined he'd keep Wallace out of the loop as much as possible. If they couldn't put the 25th Amendment into effect yet, he'd at least try to minimize Wallace's involvement. He and the President were old friends, but he had never seen him this bad off.

The concrete cellar was dour and gray, with a long corridor leading off to several rooms. Knox could easily imagine the horrors that had gone on behind their closed doors. This was a black site where Ukrainian intelligence prisoners had been taken long before the CIA's post-9/11 programs. Petrusiv led him to the end of the corridor and stopped. "So, our agreement?"

Knox handed him a thumb drive. "As requested."

Petrusiv shook the thumb drive with emphasis. "This is only the first, correct?"

"Two-way street. But again, be careful how you use that." Knox nodded toward the door. "Who's in there?"

A scuffling sound reverberated from the other side of the door.

"An arms dealer," Petrusiv explained. "Anton Bondarenko."

"What's his connection?"

"He made contact with Miroslav Slobodin last week."

"The former head of the Soviet bio-weapons program? His wife reported him missing two days ago."

"We know," Petrusiv said slyly.

"What else?"

"They're both connected to Viktor Zyuganov."

"The GRU general? How?"

"Slobodin mentioned Zyuganov when they last met. We're pressing to find out more."

"Press harder," Knox said. "Time's a factor."

Dr. Stanley Igbo stood and looked over the waiting room of his small Kenyan hospital. Normally there was an average of 60 patients waiting for treatment; today, the numbers had swelled to over 200. Worse still, many of them already had smallpox lesions breaking out on their faces and arms. His staff of eight doctors and twelve nurses were completely overwhelmed. Quarantining the smallpox patients was impossible—there simply wasn't enough space. Igbo worried the disease might spread to other patients, including two women giving birth.

The waiting room offered no protection for family members escorting the sick. After sitting an hour with his infected mother, a teenage boy broke out in lesions himself. The disease was spreading before Igbo's eyes.

Most chilling was what they had to do with the dead. Once the hospital's morgue filled up, two nurses in hazmat suits began to take the bodies to a field behind the hospital. They piled up the dead and set them ablaze in a massive funeral pyre. Igbo watched as the nurses piled on more bodies. There were over twenty of them now. Igbo stood clear of the smoke, but his nostrils still filled with the smell of cremation. Smallpox had once been eradicated from the Earth, so what caused its return? Igbo watched the flames rise and felt this was the wrath of God.

Kyle was still working over the information in the CIA's Operations Center. "So Mary Ellen Rogers looks healthy when she shakes hands with the President, and is dead less than 12 hours later."

"That's an incredibly fast course for smallpox," Dr. Kross said.

"The incubation period looks to be 12 hours instead of 12 to 14 days. And it's contagious before the symptoms appear," Kyle assessed, looking over his notes.

"How do we know that?" FBI Agent Sherman asked.

"Looking at that 12-hour window, no one else's symptoms showed up until hours after her smallpox must have been in full bloom. She's the first in Washington. That makes her the carrier."

"How could she be contagious without showing any symptoms?" Sadiq asked.

Dr. Kross pointed to the picture of Mary Ellen and the President. "Well, there would be symptoms, but they wouldn't be noticeable to others at first. Smallpox lesions begin inside the mouth."

"But how long after she was infected?" Kyle asked. It was the key to tracing the virus' origin.

"Hard to say," Dr. Kross shrugged. "Could have been only hours. She was probably infected the night before."

"That means she could have been sleeping when someone infected her," Sadiq said.

"That's a possibility," Kross agreed.

"So far we're dealing in conjecture." Larsen tried to focus the discussion. "What do we know for sure?"

"Agent Sherman and I contacted the FBI's New York office," Kyle said. "They're looking into video from stations along the 7 Express route. Based off a teenage patient's report, they found this." Kyle brought up a still image from a video on the wall screen. It showed an overhead camera's view of a subway platform. Dozens of people were exiting a train, but Kyle highlighted one in particular—a man with an N100 mask. "They tracked his movements from each camera until he boarded a train to D.C."

"Did the FBI subpoena all security cameras near the Rogers' home?" Sadiq asked Agent Sherman. "Georgetown has a lot of them."

"And a lot of them are private, close-circuit systems," Sherman said. "But yeah, we did."

"What'd it bring up?"

"This." Sherman punched up a video on the wall screen. The camera was on the side of a neighbor's house, but the vantage point included the back of the Rogers' home. Within seconds, a man appeared from the back alley and knocked on the back door. Sherman paused the video when the man's face was turned towards the camera. Zooming in, it became apparent the man was wearing an N100 mask. Parks helped bring the image into a split-screen comparison with the still from the New York subway.

"It's a match," Sherman said.

"Where'd he go after visiting the Rogers' house?" Larsen asked.

"We're still tracking that."

"Who is he?"

"New York tried identifying him and failed," Sherman said.

Parks was running a search on her computer. Within moments, she had the result. "So have we."

"The mask leaves too many variables," Sherman said. "Sure, the computer can identify eyes and the overall shape of the face, but without the nose and mouth, we can't register an ID match."

"Is it possible he's not in our databases?" Kyle asked.

"Possible. Not likely, but possible," Sherman said.

Larsen didn't like this dead end. Still, they had made progress. "Keep at it."

Petrusiv removed the thick gloves from his hands as he exited the small room. In the dim light of the corridor, Knox could see they were wet, but not what was on them. He could guess.

"And?" Knox asked.

Petrusiv sighed. It had been a long night getting this information. "Zyuganov took the bomb from Russian stock—made it disappear through an accounting error during the Soviet demise. Same with the smallpox."

"Does he have more?"

"Bondarenko doesn't know."

The two men walked up a stairwell. As they opened the outside door, the first light of dawn greeted them.

"Then we'll have to talk to Zyuganov, won't we?"

Petrusiv hesitated. It was only for a moment, but Knox caught it.

"You know where he is."

Though caught, Petrusiv wasn't about to give in. "I never said—"

"These attacks have killed tens of thousands. More could die."

Petrusiv lowered his voice. Although the courtyard was completely deserted, he looked around. He'd prefer to write this information down and burn it, but he didn't have the time. "We have a man embedded with Zyuganov. Leonid Zavin. He's extremely valuable to us. He *cannot* be touched."

"Understood."

Director of National Intelligence Maxwell Foley stepped into the elevator next to CIA Director Leslie Farrell and waited for the doors to close. Once the floor numbers began rising, Foley turned to the CIA Director.

"Have you heard from *ORACLE*?"

Farrell grimaced. "Not since the bombing."

"Then your agent could be rogue. If any of our own people could have contributed to this—to hurt us this way, it would be *ORACLE*."

"I know. But I don't think that's what's happened."

"How do you know?"

That was the problem. There hadn't been any word—any evidence of *ORACLE* since the African bombing. The agent had either been obliterated in the blast, or had disappeared like a ghost. Still, Farrell wasn't about to give up hope.

"Because if anyone could have protected us from this—stopped it before it started—it would have been *ORACLE*."

The elevator dinged and the doors opened. Their privacy gone, Foley dropped the subject. Farrell followed him down the corridor to the large and noisy conference room. Farrell still had one topic she wanted to breach before the meeting.

"When my guys came to give the President his daily briefing this morning, they told me you sent them away. What gives?"

"I'll explain in a moment." Foley took his place at the front of the room. The conference table was crowded with top- and mid-level intelligence officials, including NSA

Director Ronald Hudson, FBI Director Bill Taft, and National Security Advisor Pete Standish.

"All right, everyone," Foley said, calling the room to order. "I've just received word from the CDC. Brazil, El Salvador, and Kenya are all in the midst of an epidemic. New York now has over 3,000 cases and an 80% mortality rate. Despite quarantines, that could jump to 10,000. Washington is lower, but it doesn't look good for those that are infected."

The statistics plunged the room into somber silence.

"Now, I only want to know two things," Foley said. "One, why didn't we have any warning of these attacks, and two, what are we doing about it?"

Foley's military tone commanded attention, but the room was filled with an unsettling silence.

"Why are we playing catch up?" Foley demanded.

"We had the threads of something, but received no specific data concerning a biological attack," Farrell finally said.

"Let's hear it." Foley sat and leaned back.

Farrell turned to Kyle, who was seated in the second row behind the large conference table. Kyle stood. "Three days ago, a contact at Voice of the World received this video." Kyle cued up the video that spoke of the first vial and played it on a wall screen. "The speaker quotes the Book of Revelation in ancient Greek, specifically referencing pouring out a vial that causes a 'grievous sore.' This same group delivered another video prior to the African bombing, claiming responsibility for it."

"Has this checked out?" Foley asked.

"We've scrubbed the videos," NSA Director Hudson

said. "Technically, there's nothing noteworthy, but they seem legitimate."

Sadiq, who was seated next to Kyle, stood and spoke up. "Voice analysis indicates the speaker in the video is of Middle Eastern origin, possibly Oman, and was educated in the U.K."

"Conclusions?" Foley asked.

"Analysis suggests this is a new apocalyptic group with syncretic beliefs," Kyle said.

"So this is an unknown terrorist group with at least one nuclear weapon and a stockpile of smallpox." Foley's displeasure was clear. How this had slipped past the intelligence community was beyond him. "Where are they?"

Farrell answered haltingly. "We're working on it."

FBI Director Taft spoke up. "We identified a suspect in both the New York and Washington attacks. We tracked him to Dulles Airport, where he boarded a plane to Paris."

Farrell grimaced. "The French lost track of him."

"Great. What else do we have?" Foley insisted.

"There's no signals intelligence," Hudson said with some admiration. It was a major achievement for a modern terrorist group to launch large-scale attacks without emails, phone calls, or wire transfers.

"But if the same group is responsible for both attacks, there has to be something," Foley said.

"Every lead we track comes to a dead end," Hudson explained. "Frankly, it's like tracking a—"

"Ghost," Farrell finished the thought.

A man in a decorated naval uniform spoke up. This was Admiral Bill Judkins, head of Naval Intelligence. "We have one lead. Liaising with other intelligence agencies, we've tracked an arms dealer who met last week with Miroslav Slobodin."

"Slobodin?" Foley perked up. "We learned he went missing last week."

"And was found shot to death this morning in Kazakhstan," Farrell said, raising a murmur throughout the room.

"What else?"

"The arms dealer, Slobodin, and a GRU General Zyuganov were all wrapped up in the same business," Admiral Judkins said.

"Do we know Zyuganov's whereabouts?" Foley asked.

"We're sending a surveillance team there now," Judkins concluded.

"Good. Any more?"

Silence filled the room again.

"That's it," Farrell finally volunteered the answer.

"Thousands of Americans are dying because we failed," Foley clenched his teeth. "Now, this doesn't leave this room—but the President is lying in a bed right now, infected with smallpox. The doctors and the CDC say he'll pull through, but *everything* is riding on us resolving this threat."

Murmurs rippled through the room at the news. There had been rumors that the President had been infected, but until now, there had been no confirmation. In the hubbub, no one noticed an aide slip into the room, walk up to Foley, and whisper into his ear. "Excuse me, sir, but you'll want to see this."

The aide switched the wall screen to a TV news broadcast. The anchor appeared above a caption that read *Breaking News*. "A terrorist group has claimed responsibility for the nuclear attack in Africa and recent outbreak of smallpox throughout the world." The screen shifted to the silhouette against the blood-red backdrop. The anchor's voice continued over the video. "The group, calling themselves The Horsemen, released videos before each of the attacks. We have also learned that President Wallace is infected with smallpox, and is currently being treated in a guarded isolation unit."

"Oh no," Farrell gasped. She looked at Standish, whose mouth was agape. He was also turning pale.

Foley's face flushed red with rage as he turned to the room. "What?" he bellowed. "Who told?"

12

The Second and Third Vials

It didn't take long for news of the President's illness to ignite national discussion. News outlets on the internet, television, radio, and print immediately publicized the link between the African bombing and smallpox outbreak. As the story spread, it mutated into sensationalism. The political slants came first. President Wallace's critics said the outbreak was the inevitable result of his national security policies. Those on Wallace's side pivoted and blamed the long history of America's overreaching foreign policy. The President had turned the country's focus inward, but America's decades-long interventionist — even imperialist — actions were destined to create blowback. The first dose was 9/11. This was next.

Of course, all of this political division was typical for the media. The 24-hour news channels were filled with commentary that served their respective political bases; rather than promote real civic discussion, they entrenched their positions and helped widen the political divide in America. That wasn't the only effect. In an effort to fill broadcasting hours, non-stories became stories, and real stories were beaten to death with commentary.

Kyle, like many of his colleagues, wondered how the media would influence the reaction to another major attack.

In many ways, 9/11 occurred in another era; 24-hour news was still in its childhood. While CNN was firmly established, Fox News and MSNBC were nothing close to their present iterations. Social media was non-existent: MySpace, Twitter, and Facebook were yet to come. Most Americans' cell phones hardly took photos, and none streamed video.

When the first plane hit the twin towers, millions of Americans were still in their cars on their way to work or sitting in classrooms. They heard reports on the radio or second-hand accounts from those who had seen the news. Only those who turned on their televisions in time to watch the second plane hit could begin to fathom what was really happening. Kyle himself had been in his car when he heard the news on the radio; he, like many Americans, thought the first plane had been some small, wayward turboprop. He arrived at work in time to watch some of the first replays of the second plane crashing. He saw firsthand as smoke rose from the Pentagon some miles away, then watched with other Americans in collective disbelief as the towers fell.

The 24-hour news channels changed with 9/11. In the first hours and days, Americans were glued to their televisions, waiting for an absolution. There was a tremendous dissonance between what they wanted to believe and what their eyes saw. They couldn't grasp that the World Trade Center was gone. They couldn't believe nearly 3,000 people were pulverized in a pile of rubble; they wanted to believe that somehow there was a pocket of air where dozens were trapped alive and relatively unharmed.

As overwhelmed as the nation was by the tragedy, the event galvanized the American people. Al Qaeda ultimately underestimated the strength of the country—neither the

American economy nor the overall fabric of society collapsed with the fall of the towers. But what about the next massive attack, or series of attacks? Would the instant widespread reaction be a tool for awareness, or a weapon to spread fear? At what point would the endless theorizing on news channels and social media become a maelstrom of panic?

Kyle would know the answers soon enough. For into this world of endless and over-saturated news and information came the Apocalypse Men.

As fate would have it, this was the name that stuck with the American public, and it came about with a slip of the tongue. A TV reporter in New York stumbled over his words in a live broadcast, saying the "Apocalypse Men" instead of his intended "Horsemen of the Apocalypse." The station's top news producer encouraged the use of the term, and before long "The Apocalypse Men" was in the public consciousness.

Inevitably, the attacks also ignited religious arguments, and these were the most divisive of all. Atheists and agnostics pointed to the Apocalypse Men as one more example of religious zealotry provoking violence. The Council of Catholic Bishops took a measured approach and called the attacks "horrific acts of violence" but avoided any discussion of the group's tenants. Evangelical Christian groups varied in their response by congregation. However, several televangelists such as Ed Sheffield, whose weekly broadcasts were syndicated nationwide, were most enthusiastic in proclaiming this was, indeed, a fulfillment of Biblical prophecy. Combined with an explosion of apocalyptic theories on social media such YouTube and Facebook, these preachers stirred the public into a frenzy. Panic spread across the country. Kyle figured that might have been the Horsemen's intention all along.

In Nevada, Clive Cordell had long waited for news of such attacks. An unapologetic Prepper, Cordell anticipated this day since he first saw Ed Sheffield's sermons twenty years ago. Won over immediately by Sheffield's preaching of tribulation, he began stocking up food and supplies in his Nevada home. When his garage and spare bedrooms were overflowing, Cordell saved up and purchased a remote mountain cabin. Far from living a variation of the Boy Scout motto "Be Prepared," Cordell was convinced the world was on the precipice of self-destruction, and when the hour finally came, he'd live with the self-satisfaction of watching it burn while he thrived. Clive's devotion to Sheffield's predictions was complete. Eight years before, his wife had gotten fed up and given him an ultimatum: either get rid of all his survival gear and give Sheffield's program the boot, or she'd be gone. Cordell didn't have to think twice about his answer. What's a wife compared to being ready for the Day of Judgment?

Listening to Sheffield's latest speech, Cordell knew that day was imminent. He packed his pickup truck and trailer, then sat down to watch one last broadcast. His cabin didn't have TV reception, and Cordell didn't need it. But he would miss listening to the good ol' reverend.

Sheffield was always an animated preacher. Standing onstage with sweat glistening from his forehead, Sheffield raised his Bible high. "God's judgment is on America," he roared, sounding almost like a professional wrestler. "For decades we have preached that God would not tolerate the sins, the fornication, the lying and backbiting of this country." Sheffield emphasized each sin by pointing his finger to the ground as he named them.

Cordell cleaned his 12-gauge shotgun as he listened. "Amen."

Sheffield looked into the camera, trying to send his gaze straight through to his viewers. "Now God's judgments are here. I speak to those who have not listened. We have tried to help you, but since you wouldn't listen, you are now left to yourselves. This nation has turned from God, and God's judgments are just."

Cordell wiped down the barrel of his shotgun and snapped it back into place. Then he turned off the television and walked out to his truck. He checked the padlock on the trailer and placed the shotgun on the gun rack at the back of the cab. Clive set his shoulders back with satisfaction. He had listened to the reverend, and he was prepared. The 'civilized' world would crawl over itself as it fought its inevitable destruction. Cordell would retreat to the mountains to await the glory to come. As he drove away, he didn't bother looking back at his home. Cordell was content to watch his rearview mirror as the world was obscured in a plume of dust.

Kyle and Sadiq had been working the Apocalypse Men videos for days, but had little to show for their work.

"You know what doesn't make sense to me?" Sadiq rubbed his eyes. "Targeting Brazil, El Salvador, and Kenya. Why not just the U.S.?"

Kyle ran a hand through his hair and scratched his scalp as he thought. "I don't know. Demonstration of power, I guess. It shows the length of their reach."

"Makes sense. But why those countries specifically?"

Kyle looked at the mountain of files they had examined. They hadn't given them any answers, least of all to this question. "Dr. Hightower said we should look for the intended audience."

"So what do Brazil, El Salvador, the U.S., and Kenya all have in common that makes them the intended audience?"

Kyle typed in a search profile on his computer. "Hmm," he said. "Three countries with the highest percentage of Evangelical Christians in the world."

"Although they're all in the minority."

"In Kenya they're almost half the population. Over 25% in Brazil. Evangelicals tend to believe Revelation involves prophecies yet to be revealed."

"But they're not the only ones affected."

"True. But based on the percentage of Christians, the cultures might be aware of Revelation and End of Days prophecies."

Olivia Parks entered with a file in her hand. "Here's the follow-up on that suspect from New York and D.C."

"Did the French find him?"

"Uh huh. Dead in a villa just outside Paris."

"How?"

"French say suicide—wrists slit in a bathtub. But the autopsy showed bruising on his face and three broken teeth." She handed over the file. Kyle opened it and found several photos of the body in the morgue.

"They have an ID on him?" Sadiq asked.

"ID's a fake."

"Whoever he is, doesn't look like he wanted to go quietly," Kyle said. "Someone is tying up loose ends."

"Hey, you might want to look at this." Sadiq was nodding toward the television in the corner of the office. The news was playing with the sound off, but Kyle turned up the volume. The screen showed rows upon rows of body bags in the courtyard of a Kenyan hospital. The anchor's voice became clear. "…means the smallpox outbreak may soon reach a death toll of one million worldwide." The screen changed to a shot of New York City. "Here in the U.S., officials now say they have contained the outbreak. However, just as the Big Apple is getting back to business, new health concerns have sprung up."

The screen changed to a beach where dead fish and crabs washed ashore in the surf. The water was rust-colored, murky and filthy. "The red tide that has wreaked havoc along the eastern seaboard has now found its way into the water supply of New York City." The screen showed a hospital room, where a sixty-something woman lay in bed, wearing an oxygen mask. She seemed to breathe in pain. "Hundreds reported to area hospitals suffering breathing problems and symptoms of paralytic shellfish poisoning." The screen showed several men in respirator masks taking samples from a water treatment facility. "Scientists have confirmed the presence of *karena brevis*, the toxic algae that causes a form of red tide, in the city's water supply. Water officials acknowledge *karena brevis* cannot be eliminated through regular water treatment methods, but could not answer how the toxin entered the supply."

Sadiq sighed. "Does it ever end?"

The lines around the water trucks were worse than at a hot new delicatessen. Most waited in line patiently, gallon and five-gallon jugs in their hands. Many New Yorkers were still reluctant to venture out in public, and those that did wore respirator masks. Before long, those at the end of the line started to fear they wouldn't get any water. When one of the two water trucks left, their fears were confirmed. People jostled each other in line to get to the front. One woman grabbed the water jug from the man next to her and tossed it out into the street, forcing him out of line. A crush of people knocked over several others at the front, including a woman with three small children. The water gushed from the truck onto the pavement as the line descended into a melee. Mounted police tried to settle the crowd, but it was too late. Thirty people crowded around the gushing spout, each trying to fill what water they could. New York was beginning to descend into third world disorder.

Kyle moved through the darkened hall to his son's room. He stood in the doorway and watched Joshua sleep. His boy could be a fireball of energy when he was awake, but still as a statue when he slept. *So restful, so content.* Kyle couldn't remember the last time he slept soundly, but he was glad his son did. He watched Joshua for several minutes, then walked to the backyard.

The night air was cool and peaceful. Kyle's property went right up to the Chesapeake, and he listened to the water lap quietly against the shore. Far out in the bay, the lights of two tanker ships shimmered in the dark. Kyle stopped and watched, a thought dawning on him in the dark of night.

After hours of research the next day, Kyle reported his new theory to Larsen, Sadiq, and Parks. "The latest video spoke of poisoning waters and turning them to blood. Look," Kyle said as he cued up the Apocalypse Men video on a computer.

The silhouetted man appeared again on screen. *"Thou hast given them blood to drink, for they are worthy."* The man's voice raised in volume and took on a frightening tone. *"And the second angel poured out his vial upon the sea; and it became as the blood of a dead man: and every living soul died in the sea. And the third angel poured out his vial upon the rivers and fountains of waters; and they became blood."*

"That's this red tide," Kyle said.

Larsen, Sadiq, and Parks were confused. "Human-caused?" Parks asked doubtfully.

"That's never happened before," Larsen concurred.

"In large numbers, no," Kyle conceded. "But in places where farming has caused large amounts of nitrogen to enter the waterways, there have been algal blooms."

"This isn't just a river delta," Larsen protested. "We're talking about the entire East Coast!"

"And the New York City water supply," Kyle acknowledged. "It's easy to cultivate enough *karena brevis* to lace that. The ocean is harder," he admitted.

"Harder? Try impossible," Parks crossed her arms.

"No, not impossible. Not if they had been dumping tons of nitrogen or concentrated red tide water over many months. I checked—over the last year, there's been a series of tanker sightings off the coast. None of them made port. There were even four such sightings in the lower Chesapeake Bay." Kyle handed over his data.

"Wouldn't the Coast Guard have checked it out?" Larsen frowned.

"They did. They boarded one of the ships off the coast

of Florida. The captain claimed they had diverted to avoid a storm. The Coast Guard thought they'd find drugs smuggled aboard, but there was nothing. Another ship claimed to have made a navigational error. The rest of the ships just disappeared."

"Even the ones in the Chesapeake?"

Kyle nodded.

"The Chesapeake isn't the Bermuda Triangle." Larsen was dumbfounded. "Did we get the names of any of the shipping lines?"

"A new outfit, World's End Shipping," Kyle said, handing over a printout on the company.

"World's End? That's nice," Sadiq chuckled.

"There's not much on World's End. Small, founded three years ago. But I did some digging and found a connection to a much larger company—Mar Azul."

"Mar Azul is owned by Fernando Vasquez," Larsen said cautiously.

"The oil baron? Was a friend of Chavez; not a friend of the U.S.," Sadiq added.

"Right," Kyle said. "Six years ago, Mar Azul was threatened with takeover by the Mashiri Group. They sold off their twelve oldest ships, used the profit to hold off Mashiri, and eventually hit record profits." Kyle brought up several pictures of the ships on the computer screen. "Meanwhile, the buyer goes under, so a holding company takes the ships and puts them dry dock for a basic overhaul, hoping that would be enough to sell them. It was."

Kyle handed over a financial report on World's End Shipping. "World's End started up as a small-budget shipping line. They were glad to have even old ships to get started. But then they sent all twelve into dry dock for another 18 months—a retrofit the engineers only referred to as an 'upgrade.'"

Something didn't pass the smell test to Sadiq. "If they started off bottom-dollar, where'd they get the funds for an 'upgrade'?"

"That's what I asked," Kyle agreed. "I couldn't see how they account for it on their books."

"What are you getting at?" Larsen asked.

"I think the Mar Azul sale may be a front."

"A front? There's nothing fishy about it. No company would fake financial distress, especially when they've got a major conglomerate breathing down their neck."

"That's why it's perfect," Kyle said. "Mar Azul appears to stop hemorrhaging and Vasquez wipes his hands clean."

Larsen glared at Kyle. "You know better than that. I want a reasonable assessment, not wild speculation."

"How's this for reasonable assessment? We know whoever's funding the attacks has tremendous resources. Knox told me Viktor Zyuganov supplied the bomb and smallpox. So track Zyuganov's associates. I wouldn't be surprised if they included Vasquez."

"Won't be much time for that," Larsen said. "The chiefs going to want move on Zyuganov before he can launch another attack."

"We need to identify his connections before they nab him, or they'll just scatter."

"He's right," Sadiq said.

"You're sure about Vasquez?" Larsen probed.

"All I'm saying is we should investigate him," Kyle concluded.

Larsen considered the proposal in silence. Kyle waited impatiently, hearing the tick of the clock on the wall.

"…And soon," Kyle added.

"All right. I'll send this up. But you know what will happen if you're wrong."

Secret Service Agent Steve Chase escorted General Foley and Pete Standish into the bunker infirmary. President Wallace was more upright in bed. He looked stronger, too. His face and hands, however, were scarred from the smallpox lesions. Wallace had an oxygen tube running to his nose. Chase stood at the back of the room while Foley and Standish approached the bed.

"Mr. President, I'm glad to see you're doing better," Foley said.

"That's not what the rest of the country will say when they see me," Wallace scoffed. "Can you believe it? A president infected with smallpox."

"…Surviving smallpox," Foley corrected him. "That's something we should be grateful for."

Wallace shrugged. It would have been better if he hadn't been infected in the first place.

"Well, Mr. President, you always wanted to have something in common with Washington and Lincoln," Standish said. "Now you do. They also survived smallpox."

"Yeah, so did Stalin," the President said flatly.

Chase suppressed a laugh with a smirk. Standish gaped at the president's response.

"Look, I appreciate the support, but I don't think comparisons to Washington and Lincoln will play with the public."

"They just might," Standish said. He turned to Foley. "What do you think?"

"Run with it," Foley nodded.

Wallace looked at the folder in Foley's hand. "What have you got, Bumpy?"

"Viktor Andropovich Zyuganov. GRU general, retired six years ago. Had access to nukes and connections to the Soviet bio-weapons program." Foley held up a photo for the President to see.

"He's our man?"

"One of them, for sure."

"We know where he is?"

"Our Ukrainian contacts have an agent embedded with them."

"Then let's get him."

Standish could see the President was chomping at the bit, and he didn't like it.

"It's not that simple," Foley said. "We know he's one of the main actors, but if we seize him without confirming and containing the other organizers of these attacks, we could be more vulnerable."

"What else is there?"

"The red tide, for example. Videos link that to the other attacks. And if it was man-made, this red tide took tremendous resources."

"How many people have died from this?" Wallace asked.

Foley knew he was about to get dressed down, but he remained professional and answered the President's question. "Thirty-six so far, Mr. President."

"Thirty-six?" Wallace repeated, his words dripping with scorn.

"It's also cost the fishing industry billions of dollars."

"Thirty-six people. How many have died from small-pox?"

"With most of the casualties coming from Africa, Brazil, and Central America—almost 2 million."

"And the African bombing?"

The President had already belabored the point, but Foley answered, keeping his voice as calm as possible. "Some 40,000."

"Get Zyuganov," Wallace ordered. "He's the lynchpin. I'm not waiting until he launches his next attack and kills another 2 million."

13

Ambush

Larsen led Kyle into the CIA's Operations Center. The room was lit by large wall screens and over a dozen computer monitors. The room was similar to the Combat Information Center of a warship—dark, quiet, and businesslike. Technicians manned each of the computers, bringing up various information and video feeds. The wall screen showed an infrared image from a drone. The image was grainy and plagued with constant interference, but just clear enough to discern an upscale villa at night.

"Eagle Eye in place," a technician called out as he cleaned up the signal.

Kyle noticed Knox and Petrusiv standing at the back of the room, watching the screen. Kyle made his way over to them.

"We should have waited," Kyle whispered in Knox's ear. "That contact could have helped us identify every major player in the Apocalypse Men organization."

"I know," Knox sighed. "But it's out of our hands now."

"Approaching target," one of the technicians at the computers called out.

In a distant country, two stealth-modified Black Hawk helicopters skimmed over the treetops of a forest, heading for the villa on top of a hill. Two SEAL teams, dressed in full gear, sat in the helicopters. The team leaders gave hand signals, and the SEALs flipped their night vision goggles over their eyes.

Zyuganov's villa was Roman in design, but he added a few of his own flourishes to uniquely modernize it. He sat at dinner and poured a fine claret. Zyuganov raised the glass and closed his eyes as he savored the aroma. Something caught his attention. Zyuganov opened his eyes and listened. There it was, just above the silence of night—a faint sound far in the distance. He stood and walked to the open window, listening. Zyuganov caught it again—a strange reverberation. He picked up his cell phone and dialed.

President Wallace was well enough to join his key intelligence and military advisors in the White House Situation Room. They all sat with their eyes glued to the same video feed as the one in the Pentagon Operations Center. Wallace wore a zip-up nylon president's jacket and khakis. He was the most casually dressed person in the room, but given his scarring, no one begrudged him his ensemble. Though weak from his ordeal, Wallace appeared more animated than he had been in days. He was eager to see justice meted out.

In the villa, Leonid Zavin and Zyuganov's driver sat in a lounge and heard a noise pierce the silence of the night. Zavin and the driver looked up toward the source of the sound. It was strangely, of all things, like a lawnmower. Zyuganov passed the two men as he headed for his panic room. With his phone in hand, Zyuganov locked the door and sealed himself inside. Zavin strode to the door and banged on it. "General!"

Outside, the first of the stealth-modified Black Hawks hovered high above the compound. The pilot looked at the sloped ground below and assessed it was too steep to touch down. The SEAL team leader shouted to him, "Slide it right and we'll hop off into the grass!"

"Got it." The pilot maneuvered downward.

Inside the villa, Zavin and the driver now saw the helicopter. Zavin banged on the door more urgently. Zyuganov did not answer. Locked in his panic room, he connected his call.

"Yes?" a Middle Eastern voice answered.

"I won't be making it tomorrow," Zyuganov said.

"Oh?" the voice was surprised.

"It's Slobodin," Zyuganov explained. "I thought I had taken care of him in time, but...I was wrong." The words came slowly. Zyuganov hated to admit failure. "I'm sorry if I have let you down."

"There's no need," the voice on the other end of the line said generously. "Everything is in place, as you've seen to it."

There was a long pause. Zyuganov didn't know what else to say.

"We will miss you, comrade," the voice on the other end of the line said. He usually used the term 'brother,' but knew 'comrade' carried more meaning for Zyuganov. It was an expression of the highest respect.

Zyuganov straightened his shoulders, buoyed by the compliment. "Thank you." He hung up. Zyuganov opened a safe and pulled out a lock box. Inside, there was a device with a switch.

Zavin was banging loudly on the door, his call more insistent. "General!"

The first helicopter hovered just three feet above the ground, the pilot keeping the rotors clear of the nearby trees and stone wall. He turned to the SEAL team leader. "Go!"

The first SEAL hopped out. Just as his boots touched the ground, the compound exploded in a blinding flash. Shrapnel hit the helicopter's rotors and body. A large piece flew through the open cabin door, barely missing three SEAL team members before it embedded itself in the underside of the roof. Shrapnel also shredded the engine, sending up a shower of sparks, the screeching sound of scraping metal, and a plume of smoke. The pilot frantically tried to crab the helicopter away from the fireball, but with the engine damaged, the Black Hawk struggled, shrugged, then dropped to the ground.

As the rotors hit the earth they shredded the dirt like a tiller, then broke away. The SEALs in the cabin slid to the lower side of the craft, frantically trying to hold on. The Black Hawk's fuselage rolled onto the ground, rocked backwards, then settled. The SEALs had been thrown violently, but all survived. The pilot's fingers were tightly gripped on the stick when the helicopter came to rest.

Inside the CIA Operations Center, the greenish night vision screen suddenly blew out to bright white. Gasps sounded. One of the technicians calmly tried to reestablish contact.

"Giant Killer One, Giant Killer One, do you read?"

In the White House Situation Room, Foley was aghast. "What just happened?"

The room was silent as everyone held their breath in anxiety—all except Wallace. His eyes gleamed with a budding sense of elation.

Back in the CIA Operations Center, Petrusiv was stunned. Breaking decorum, he shouted, "Who fired?"

The screen readjusted as the explosion faded. The bird's-eye view from the drone became visible again. Black smoke billowed from the hollow shell of the villa, largely obscuring the top of the screen. In contrast, white splotches blew out the screen where hot spots burned. At the bottom of the screen, the crippled helicopter lay on the hillside. The SEAL team members could be seen climbing out of the wreckage. The second helicopter, having completed an evasive maneuver, now circled over the compound. The pilot's voice crackled over the radio. "Target detonated a device."

The technician still tried to contact the other helicopter. "Giant Killer One, do you read?"

A weak audio signal carried the first pilot's voice. "We're still here, Center. A bit shaken, but still here."

Wallace sat on the edge of his chair as he watched the screen. "What about Zyuganov?"

The SEAL team leader's voice came over the radio in response. "The whole compound is gone. Target's destroyed, sir."

"Can you confirm?" Wallace asked over speaker.

A military aide typed a command into his computer. "Drone shows no life in the villa. Scan showed there were three subjects before the blast."

The second helicopter flew over the smoldering ruins of the compound. The second SEAL team leader leaned out of the cabin and looked down with his night vision goggles. There was nothing left but rubble. "Target is expired," he confirmed.

"We got him!" Wallace shouted as he sprang to his feet, jubilant. Standish averted his eyes. He was glad Zyuganov was no longer a threat, but didn't feel like celebrating revenge.

The Chairman of the Joint Chiefs of Staff leaned toward the speaker. "Copy. Search the compound for any data and make sure you fully demo that bird. Then get your butts back to base."

"Roger that," the second pilot's voice came over the radio.

Wallace grinned. "One lost chopper, none of our men. I'll take that."

Petrusiv watched the screen in stunned silence. He turned and stared coldly at Knox, fuming silently. When it looked like his anger would boil over, Petrusiv left the Operations Center. Knox followed, catching him in the corner of an empty corridor.

Petrusiv could no longer hold his tongue. "I told you he wasn't to be touched! That was the agreement!"

"I know," Knox said quietly.

"It wasn't just about Zyuganov. Leonid established a pipeline of intelligence that we could have kept going for years. We could have stopped dozens of arms dealers." He screwed his lips in frustration. "Now all up in smoke."

"I'm just as upset as you are," Knox said, keeping his

voice low and calm. "But it wasn't my call. It was my superiors'. And I have to follow them, even if their judgment here was completely wrong." Knox knew speaking like this was insubordination, but he was angry. He feared he was losing Petrusiv's partnership and hoped the unvarnished truth might keep him on. It didn't work.

"That may be true," Petrusiv said. "But there's a price to be paid." He turned and walked away.

14

The Fourth Vial

White House Chief of Staff Sharon Mattice called Pete Standish and Steve Chase into her office. Always a fireball, Mattice was even more animated than usual. "Now we've scored a victory, it's time for the President to go public again."

"Is he ready for it?" Standish asked doubtfully. "I saw him yesterday, and the scars are still—"

"Huntington is killing us on this smallpox issue," Mattice cut him off. Neither Chase or Standish liked her choice of words, given the President's close call with mortality, but winning the election was a matter of life or death with Mattice. "She'll say the proof of our national security failure is on the President's face."

"Are we sure she'll say that?" Standish countered. "Huntington's fierce, but I don't think she'll kick a guy when he's down. Not like that."

"You really believe that?" Mattice snarked. She let the question hang, showing as much contempt for Standish's judgment as for Huntington herself. "I wouldn't put anything past her. But if we don't go public now, when we've eliminated the threat, we may not win the election. We're going to have to face—" Mattice caught herself in a painful slip of the tongue. She cleared her throat and started again.

"We're going to have to own up to the President's condition now or later. Better now."

Chase had kept silent until now, standing at the back of the room with his arms crossed. Mattice hadn't offered him a seat, as always. Mattice had been frosty towards Chase from the beginning, treating him more like hired help than the head of the President's protection detail. In Mattice's view the Secret Service were cumbersome and a burden that had to be tolerated. She never held back in expressing her displeasure with them.

In the first hours of the President's illness, he thought Mattice blamed him. He'd expected as much from her. But Mattice didn't lay the blame on the Secret Service. Mary Ellen Rogers had been invited to the breakfast by Mattice's friend. It also looked, by all appearances, that the poor woman had been as much a victim as the President. Mary Ellen Rogers apparently didn't know she was infected when she attended the event. She had been held captive and suffered a horrible death. Mattice and Chase both shouldered the blame, and now both had to move on—he just didn't like the way she was doing it.

"What do you have in mind?" Chase asked.

"A symbolic speech. Bigger than the Oval Office or East Room."

"Not the Lincoln Memorial, I hope." Chase didn't mind needling Mattice's enthusiasm, but he also wanted her to know anything too grand would be a logistical nightmare.

"I was thinking the Washington Hilton. It's where Reagan was shot and survived." Mattice loathed President Reagan, but she didn't mind seizing on history when it fit her narrative. Reagan had not only been the last president to survive an assassination attempt, but went on to preside

over an era of prosperity in America and played an influ-
ential role in ending the Cold War. The spin was clear—re-
elect Wallace, a man of similar fortitude, and America can
look to good days ahead. "Fitting, huh?"

Chase shrugged. "Well, it's better than the Watergate."

Mattice's look cast daggers at Chase, but he didn't
mind. He liked getting under her skin.

Standish wasn't ready to talk locations. "The question
remains, can Wallace handle it?"

"He has to," Mattice said. "But you know Wallace,
he's chomping at the bit to get out there. And taking out
Zyuganov—we need to be shouting this from the rooftops."
Mattice felt that settled the issue.

Chase could live with the choice of venue. It was no
more dangerous than the usual public appearance, but like
Standish, he had reservations about the President's fitness.
Mattice was moving to the door, ushering them out. She
wasn't one for manners.

"One more thing," Standish said as he stood his ground.
"I hear he's dropping Townsend and putting Barish on the
ticket."

Mattice swiftly closed the door, afraid Standish would
be overheard. "Where'd you hear that?" she asked in a
hushed tone.

"It's the talk of the West Wing," Standish answered.
Mattice's desire to keep it quiet was like defusing a bomb
that had already gone off. It was no surprise—Townsend
was considered by most to be a joke. A former congress-
man from Philadelphia, Earl Townsend had a reputation
as a blabber, one that only worsened as Vice President. In
2012, a political commentator claimed he had 'more blus-
ter than Hurricane Sandy'—a quote that soon saddled him

with the nickname 'The East Coast Windbag.' Townsend held enough clout to prove an asset on Wallace's ticket the first go-around. Now even members of his own party were happy to have him sidelined in a largely honorary position. Some presidents make their second-in-command an integral part of their administration, while others leave the Vice President out in the cold. Wallace was in the latter category, which only fueled rumors that Townsend was getting the boot. Though Lisa Barish was young, she was experienced, energetic, and could add value to the administration. As a woman veep candidate, she could also counter Huntington's strong challenge for the presidency.

"That's just a rumor," Mattice said, "But if word gets to Townsend before Wallace can talk to him, it'll be a disaster." She knew as well as anyone that Townsend was a goner. Mattice had even proposed Barish as a running mate, though Wallace was already considering her. But no plans had been finalized, and Townsend needed to be sent off gently.

Standish nodded. "Loose lips sink ships." A veteran, Standish found a military phrase now and then apropos. But now he began to wonder—was Wallace's ship going down too?

"Right," Mattice said. "I'll talk with the staff and tell them to put a lid on it."

More than ever, Chase was glad Mattice wasn't his boss.

Kyle rubbed his eyes and tried to focus once more on the blur of text in front of him. He had been researching and reading for hours. Parks tapped him on the shoulder and handed over a cup of coffee. "Looks like you could use this."

"Thanks," Kyle said, taking a large sip. "We get anything from the raid on Zyuganov?"

"One of our satellites caught what looks to be a sat phone transmission. It came from the compound just before it exploded. The transmission was encrypted, but it called a cell phone in France. That phone hasn't been used again."

"It won't be." Kyle knew Zyuganov's call had been a warning. Other than the videos, which hadn't turned up much, there wasn't any electronic trail to the Apocalypse Men. That was unlikely to change. "What about the encryption?"

Parks shook her head. "Haven't been able to break it yet."

Kyle was surprised by this response. One of the NSA's top objectives was breaking codes. How had this one been so tricky? It only proved the resilience of the Apocalypse Men.

"So here's what I don't get," Parks said as she took a seat across from Kyle. "If they're using oil tankers to dump algae-laced water, wouldn't there be oil residue?"

"They retrofitted the tankers in dry dock. Most likely, they've put in new bladders and added a drain that allows them to dump water without being noticed."

"The average oil tanker moves about two billion metric tons of oil a year. How could they cultivate that much concentrated red tide water for twelve ships?"

"They'd need a manufacturing facility. Probably use chemical fertilizer to stimulate the growth of *karena brevis*."

"Yeah, but where?"

"I tracked the ship the Coast Guard boarded off of Florida." Kyle pulled up a map on his computer. Criss-crossing lines tracked the path of each voyage. "Last year it made three stops in Jakarta. But each time it only made port there to pick up supplies. Then it would show up in the Panama Canal 45 days later. No sign of it in the interim."

Parks shook her head. "It shouldn't take 45 days for a large tanker to go straight from Jakarta to the Panama Canal."

"Right. Probably stopped somewhere in between. I checked for private industrial ports on offshore Indonesian islands and found three." Kyle zoomed in on the map. "Get this—they're all owned by the largest supplier of oil and chemical fertilizer in Asia—Aaban Assad al-Mashiri."

"Mashiri? He's one of the ten richest people in the world. Owns a fifth of the oil fields south of Russia from the Middle East to East Asia. He'd certainly have the resources to generate these attacks, but he's apolitical."

"Maybe he's not as much as we think."

"Okay, but would he risk everything for such an obscure attack? I don't—"

Sadiq rushed into the room, a flash drive in his hand. "There's another message." He put the drive into the computer and cued up the file.

"When did we get this?" Kyle asked.

Just now. But it was recorded two days ago."

"Two days? It wasn't posted online?"

Sadiq shook his head. "It came in a package to Voice of the World, but sat on a reporter's desk for two days while he was out on assignment. We didn't learn about it until he returned."

"The last video was released directly online. Why go back to hand-delivery?"

"Keeping the delivery methods random makes them harder to track," Sadiq said.

"Unfortunately, even the direct upload was a dead end," Parks confirmed.

"We were too late to stop the previous attacks by the time the videos arrived. Let's hope we're not even farther behind."

The silhouetted man appeared on the screen against the blood-red backdrop, just as before. *"And the fourth angel poured out his vial upon the sun; and power was given unto him to scorch men with fire. And men were scorched with great heat, and blasphemed the name of God, which hath power over these plagues. For the judgment of God is like a great star Wormwood, falling from heaven, burning like a lamp."*

Kyle inhaled sharply. Something told him what was coming was much worse.

The Boeing 747 began its descent from 35,000 feet as it prepared to land in Jakarta. Despite leaving Paris over 15 hours ago, Aaban Assad al-Mashiri was quite comfortable. Only twelve 747s in the world were privately owned, and Boeing kept the names of the owners strictly confidential. Mashiri was one of the twelve. Boeing 747s cost half a billion dollars with standard fittings, but Mashiri's jet was furnished in luxury that made Air Force One pale in comparison. The bed was king-sized in a standard hotel-sized bedroom. Mashiri slept soundly, and had plenty of room to stretch his legs in the wide-body aircraft that contained only a dozen first-class luxury seats. The rest of the aircraft was fitted with lounges and even a jacuzzi.

Though born into a wealthy family, Mashiri exponentially increased his fortune through hard work and shrewd business decisions. His father had been part of a Middle Eastern oil empire that gradually expanded eastward. His mother was part of a wealthy Pakistani family. When Aaban was nine years old, his father moved the family to Indonesia. There, his father began to assert his independence from his family's company, eventually earning enough to start his own company. Using the profits he made in Indonesia, his father bought his family's Middle Eastern oil fields outright. Now his company stretched over nearly half the globe.

Mashiri's parents were devout Muslims, and he was raised well within the confines of the faith. His name, Aaban, meant 'iron angel'—and though his parents could not have known it when he was born, the name was fitting. Aaban was a man of dual nature. He had the capacity for deep religious thought, but also an iron will that could manifest itself in absolute ruthlessness.

That ruthlessness found direction in his hatred of two countries, born from political indoctrination and visceral experience. In his teenage years, Aaban witnessed upheaval in Indonesia and the war in nearby Vietnam. These events helped plant his deep distrust of America and its politics, but this was also tempered by his father's business interests. General Suharto's coup of Indonesia led to more foreign investment, a boon to his father's company. But to Aaban, the American support for Suharto's government and the bloody Vietnam War smacked of a new brand of colonialism. Aaban had come to this conclusion through associations with friends and teachers, who all supported Sukarno. This anti-colonial sentiment resonated with the young Mashiri, as he had learned of the plight of Palestinians in his earliest years in the Middle East. He learned that Palestinians had been displaced by Jewish settlers who created the nation of Israel, and felt that had been equally unjust.

Aaban's father forbade him to make any open political statement. At first, the young man felt this was unfair and selfish, but in time, he came to realize the wisdom in this decree. Aaban would inherit his father's empire, and if managed well, it would give him the means to do anything he wanted. Men with wealth are not limited to power in business—they can have political power too. On the other hand, men who only hold political power are beholden to those who will financially support them. The young Mashiri also came to understand another vital truth—holding his own political views secret kept him from the scrutiny and opposition that those who profess their views openly experience. He could do far more if he operated his political agenda in secret.

Aaban knew he'd have to understand the West to expand his father's empire when he inherited it, so he attended Oxford University. In England, he discovered new passions as he learned about Christianity. Though he never forsook his Muslim roots, Mashiri continued to build his religious understanding as he learned about Western culture. He also learned how Western beliefs and capitalism could be as powerful as Western politics.

When Mashiri took over his father's empire, he shrewdly expanded it and broadened its scope. Mashiri foresaw the decline in the Indonesian oil market and diversified into fertilizer manufacturing well before oil sagged.

Mashiri had a talent for seeing the direction the future was heading, and his business choices eventually gave him the ability to influence it.

Mashiri, however, wasn't satisfied with his influence as a billionaire businessman. Eventually he became convinced that there were two sources of imbalance in the world—first and foremost, the United States, and second, as a regional power in the Middle East, Israel. Both countries had wreaked havoc—the imperialist policies of America, with its wars and covert operations, had wreaked a swath of destruction over the globe—and Israel had been a thorn to all Muslim people, particularly the Palestinians they displaced and abused. There had to be a reckoning. There had to be a restoration of balance.

Mashiri had seen the U.S. War on Terror coming since the 1996 bombing of the Khobar Towers complex in Saudi Arabia. But what organizations such as Al Qaeda and Hezbollah gained in enthusiasm, they lacked in patience. Mashiri knew 9/11 would not bring the collapse of America that Al Qaeda had predicted. It would take massive and coordinated attacks, coupled with smart procedures that would elude the Americans' intelligence capabilities, to strike a crippling blow. Psychology was also an important factor. Mashiri, a man of infinite patience, had looked at Al Qaeda's failures and seen where adjustments needed to be made. The plan was well underway, but the greatest components were yet to be realized.

Earth is for burying, and they will do their share. The young man was right, Mashiri thought. His plan would restore balance to the world. It would usher in a new age. But first, Earth must be cleansed with blood and fire.

That night, Kyle tossed and turned for hours. His bedroom was sweltering, but his mind was too troubled to sleep. When Kyle finally drifted off he had a terrible nightmare. At first, there was an oppressive darkness—absolute and impenetrable. Then, with a terrifying and ghastly roar, an orange blaze erupted like a furnace. Kyle saw the waves of an ocean undulate out of the blackness. Flames spread over them, tossing large ships aside like toys. The inferno engulfed a bridge and knocked cars off like matchsticks. The dream moved to another location, where a large concrete wall rose out of the darkness. There was a loud cracking noise. Then, with an earth-rattling shudder, the wall began to break apart. A deluge of boiling black water pushed the tumbling pieces of the wall toward Kyle. Just as he felt he was going to be scorched, drowned, or crushed by the concrete, the dream moved to a final location. Here, he was in a city. The inferno returned, obliterating buildings and sweeping everything in its path. The flames rushed on, lapping at a large Egyptian obelisk.

Kyle awoke with a shudder. He sat at the edge of his bed for a moment, trying to shake the horror of the dream from his memory. Finally he slowed his racing heartbeat, but he couldn't shake the images from his mind. Sleep was out of the question. Kyle got up and silently moved down the hall. He stood at the doorway of his son's bedroom and watched him sleep, making sure he was all right. Kyle also passed the guest bedroom where his mother Lyla was sleeping. Seeing both were fine, he went out to his deck and watched the water. It was a quiet night. The heat seemed too much for even the crickets—everything was bathed in silence. Kyle tried to relax and take in the calm scene, but his mind turned back to the dream. What did it mean? He knew the dream was provoked by the latest video—but was it his imagination, or could there be a warning in the imagery? A boat horn sounded far in the distance, breaking the silence. To Kyle, it was a harbinger, and the sound coursed through him like a shot of electricity. He dressed quickly and climbed into his car. As he drove north onto the freeway, Kyle glanced at his watch. It was barely 4 A.M. He'd call his mother in three hours and let her know he was on his way to Princeton.

15

Dawn of the Apocalypse Men

The island in the South Pacific was little more than a postage stamp in the middle of the ocean, barely a mile square. When Amelia Earhart disappeared in 1937, she was aiming for Howland Island, no larger than Mashiri's own retreat. Despite the advance in navigational techniques since Earhart's day, Mashiri prided himself on his island's near anonymity. The island, in fact, had no name. It was simply the most secluded of Mashiri's many properties.

There were low sloping hills no higher than 40 feet on the western side of the island. Trees and jungle vegetation grew thickly across its surface. On the eastern side lay a golden sandy beach and a large reef, creating a natural harbor. Mashiri had the reef dredged to allow yacht access, then subsequently turned the reef into a breakwater. If environmentalists knew of this, they would have been outraged, but Mashiri's security kept the island a closely guarded secret. Mashiri was indifferent to environmentalists, although he was high on their lists as one of the biggest producers of both oil and chemical fertilizer in the world.

The house Mashiri built in the center of the island was not large, but was comfortable. In front of it, he had cleared the jungle, enclosed a natural lagoon, and redirected a spring from the hills so it flowed in a small waterfall to the pool. It was crafted tropical luxury, but one that would leave most resorts envious. Mashiri had perfected every detail down to the sparkling crystal-clear water and variety of flowers.

Only the most exclusive guests were allowed to visit. The two men who arrived for the meeting were no different. One came by seaplane, landing in the harbor; another arrived on Mashiri's own yacht, a gesture of hospitality that alleviated the slower voyage. Both the seaplane pilot and yacht captain were Mashiri's own. This maintained his security regarding the exact location of the island.

The man who arrived by seaplane had come from the west, flying over a dozen offshore oil rigs. "I take it these are all his," he told the pilot.

"Every one of them," the pilot answered. They had flown until the rigs were no longer visible and there was only the wide expanse of ocean before they had finally seen the island.

Once gathered together on the island, the two guests waited on a shaded veranda by the pool. Within minutes, Mashiri arrived by helicopter, landing on the small pad just outside the house.

Mashiri walked to the veranda and smiled as he greeted the men. "Welcome, brothers." He motioned to a table where drinks were available. All seated, the men represented one of the most powerful meetings on earth. They were three of the most wealthy men in the world. They were also three of the four Horsemen. Only Viktor Zyuganov, the Red Horse of War, was absent. One of the guests was Fernando Vasquez, the oil baron and shipping magnate from South America, the Black Horse of Famine. The other was Amir Anwar Al-Salameh, a tech mogul. He was also known as the White Horse of Conquest. Mashiri, the leader, was known as the Pale Horse of Death.

Mashiri's attitude was decidedly more upbeat than his guests. Sensing their hesitation, Mashiri waited for them to speak.

Vasquez finally broke the silence. "So, we've been dealt some setbacks."

"Zyuganov is a loss, but not in vain," Mashiri said as he reached for a drink.

Salameh and Vasquez looked at each other. "I'm not sure if everything's been in vain to this point," Vasquez said. "I've spent half my fortune, but what do we have to show for it?"

"What do we have to show?" Mashiri echoed the question.

"The bomb in Africa targeted people we could care less about. We've poisoned the waters around America, but that hasn't made it collapse. We've spread smallpox around the world—perhaps our most successful move—but our main targets, including the American President, have survived. So again, I ask, what have we accomplished?"

Mashiri leaned back. "Brothers, we are united in purpose, even if we bring different causes to our union. You ask what we have accomplished? I tell you—confusion."

Vasquez and Salameh were also confused. Salameh lowered his chin toward his chest while Vasquez's eyes widened.

Mashiri expected this reaction from his colleagues. He hadn't shared the full breadth of his vision or the extent of his operations. Vasquez and Salameh didn't know the African bomb had also taken out a CIA agent who had threatened their whole operation, or that Mashiri had worked with Zyuganov to put the next phase of their attacks into play. Even with Zyuganov's death, the operation was secure. Mashiri had seen to that—even by ordering Zyuganov's suicide.

"The intelligence services are confused by our attacks," Mashiri explained, "because they seem random and illogical in their targeting. We've pulled them in so many different directions that they cannot see the next attack—the one that will bring them to their knees."

"You're confident of this?" Salameh asked skeptically.

"Brothers, we have been patient in our preparations. They have stretched decades. We have learned from the failures of others and taken precautions. Despite Zyuganov's death, his great work is accomplished. Brothers, this is our great day. Al Qaeda brought fear on 9/11. But they failed because of what they did not take from the Americans—hope." Mashiri smiled with satisfaction. "Take away their hope, and they will fall."

The Maryland countryside was still dark when the two men left the farmhouse. Sliding the barn doors open, they could see the vehicle loom like a beast in the darkness. They drove out onto the main road and were soon on the highway. As the darkness faded just before dawn, the armored car's headlights cut through a blue haze of fog.

Out west, it was still the middle of the night. Only the black outline of the mountains cut against the star-lit sky. Here was one of the largest and most popular man-made lakes in the United States, but the driver saw no one as he pulled up to the boat ramp. Backing up his trailer, the driver let his tail lights shine red on the water. It was the only illumination in the darkness. The driver and his passenger hopped out of the pickup truck and climbed onto the trailer. The men untied the canvas covering and pulled it back, revealing a personal submarine. The driver embraced the passenger, the two men whispered goodbyes, and the passenger climbed into the submarine.

The Port of Los Angeles was not so silent. Here, it was just as late, but the busiest container port in the United States never sleeps. Lit by large floodlights, the cranes offloaded containers from two freighter ships and lowered them to the cradles of waiting semi trucks. Offshore, another large container ship, *Last Horizon*, came just within sight of the port. Soon it would enter the breakwater. Within an hour, the ship would be offloading at the dock. Deep within the stacks of containers was one box that held a most volatile cargo.

By dawn, the armored truck was crossing the Theodore Roosevelt Bridge into Washington. Inside the truck, the protective steel plating had been replaced with lead, just like the lining of the container box outside Los Angeles harbor. The heavier lead made the truck ride lower, but it shielded its cargo from detection.

Kyle reached Princeton's campus just after 7:30. He ran over to 1879 Hall, catching Dr. Hightower just as he was entering the building.

"Mr. Ferguson," Hightower said in surprise. "I don't believe we have an appointment this morning."

Kyle was nearly out breath. "I need to show you something."

Hightower could see the urgency in Kyle's eyes. He had a graduate consultation scheduled for 8:00, but still assented. "Come," he ushered Kyle to his office.

President Wallace entered the ballroom in the Washington Hilton and moved towards the dais. Murmurs filled the room at the sight of the President, still scarred from his ordeal. Wallace moved slowly, but when he took the podium, he spoke with vigor.

"My fellow Americans, the last few days have been dark indeed. They have affected all of us—have taken loved ones from many of us, and left us deeply shaken. But I come to you today with great news." Wallace paused, pulling the audience in with baited breath. "Following my orders, Navy SEALs conducted an operation that brought the perpetrators of these heinous attacks to justice."

The room erupted in rapturous applause. Cheers were scattered throughout the crowd. Wallace nodded in acknowledgment, but the applause continued for a full minute. He waited patiently. This was a moment to bask in. Finally, when the applause subsided, Wallace continued.

"Let those who would plan such attacks against us remember this day: justice will always prevail." Applause followed, more thunderous than before. Wallace broke into a smile, but he kept his mouth closed. Baring his teeth would have been inappropriate. Still, he thought to himself, "Game on, Huntington."

Kyle showed the most recent video to Hightower, who sat in silence and frowned.

"What?"

"These messages predicting future attacks—they've

always spoken of vials and quoted from Revelation 16," Hightower explained. "But the second part of this message quotes Revelation 8. See, here: *For the judgment of God is like a great star Wormwood, falling from heaven, burning like a lamp.*"

"Great star Wormwood—what does that mean?"

"Many scholars interpret the idea of 'a great star falling' as a comet or meteor hitting the earth. Not all, but many do."

"Okay. What about this name 'Wormwood'? What does that mean?"

"You've heard of it," Hightower said.

Kyle shook his head, dumbfounded. "No."

"Of course you have. Everyone in the civilized world has heard of it. You just know it by its Ukrainian name—*Chernobyl.*"

16

Hunting

The man stood at the sixth floor window and looked out toward Connecticut Avenue. The President's speech had just ended on television, and he knew in minutes the motorcade would be heading down the street. The man had a number dialed into his cell phone, ready to call as soon as he caught sight of the President's limousine.

Several blocks away, just outside Scott Circle, the armored truck sat in the Holiday Inn's underground parking garage. The driver leaned back in his seat and waited while the man in the passenger seat kept vigil. Both were dressed in company uniforms, but the passenger didn't like waiting here in the garage. To him, it was taking too much of a risk.

As Kyle drove towards Washington, he thought about his dream again. This was the fourth time he had some sort of premonition. Now he knew what the flames meant. But what about the locations? He pondered this question as he drove past Philadelphia and Baltimore, but couldn't find the answer. At first, he thought the bridge was the Golden Gate in San Francisco, but the bridge in his dream wasn't the Golden Gate's iconic orange. Perhaps it was the Verrazano Narrows Bridge in New York. The concrete walls totally stumped him. He moved on to the Egyptian obelisk. The first thing that came to Kyle's mind made him kick himself. It was obvious—he saw it all the time—the Washington Monument. Kyle's cell phone wasn't a secure line, but he still called Larsen's office. It did no good. Kyle could only reach his voice mail. He hung up and called Sadiq, but the phone just rang. Kyle slammed the steering wheel and floored the accelerator. He was still 45 minutes from CIA headquarters.

The second spotter watched another motorcade pull up to the Hilton. For a moment, he worried all of their plans would be in vain. What if the President had called a decoy motorcade? Then they wouldn't be able to discern which one carried the man himself. This was a common security measure with Marine One, the President's helicopter. When flying to Andrews Air Force Base, Marine One would be accompanied by two identical helicopters, a high-tech shell game designed to keep the President safe. But the spotter's concerns proved unfounded when the second motorcade left while the President was still on television. Now the spotter's fear turned to glee. *Two birds with one stone*, he thought.

Wallace climbed into the back of his limo, still grinning. This was his best appearance in months—smallpox scars and all. Now he had a real chance at re-election. Wallace's grin faded as he looked at the man sitting across from him. It was Vice President Earl Townsend.

"Earl. Well, this is a surprise."

Riding in the limousine behind the President's, Secret Service Agent Steve Chase was troubled. The President's speech had gone better than hoped—Wallace showed more strength than Chase expected, and the event occurred without a hitch. However, the news that Vice President Townsend had arrived unexpectedly was most unwelcome. Whatever Townsend wanted, it would have been better if he had waited until they were inside the relative fortress of the White House. It would only take five or six minutes to reach the presidential mansion, but Chase would be on edge for every one of them. Across from him, Mattice was elated. The President's speech had gone just as she expected.

Mattice chatted excitedly on her phone with the President's campaign chief. "I want us to go full speed. There'll be nothing to stop us."

In the Holiday Inn parking garage, the driver of the armored truck drummed his fingers on the steering wheel. The passenger looked at him, a glance that asked him to stop, but the driver ignored him. The shrill tone of a cell phone pierced the air.

"Yes?" the passenger answered.

"They're coming," the first spotter said curtly over the phone.

The line clicked off. The driver turned the ignition and the truck's diesel engine boomed in the cavernous garage. Within moments, they emerged into daylight, pulling onto the streets of Washington.

The personal submarine made its way through Lake Mead to a barrier net. Only a few hundred feet away, the intake towers of the Hoover Dam loomed from the depths of the water. Hoover Dam had long been considered a target.

Troops had manned bunkers high up Black Canyon's walls throughout World War II to protect against sabotage. Following the 9/11 attacks, a high overpass bridge was built south of the dam to divert tractor-trailer traffic. Homeland Security patrolled and monitored every inch of the dam. In a control center hidden deep within the dam's walls, a Homeland Security guard watched a wall full of monitors. One monitor showed the underwater view from the lake, where the submarine now came into view. The guard turned to his supervisor. "Uh, sir?"

The sun was now rising on the Port of Los Angeles. The giant container ship *Last Horizon* had been delayed and was forced to wait inside the breakwater. The dockworkers' contract was up for renewal again, and though they weren't planning another strike, they had slowed their output to show just how valuable they were. The last two ships had taken nearly twice the average offload time. Now *Last Horizon* was cleared to approach the docks and massive cranes. As *Last Horizon*'s engines churned, the ship moved slowly into the channel. The pilot stood on the flying bridge, helping guide the ship toward shore. Little did he know, *Last Horizon* would not make port.

Townsend didn't waste time with pleasantries. "Mr. President, you're dumping me."

"I never said anything about—" Wallace lamely tried to deflect Townsend's attack.

"I've stood by you every step of the way," Townsend cut in. He wasn't having any of it. "Even when you had smallpox. When Hodge and Standish wanted to invoke the 25th Amendment, I backed you up."

"I didn't hear you say anything in that room," Wallace sneered. Townsend seemed more cowardly than he had ever seen him, and he detested this kind of weakness. He had little tolerance for groveling.

"The discussion continued outside," Townsend said, trying to stand firm. "Behind your back. And I had it the whole time."

Wallace regretted ever putting Townsend on his ticket. Sure, he helped secure victory, but he had suffered too much grief at this man's hands. He had already been planning to dump him for Barish, but now he didn't want to wait for the election. Next week wasn't fast enough, but he knew he should wait at least until then to not ruin the momentum his speech had given him. He'd tell Mattice his decision when they arrived at the White House.

"I've been for you since day one!" Townsend shouted, indignant. "And now you want to put me out to pasture because a young female face is more important to your campaign than loyalty." Townsend was frothing at the mouth with anger. "That, Mr. President, that is a betrayal of the highest—"

He would never finish the sentence.

17

Chaos

The bomb detonated just over a mile away, instantly obliterating the armored truck and four city blocks with it. The President's motorcade had just reached Lafayette Square Park when it was hit by the blast wave, tumbling the limousines end over end in a violent spin. The explosion was not as large as the 'Little Boy' bomb at Hiroshima, but the ground burst still caused a massive firestorm that swept everything in its path. The blast spread southward, charring the north facade of the White House black. One of the columns on the iconic north portico was ripped away, revealing a bone-like steel support.

The White House had suffered major fire damage before: the British burned the mansion in 1814, less than 15 years after its completion. A single brick on the south balcony remained unpainted in remembrance of that event. Now the White House was scarred in a way that might never see recovery.

The flames rose over the facade of the White House and hit the Two Secret Service sharpshooters stationed on the roof. Both suffered third-degree burns from the blast wave before it knocked them off the roof, falling to their deaths. But now the blast wave was weakening. The south facade of the White House remained relatively unscathed.

Strange things happen when a nuclear detonation occurs in a metropolitan area. While the ground burst did significant damage in the immediate quarter-mile vicinity of the detonation, the blast wave lessened quickly. Still, as it spread southward and reached the National Mall, the heat set every American flag surrounding the Washington Monument on fire. The flames only lapped at the obelisk itself, dying out by the time they reached the Tidal Basin. The Capitol, situated on the other end of the Mall, suffered no damage at all.

In the Port of Los Angeles, the second bomb detonated in its container, incinerating the *Last Horizon* and the surrounding docks. This bomb was much larger than the one in Washington, and it easily demolished the stacks of metal containers and large cranes. Those few that remained became a glowing mass of melted iron. The blast wave spread and hit the Vincent Thomas Bridge, snapping suspension cables and tossing cars and buses into the water a thousand feet away. Freed from its support cables, the bridge collapsed. Only the massive green pillars stood. Like the facade of the White House, the pillars were now scorched black.

At the Hoover Dam, the submarine exploded, sending out a huge blast wave. Hit with the force of the detonation, the dam's walls shuddered, cracked, and abruptly collapsed. Lake Mead began to gush out, but hit with the nuclear explosion, the water closest to the blast turned to steam. The narrow walls of Black Canyon sheared off and slid into the Colorado River. The blast hit the overpass bridge and broke it apart, sending tractor-trailers and cars flying.

The remnants of Lake Mead now surged over the destroyed power plant, bringing death downriver.

The President's limo was no match for a nuclear blast. Though the chassis remained intact, the windows were cracked and the roof was half caved-in. Neither the President or Vice President were buckled in. The blast tossed them like rag dolls. Townsend's chest collapsed from blunt-force trauma, but he retained consciousness. The limo came to rest on its roof. Wallace lay face-down against the far seat. Townsend could see the President's spine had been violently compressed. He was dead. Still in shock, Townsend struggled to speak, though there was no one to hear him.

"Wha— What?" Townsend's voice was nearly a whisper. He shuddered, then exhaled for the last time as his eyes grew still and dull.

In the second limo, Chase's body was crushed, but he too had retained consciousness. The synapses in his brain seemed to fire randomly as he struggled to understand what had just happened. He looked over at Mattice, whose head was thrown backward. Her neck was broken. Mattice's mouth flapped open like a dying fish. Chase thought she was trying to say something, but then he heard her choking on her own blood. It was horrific sound, and Chase wanted it to stop. He wanted the whole thing to stop. He had failed to protect the President a second time, and couldn't bear the disappointment. He listened to the last of Mattice's gargling, then drifted into blackness.

Kyle reached the Beltway when he saw a flash of light, heard a deep boom, and then saw the mushroom cloud rise above Washington. The sight caused an extreme feeling of futility. This had been the worst fear of every intelligence agency, but for Kyle, it was much more personal. He saw the haunting visions of his dream realized once again. He remembered seeing the smoke rise from the Pentagon on 9/11, but this was far worse. The mushroom cloud looked much larger, and it was rising from the middle of the city. Half a mile of the city could be gone, and tens of thousands were probably dead.

Kyle called his house. He waited as the phone rang and rang, his unease growing. His home in Mayo was far away from the blast, but his mother should have answered. Kyle called his parents' home.

"Kyle?" his father answered.

"Are mom and Joshua there?" Kyle tried to remain calm.

"No, they left for the Air & Space Museum 15 minutes ago."

"I'll try her cell phone. Turn on the news and stay inside. I'll call you again."

Kyle was more terse than usual.

Jack caught the urgency in his son's voice. "Kyle—"

Kyle hung up and called his mother's phone. After ten rings, he dialed again. Lyla didn't answer. Kyle tried over and over, but by the fourth call, the phone stopped ringing and gave a dead tone. The explosion hadn't knocked out many cell phone towers, but the flood of calls in the wake of the blast quickly overloaded the system. Kyle kept dialing.

Ahead, the cars on the highway began to slow down. Police lights flashed as cruisers blocked the road. Kyle inched forward and stuck his head out the window, showing his CIA identification.

"Road's closed!" a Highway Patrol officer shouted at him, annoyed.

"I work at CIA," Kyle replied.

"Not today, you don't."

Kyle was only ten minutes away from CIA headquarters, but the mushroom cloud was still rising above Washington. It had begun to morph and dissipate, but the shape was still discernible.

"All non-essential personnel are evacuating Washington, even over the river in Langley," the officer explained. "Now please, turn around; we're going to need these lanes for evacuation."

Kyle looked over his shoulder. Behind him, police were already directing traffic to turn around.

Supreme Court Chief Justice Thaddeus Wilson had seen the blast from his office window and ducked below his desk. His clerks also hit the deck. Just as he got to his feet, the door flung open and two Secret Service agents charged into the room.

"What's going on?" Wilson asked, somewhat bewildered after the explosion.

"Please come with us, sir," one of the agents blurted as they carried him out.

Outside the Supreme Court building, a Sikorsky UH-60 Black Hawk helicopter waited, its rotors spinning. The Secret Service agents rushed Justice Wilson to the helicopter and pushed him on board. Within seconds, the helicopter was airborne, heading away from the destruction that lay north of the Mall.

The town of Allendale, South Carolina, has a population of less than 3,500, but close to a third of that was crowded into the gymnasium on the University of South Carolina Salke-hatchie's campus. The Speaker of the House sat on the dais and looked out at the crowd. It was good to be back home in South Carolina; he was well-loved here. Allendale's mayor was just finishing up his introduction.

"Ladies and gentleman, the Honorable Russell H. Barnes!"

The crowd erupted in an applause that shook the walls of the gymnasium. Barnes stood and grinned as he waved to the crowd, taking his place at the lectern. Before Barnes could utter a syllable, a Capitol Policeman stood next to him and covered the microphone.

"You need to leave right now, sir," the policeman whispered in his ear.

Barnes didn't have time to react. A surge of policemen and security officers surrounded him and escorted him from the gymnasium. Unaware of what had just happened in Washington, the crowd reacted with murmurs of confusion and groans of disapproval.

Outside, the policemen pushed Barnes into a waiting car. The motorcade rushed off, heading for the airport. In the back seat, Barnes leaned with the torque of the high-speed cornering. He shoved the Capitol Policeman who was nearly on top of him.

"Someone want to tell me what is going on?" Barnes shouted over the roar of the car's engine. Another Capitol Policeman in the front passenger seat turned and looked at him, but didn't respond.

The motorcade raced onto the airport tarmac. Police cars had already surrounded the Speaker's jet. The car screeched to a halt and the Capitol Police officers rushed Barnes out of the car and onto the waiting plane. Inside, Barnes' Chief of Staff, Andy Rask, stood in the aisle. Barnes saw Rask was pale.

"Andy, what's happened?"

"A nuclear bomb went off in Washington," Rask said, his voice hoarse.

"What?" Barnes paused, trying to fathom the unfathomable. "What's left?"

"It was a small detonation. Maybe half a mile is totally gone. Definitely ground-based."

Barnes immediately thought of his family. "Missy and the kids?"

"I just talked with her—they're fine."

Barnes shook his head in disbelief.

"But Rusty—" Rask called his boss by a nickname he'd long used, bracing himself, "the President and Vice President were both killed. We're flying to a secure location where you'll meet Chief Justice Wilson. He'll swear you in as president."

Barnes was dumbstruck. He knew the constitutional line of succession, but he was not ready for this. No man wanted to become president in the middle of a national crisis.

Kyle crept through traffic outside Washington. He called his mother again, but there was still no answer. His call to Sadiq's office, however, was successful.

"Kyle!" Sadiq exclaimed. The reception was snowy, but his voice came through distinctly.

"What happened?"

"They got us with a tripleheader. All of them nuclear. Here, Hoover Dam, and the Port of Los Angeles."

The news was even worse than Kyle had expected. He laid his head on the steering wheel. "What's the damage?"

"We're still getting assessments, but the damage in Washington seems to be less than a mile in diameter."

"Where's ground zero?"

"We're still working on that, but it looks to be somewhere around Scott Circle."

Kyle exhaled and closed his eyes, hoping his mother and Joshua weren't close to the blast.

"We just heard—the President's motorcade was hit," Sadiq said. "He and the VP are dead."

Kyle shook his head, anger building. "I've got to get back there. They've blocked the highway, but—"

"Forget it," Sadiq interrupted. "They're evacuating."

"Not counter-terrorism personnel," Kyle asserted. Safety precautions or not, pulling out counter-terrorism analysts at a time like this would be insane.

"I doubt you'll get in," Sadiq said. "I'll update you as I can."

Raymond Westerhouse sat in his Whittier home glued to the television. He had been wakened by a large boom this morning, and looked out and saw smoke and a strange glow to the southwest. Now, forty minutes later, news of the massive attack across the nation was dominating the airwaves. Raymond knew fallout might blow their way, but he was just as concerned about the destruction of Hoover Dam. Much of Southern California's water and electricity was supplied by the dam, and now, with it gone, their utilities might falter. If there were massive blackouts and water shortages, it wouldn't be long before everything fell apart.

"Residents in all the greater Los Angeles area are urged to stay inside and close windows and doors," the television anchor said grimly. "Residents in the San Pedro and Long Beach areas are to follow orders from emergency personnel."

Raymond's ten year-old daughter, Sarah, came and sat down next to him. "What do you think, Daddy?"

Raymond wrapped his arm around his daughter and hugged her. Then he walked to the kitchen and began to gather up supplies—food, water bottles, matches, candles, and flashlights. "I think if we wait around here, we'll never get out. In an hour, traffic's going to be jammed on every freeway." Raymond carried the supplies in his full arms to the bedroom, where he started putting them in a large duffel bag. He grabbed blankets from the bed and pulled clothes from the closet. "We better go, baby," he called to his daughter. "Get a change of clothes, a blanket, and your small suitcase."

"The one with rollers?" Sarah asked, still lingering by the television.

"Yeah, that's the one." Raymond brought his packed bags into the living room.

"Can I bring Chester?" Sarah looked at their Chocolate Lab dog.

"No baby. We'll leave Chester some food and water."

"But he'll get lonely," Sarah protested, almost whining.

"When things clear up, Chester will have all his animal friends in the neighborhood to play with." It wasn't a convincing argument, but Raymond was too anxious to bother with a real answer. He ushered his daughter to her room. "Now let's go, honey."

Minutes later, their Toyota Four Runner loaded, Raymond guided Sarah over the driveway. Both shielded themselves with their coats over their heads until they were safely in the SUV. Raymond put the Toyota in gear and sped out of their neighborhood, hoping to stay ahead of the exodus that was sure to come.

Speaker Barnes' jet landed at Offutt Air Force Base in Nebraska and taxied to a stop. Barnes nearly tumbled down the stairs as Capitol Police pushed him toward a large convoy of military vehicles. The convoy took him to a small brick building on the other side of the tarmac. Military Police stood guard at the entrance. The building was about the size of an equipment shed at a public park, but this was the entrance to an underground bunker. Two Military Policemen joined the Capitol Police and escorted Barnes into the bunker.

The police led Barnes down a corridor into the situation room, where a conference table and three wall screens were set. Offutt is the headquarters of United States Strategic Command (STRATCOM), formerly known in Cold War days as Strategic Air Command. As such, the base is well equipped with the communications equipment and resources for the President to understand and respond to a major security crisis. Barnes was acutely aware this was the same bunker where President George W. Bush spent half the day on 9/11. The sense of historical déjà vu made him uneasy.

The wall screens showed news broadcasts from Washington, Las Vegas, and Los Angeles. Most of the shots were from afar, taken from the rooftops of each station. The Washington feed showed the wall of fire that scorched the White House, though no cameras were focused on ground zero. The Los Angeles feed replayed the moment just after detonation, when a helicopter covering traffic over Hollywood turned its camera toward San Pedro. The mushroom cloud and swath of destruction were clearly visible, though the image shook violently with the force of the blast wave. The Las Vegas feed was farthest from the explosion; only a distant column of smoke from rugged Black Canyon showed what remained of the Hoover Dam. Police were keeping reporters at bay, and the helicopters had been ordered to land—the footage wouldn't get any clearer. On the ground, reporters stood at police blockades. Behind them, the scenes were utter chaos—smoke, flames from secondary fires, and flashing emergency lights. The cacophony of sirens made it difficult for any of the reporters to be heard. In the bunker, the sound on all the feeds was turned low, making the reports even more difficult to hear. Barnes watched the carnage, stunned.

Before he could get a hold on what had exactly happened across the whole country, Barnes' attention was drawn to a new entourage that entered the bunker. Secret Service agents escorted Chief Justice Wilson into the room.

Wilson dispensed with any pleasantries. Given the situation, they would be highly inappropriate. "Mr. Speaker, are you ready to take the Oath of Office?"

Barnes took a deep breath and nodded.

Just about every high-ranking official in the U.S. dreams of becoming president, at least once. This wasn't at all how Barnes had imagined. This wasn't standing on the steps of the Capitol, with a million people on the Mall and the rest of America stretching out before you. Barnes was secluded in a utilitarian bunker. Lyndon Johnson might have had similar feelings on that fateful day in Dallas, 1963. He took the Oath of Office aboard Air Force One with former President Kennedy's body lying in the back of the plane. Widowed Jacqueline Kennedy stood beside the new President as he was sworn in, her husband's blood spattered over her beautiful pink Chanel suit. But as awkward as that moment had been, Johnson always knew he was a 'heartbeat away from the presidency.' Before today, eight presidents had died in office. Vice presidents succeeded them every time. They knew they might have to take on the mantle of the presidency. Despite being third in succession, it never seemed a realistic possibility that the Speaker of the House would ascend to the office.

In the brief moment that Barnes dreamed of becoming president, he imagined using a family Bible that had been printed in 1835. Rask would have retrieved it from Barnes' South Carolina home, but there had been no time. In fact, no Bible was available at all for Barnes' swearing in. The MPs tried to send for the base chaplain to secure one, but Barnes resorted to placing his hand on a cheap booklet copy of the Constitution instead. There was no time for ceremony.

The traffic now snarled the entire length of the beltway. Kyle craned his neck to see far down the road. It was thick with cars, with no end in sight. None of them were moving at all. Kyle stepped out of his car and looked up at the sky. The smoke was blowing off to the southeast. That meant Kyle might be able to enter the city from the north. He had no way of knowing whether his mother and son were in harm's way.

Just then, an army truck roared past in the empty median and skidded to a stop. Soldiers poured out of the back at the order of a sergeant. "All right, everyone, suit up!" the sergeant ordered. Each of the soldiers pulled out their NBC suits and began to put them on.

Kyle pulled his Prius onto the shoulder and left it there. He strode over to the sergeant, holding his CIA identification in front of him. "I'm with counter-terrorism," Kyle explained. "You heading into the city?"

The sergeant saw exactly what Kyle was thinking. "We can't take you unless you're suited up."

Kyle motioned to the truck. "Got an extra one?"

Moments later, Kyle sat in the back of the truck with the soldiers, his NBC suit already feeling hot and clammy against his skin. The ride through the median was rough, and Kyle had to grip onto the bench to not go flying on the bumps. Holding on tightly, Kyle watched as the truck zipped past the line of cars. When the truck raced through an underpass, the noise of the engine reverberated loudly off the concrete. The truck slowed, then honked its horn as the driver shifted into second gear. Creeping now, the truck pulled through the maze of cars and exited the Beltway onto Route 190/River Road NW. The truck picked up speed as it headed southeast. There was no traffic on this side of the road; all cars were evacuating on the opposite side, leaving room for emergency vehicles to enter the city. Kyle paused to consider this was the fastest he'd ever gotten into the city. The truck passed through Cathedral Heights and turned onto Massachusetts Avenue. As they passed the Naval Observatory, the smoke began to hit them.

Even through his gas mask, Kyle could smell burning and the felt the slightest taste of metal. He knew he was taking a risk entering a radioactive zone, but he had to find his mother and son.

18

Response

Over 18.5 million people live in the Greater Los Angeles Area. Every one of them was now living on edge. Despite orders to stay indoors, millions had flooded the freeways, seeking to flee Southern California any way they could. The wind was carrying fallout north and west over Long Beach, Lynwood, and Downey. Angelinos had also taken to the water. The ports in San Pedro and Long Beach had been destroyed, and the harbors at Redondo and Seal Beach were dangerously close to the hot zone, but nearly a million people now flooded Marina del Ray. Lying well north of ground zero but close to the major population centers in the west of Los Angeles, Marina del Ray seemed the ideal place to stage a water-bound evacuation, but authorities couldn't handle something like this.

A deluge of people forced their way onto the docks, trying to find passage on any boat. One boat owner, fearing that his sailboat would be sunk after a dozen people jumped aboard, started fending them off with a gaff. With the boat cleared of half the passengers, the owner wielded the gaff to keep others on the dock at bay.

A double-decker sightseeing boat owner was more enterprising: he charged $1,000 for each passenger while his two mammoth sons, who were bouncers at Hollywood

nightclubs, kept the crowd at bay. It was shameless oppor-
tunism, but it worked with the upscale West Los Angeles
crowd. The owner had thirty passengers in five minutes.
One father, having paid $1,000 for each of his three chil-
dren, found himself with an empty wallet. The boat owner
tried to wave him off, but the man pulled the Rolex off his
wrist and offered it in exchange for his wife's passage.

Seeing the money exchanging hands nearby, the owner
of a 30-foot sailboat started charging $500 per passenger.
He crowded 27 passengers on board when the Harbor Master appeared over his mooring and shouted down to him.
"That's too many! Too many passengers!" The boat owner
ignored him; perhaps he never heard the Harbor Master's
voice, barely audible above the clamor.

A sudden jolt from the crowd pushed the Harbor Master
toward the water, but he caught himself on a pylon. As he
turned, he caught sight of two men stealing a sailboat at
gunpoint. One of the men drove the boat's owner overboard
while the other began to motor them out into the channel. The boat owner swam toward the hull and reached up
to grab hold of a cleat, but one of the men saw him and
opened fire. The owner dove down and swam away, somehow missing the five bullets at point-blank range. He rose
again to the surface twenty feet away in the middle of the
channel. The man only had time to register the low roar
behind him before he turned and saw a speedboat. Ignor-
ing all navigational rules of the harbor, the speedboat was
racing through the channel, frantically trying to make open
sea to leave the chaos behind. The sailboat owner tried to
dive down again, but the speedboat was bearing down on
him too fast. The speedboat driver didn't bother to swerve.
He might not have even seen the man in the water, and he

didn't slow when the boat met with a dull thud. As the wake of the speedboat subsided, the sailboat owner's body rose to the surface. He was face-down in the water and not moving. His body bobbed in the foam as an expanding cloud tinged the water red.

Barnes sat before a wall of screens in a video conference with DNI Foley, CIA Director Farrell, and FBI Director Taft. Secretary of Homeland Security Mike Tibbetts was also on a screen, but his was cutting out. After several seconds of digital blocking, greenish shapes, and a cringing electronic scream, Barnes shut Tibbetts' screen off and turned to the other three. It only added to the agitation in his voice. "Who's responsible for this?"

"We received a message yesterday that predicted the attacks," Farrell said, the static making her feminine voice sound slightly robotic. "It was from the so-called Apocalypse Men."

"The Apocalypse Men?" Barnes couldn't hide his confusion. "I thought that was all wrapped up. Wasn't Wallace celebrating that this morning?"

Farrell hesitated. She expected Foley to answer, and after all, he was the one who had been there when Wallace had made the decision to take Zyuganov out. She had listened to her analysts and agreed it would have been better to wait. Barnes, however, continued looking at her screen. She swallowed and spoke low. This was a bitter pill. "It appears their capabilities were underestimated."

"So how do we fight back?" Barnes asked, moving the conversation to the key issue.

"We're doing the best we can to track them, Mr. President," Foley said. He put a slight emphasis on the title to bolster Barnes' confidence. On the other hand, he knew it might put added pressure on the new President, given how quickly he had been thrust into the role.

Barnes exhaled slowly as he looked at the screens. The peripheral ones still showed news footage from across the country, though the sound was muted. Foley, Farrell, and Taft waited on the President. *This is my first decision*, Barnes thought, *and I better not screw it up.*

"Here's what we do," Barnes said, his tone exuding authority, "All military leaves are canceled. Worldwide. Every reserve soldier will be called up immediately. I want an aerial cap over the entire country. No civilian traffic—air, sea, or ground—comes into affected areas except to help evacuate the population as necessary." That order was already taking place in Washington, but in Los Angeles, things were more disorganized. Barnes glared at the faces on the screens. "And every intelligence branch is going to do this right this time, and get those bastards. Understood?"

Foley, Farrell, and Taft's answer was unanimous. "Yes, sir."

The truck reached the edge of the destruction. It continued on for three blocks before the engine shuddered and the truck ground to a halt. The soldiers hopped out of the truck and began following the orders. Officers in NBC suits shouted to the men as they divided them into two groups, heading off in different directions. Several of the soldiers held Geiger counters that crackled at the radiation in the area. Kyle hopped off the truck and looked around. Ahead, the road was blocked by rubble. Smoke and ash obscured the view a block south. The buildings on this street still stood, but a few were nothing but shells. The fire of the initial blast wave had long died out, but now secondary fires were burning from gas lines. While Kyle's suit made him look identical to the soldiers, his bewildered body language made him stick out. Kyle couldn't understand a muffled word the officers had shouted behind their masks. One of the officers approached Kyle. Although his face was hidden behind his mask, Kyle could see the man's eyes were wide with rage. "Who are you?" the officer hissed behind his mask.

Kyle hesitated as he processed the officer's muffled question. "CIA."

"Get out of here!" The officer shoved Kyle, hard enough to bruise his chest under his suit. "This is no place for tourists! We'll report to your people when we have something!" The officer shoved him again, knocking him against the truck.

The blow knocked Kyle's mask forward. By the time he adjusted his headgear, the officer was gone, shouting orders at another group of soldiers. Kyle wondered how the officer intended for him to leave since the truck's cab was empty. There was no one in the back either. Kyle wasn't about to head back on foot, at least until he had looked for his mother and son. Seeing the soldiers occupied with their duties, he slipped away and headed east.

It wasn't long before Kyle was out of the soldiers' sight. The trees on this street were charred black skeletons; their leaves had been burned or ripped away. Several cars burned. Ash fell through the air like snow. On the corner, the facade of a three-story brownstone had collapsed, giving the building the strange appearance of a doll's house. Several civilians, blackened with soot and unprotected from radiation, were pulling survivors from the rubble. Kyle ran over to help, but slowed when he nearly tripped in his suit. He tossed brickwork aside and climbed into the open first floor. Shuffling through rubble and broken furniture, Kyle reached a middle-aged woman who had been buried under her kitchen table. Though covered in scratches, the woman was in relatively good condition. Once he had lifted the table off of her and helped her to her feet, the woman was able to walk to another rescuer who guided her out of the rubble.

Kyle heard shouts coming from the other side of the building. Making his way around a wall and the remains of the main hallway, he entered another apartment. Following the sound of the cries, he located an elderly man in the remains of his living room. The man had a bleeding laceration on his head. Kyle put a gloved hand on the wound to apply pressure and cleared debris off the man with his other hand. Another rescuer came and finished tossing aside the fragments of wood and brick that covered the man. Together, Kyle and the rescuer helped the man to his feet, and carrying him with his arms over their shoulders, escorted him from the ruin of his home.

When they reached the street, another army truck with a covered bed pulled up. Several wounded civilians rode in the back. Their injuries ranged from burns and lacerations to broken bones. The floor was covered with stretchers bearing the more heavily wounded. Kyle began to help the elderly man up into the truck when he heard a shout behind him.

"Dad!" A man not much older than Kyle ran up to them and took hold of the elderly man. Kyle stepped aside, letting the man examine his father.

A soldier in an NBC suit helped others into the truck, then turned to the father and son. "Time to go."

The man helped his elderly father take the last seat in the truck. Stepping back, the man turned to the soldier. "Which hospital are you going to? George Washington? Howard?"

The soldier shook his head. "Too close to the blast. All the windows were blown out at GW and there's a power outage at Howard." He motioned to the truck bed. "We're taking everyone to Washington Hospital Center. They're ER-One for major trauma response." The soldier headed toward the cab. Kyle followed. He could see there would be no way of finding Lyla or Joshua out here. They'd be at the hospital, if they were still alive.

"Got space for one more?" Kyle asked the soldier.

The soldier stopped and looked at him. "You a medic?"

"Sure," Kyle lied.

"Get in the back and see what you can do," the soldier said. "We're short of medics."

Kyle hopped in the back of the truck. There wasn't a place to sit, so he crouched over the wounded as the truck pulled away. Keeping his balance was tricky. He didn't want to fall into any of the wounded. There was a small first aid kit at the front of the truck bed. Kyle opened it and went to work. He started with bandaging the elderly man's head, trying to hold the skin on either side of the laceration together to stanch the blood. It was clear the man needed stitches, but Kyle didn't have those skills and the kit didn't include a needle or surgical thread. One man on the floor was moaning as he held his swollen leg. It was clear it was broken. Worse still, he had a second degree burn just below the break. Kyle took a chemical cold pack and pressed it gently against the swollen leg. The man grimaced with the smarting pain of the pack, then relaxed as the cooling compress started to work.

Twenty minutes later, they were half a block from Washington Hospital Center. There, over forty fire trucks, tarps, and tents were lined up side-by-side in a mass decontamination station. Kyle helped the wounded out of the truck and followed the booming orders policemen yelled over bullhorns. Everyone, including the ambulatory wounded, was funneled into lines before the fire trucks. All were required to strip to their underwear behind large yellow privacy tarps and leave their clothes in a pile for decontamination and disposal. Kyle was grateful for his NBC suit. Unlike the rest of people heading through the decontamination station, he didn't have to strip down. As he stood beneath the shower from the ladder hose and side spray from two trucks, he had the distinct feeling of going through a car wash. Even at low pressure, the water stung slightly. The workers scrubbed his NBC suit down with brushes and waved him on. Once through the washing station, he removed his NBC suit and let a technician wand a Geiger counter over him. His clothes had remained free of radioactive dust, and were a good sight better than the disposable paper suits being handed out.

Kyle looked out at the mass of thousands of wounded and medical staff that covered the lawn outside the hospital. The doctors, nurses, and EMTs worked calmly, but with the massive crowd the noise was still chaotic. The ER-One designation meant Washington Hospital Center was D.C.'s primary site for treatment following a massive catastrophe. Kyle watched the doctors and nurses performing triage and quickly deciphered the color-coded wrist bands they placed on each patient. Red meant serious life-threatening injuries that demanded treatment. These victims were the first to be taken inside the hospital. Yellow meant serious injuries, but the patient's condition was stable and unlikely to deteriorate for hours. Green meant minor injuries. These patients were the last to receive treatment, and waited outside. Black was reserved for the dying—those whose condition was beyond hope. Most of these patients were carried to a far corner of the lawn, where three nurses tried to comfort them in their last moments.

Kyle wove through the mass of people, looking at the children in each of the areas. He searched frantically for his son, but it was difficult to find recognizable features on many of the children. Some had their faces obscured with bandages; others had their skin, face, and hair blackened by soot and burns. Kyle started to look for children around Joshua's size. He cringed at the sight of children who were badly burned or missing limbs, but despite the pit in his stomach, continued searching. He felt some relief when he didn't find Joshua or Lyla among the wounded. He pulled out his phone to call Lyla again, but there was still no cellular service.

Kyle made one last look over the grounds as he moved toward the hospital entrance. Besides the medical staff, there were few uninjured civilians outside. Satisfied his mother and son weren't on the lawn, Kyle entered the hospital lobby and looked around.

Hundreds of injured people lay on gurneys, cluttering the lobby and lining the hallways. Despite smaller numbers than on the grounds, the walls amplified the sound of the crowd. Kyle had to keep clear of the narrow pathways as nurses and doctors darted through to treat the wounded.

Despite the chaotic scene, there was a clear system and certain efficiency processing patients. Nevertheless, the hospital was inundated.

Kyle pressed himself against the wall as he took in the scene. Nearby, a mother stood over a gurney where her child lay, gently stroking her face. Kyle leaned over to the mother and gently asked, "What part of the city did you come from?" The mother, too absorbed with her child, did not reply.

Down the hall, a child vomited, then slumped over the edge of his gurney. A nurse rushed over to help. Not far away, a doctor started chest compressions on another child who had gone into cardiac arrest. Kyle watched, a sense of hopelessness growing within him. Another nurse breezed past with an IV bag and tubing in her hands. Kyle caught her arm. "Any patients come in from the Mall?"

The nurse shook her head. "I don't know. They're from all over." Then she continued to breeze down the hall.

Kyle gazed over the lobby and decided it was useless waiting here. He followed the signs down a corridor to the burn unit. He walked carefully past the rooms, but didn't see his son. The hospital staff here were too busy to take notice of him.

Kyle decided to head to the Intensive Care Unit, which lay in another wing of the hospital. Following signs down a maze of corridors, Kyle eventually made his way to the ICU. Here, just as in the hospital in New York, the patients' rooms were isolated but visible through glass. The first two rooms he passed contained a middle-aged woman and a teenage girl, but the third room held a young boy. He looked to be about Joshua's age, but with heavy bruising about his eyes and face, it was difficult to distinguish his features. The boy also lay in a myriad of bandages. There was no name on the white board by his bed, and no definitive identification. Kyle watched him carefully. *It could be Joshua*, he thought, but he wasn't sure. The longer he watched the boy, the more fear welled inside him. He could not lose another son. This wasn't, after all, the first time he had almost lost him.

Five years earlier, Kyle stayed in Adam's hospital room long after the staff had taken his body away. Kyle stared at the empty bed, unable to reconcile what had happened. Why had God abandoned him in the very hour he reached out to him? A nurse walked into the room, but seeing Kyle's grief-stricken form, left without a word. Kyle sat for nearly an hour, then stood and went to the window. He gazed outside, his eyes focusing on only the gray overcast sky.

Presently, his wife Krissy slipped into the room. Her abdomen was swollen in her 27th week of pregnancy—she had always had a slight and short frame, and her belly showed more than most women at this stage. She sat down with some difficulty. It was the first time Krissy sat in the room. When she first saw Adam in the hospital bed, she suffered a nervous breakdown. She couldn't bear to watch her boy suffer. Thus Kyle maintained his solo vigil until well after the boy expired.

Krissy looked at the empty bed and began to weep. Kyle kept his eyes directed out the window. He could hear her crying, but he didn't turn. A long silence passed between them.

"I can't," Krissy finally said.

"What?" Kyle turned from the window, drawn from his reverie.

Krissy exhaled slowly. "I can't do this again. I can't bring a child into a world like this."

Kyle couldn't believe what he was hearing. "What? …No."

"I can't do it," Krissy said, more resolute. "I don't want to worry every day he goes out the door. I'm not ready for that."

Kyle's face twisted in pain. "No. You can't."

Krissy straightened, more resolved. "I can. I've thought about this, and I've decided." Washington, D.C. has the loosest abortion laws in the nation—unlike most states, it has no deadline for terminating a pregnancy. In her mind, she had thought it through, but Kyle couldn't believe how she could make a unilateral decision on such an important issue.

"I can't believe you—" he seethed in anger. "How selfish—"

"You're not the only one in pain!" Krissy exploded. That was the heart of the matter. She was in pain, and she wanted to end it. The life growing inside her reminded her more of her loss than the solace having another child could bring.

Kyle advanced toward his wife, his shoulders tensed aggressively. "And this is your out? You can't take it so this is your plan?"

Both their tempers had flared beyond reasonable discussion, but Krissy wasn't about to back down. "It's my body and my pregnancy." Krissy had never been a conscious advocate for women's rights or abortion, and Kyle had never been overtly for or opposed to it either. They simply hadn't given it much thought. But now, when the tragic death of their son put a wedge between them, their means of handling their grief was tearing them apart. "Legally, it's my choice," she said, trying to end the argument, "so accept it."

Kyle felt powerless, but for all the grief he felt for Adam, this news was ripping out his heart. Now Krissy became an object of all his anger. He loomed over her, and though he had never once laid a hand on his wife, he was now tempted to strike. "Don't take another child from me!" he boomed.

Krissy shrank, but when Kyle turned to fume, she looked up with fiery eyes. There was no changing her mind. Kyle paced like an animal in a cage, trying to think of a way out of his predicament.

"Here's what I'm going to do," he said finally. "I'm going to every TV station within a hundred miles, and I'll tell them about Adam. And then I'm going to tell them how you want to murder our other child!"

Krissy's mouth dropped open in shock. It took her a moment to realize just what her husband was saying. Although he had no legal right to stop her from having an abortion, he was willing to make their marriage a media circus, to drag them through a public and politically charged battle to see his way. It was a scorched earth tactic, one he knew that would destroy their marriage, but he was willing to do it to save his child.

But it wasn't an abortion that was tearing their marriage apart. It was that they had both neglected the needs of their spouse for too long. In many ways, Kyle and Krissy had lived parallel and separate lives. Most young couples mature together through combined hardships in the early years of marriage. Kyle and Krissy forged less of a bond. Their dual-career marriage shielded them from financial struggle, and Kyle had little interest in arguing over issues Krissy felt were important. He let her choose what she saw fit. Their careers also took up a tremendous amount of time, so they weren't always together. For Kyle and Krissy, life had fallen into an easy routine. They had deluded themselves into thinking things left undone today, including tending to their marriage, could be done tomorrow. Nothing was immutable. But life isn't like that. Every now and then, certain moments will pose a choice—and that choice will forever determine your course. These moments often come without preparation, and for those who have fallen into the trap of thinking anything can be amended tomorrow—as Kyle and Krissy did—they often don't see them coming. This was such a moment. There was no bringing Adam back. They couldn't bolster a marriage that had been neglected when it was buffeted with such a crisis. Now their decisions would determine their course.

Krissy's face slowly turned from astonishment to fear, and then frustration. "You wouldn't," she said, tearing up again.

"You're not giving me a choice." Kyle's face darkened.

Krissy looked at her husband, hot tears streaming down her face. There was no love here, no comfort. "I hate you. I *hate* you," she cried through clenched teeth.

"Feeling's mutual." Kyle glared at Krissy. He no longer saw the vivacious girl he had fallen in love with in college. Now he saw only a cold-hearted woman. Anger had clouded his vision, for Krissy didn't mean to be cold-hearted. Her decision was born of a pain he did not see and would not share. But it was too late. Each of them would suffer alone.

Kyle won the fight to save Joshua's life, but the marriage was over. Two days after their second son was born, Krissy left the hospital and never spoke to them again. Kyle hadn't heard a word from her until his mother mentioned her call.

In time, Kyle recognized his fault in what had happened. He hadn't acknowledged Krissy's pain, let alone given her any comfort. Had he not failed in that crucial duty of any spouse—to give emotional support and comfort—their argument might never have happened. Part of him wanted to admit this to her, to confess his own failings, but he knew it wouldn't change anything. Kyle knew the marriage couldn't be reconciled, and even if it could be, he had no desire to do it. Even though he had emotionally abandoned her, Krissy had still chosen her own feelings over the welfare of their child. Although she had caved under his threats, Kyle didn't want to be married to a woman like that. In the end, he felt any contact would be pointless.

Kyle's life changed after the divorce. Though he was overjoyed with his new son, life as a single father was difficult. His work hours were long, and his parents often became surrogate guardians. Although his home in Falls Church, Virginia, had been lovely, it reminded him too much of his wife. Worse still, his neighbors, who loved Krissy, regarded him as the local pariah. Change was necessary. Kyle moved to a house in Mayo, Maryland, on the Chesapeake Bay. While it made for a long commute to Langley, the new house on the water offered secluded respite. Kyle sold his Jeep Grand Cherokee and bought a Toyota

Prius to handle the commute. In the long hours driving to and from work, Kyle often thought of his new son. Joshua was the joy of his life. Now he might lose him too.

A voice pulled Kyle back to the ICU. A woman stood next to him, her face and neck covered in burns. Her arms were heavily bandaged. "We were looking forward to this trip," the woman said. "Our daughter was presenting at a civics convention," she explained. "We told her we couldn't afford to come. We wanted to surprise her."

Kyle turned away from the woman. He discreetly wiped the tears that had formed as he thought about Joshua. He felt compelled to shield his pain from this woman's strange intrusion.

"I shouldn't have brought Timmy," the woman said. "You prepare to send him off to school. You're never prepared to have to say goodbye."

Adam flashed into Kyle's mind. He closed his eyes to bolster himself. *You don't know if you've lost another one yet*, Kyle thought. *There's still hope.* When he opened his eyes and looked through the glass, he saw the boy clearly for the first time. This wasn't his son. It was the woman's. He knew her pain, but Kyle wasn't ready to commiserate. A shot of adrenaline ran through him, and with it, a message—*Joshua is alive, and you have to find him.* Kyle excused himself and headed down the corridor. His search continued with renewed purpose.

For all its maze of freeways, Los Angeles has only four main arteries that lead to points north and east. U.S. 101 and I-5 are to the northwest and north, I-15 and I-10 to the northeast and east. All of these were now jammed as millions evacuated Southern California. Police directed both sides of the freeways for outgoing traffic, leaving only one lane to head back into the city. Still, the roads were flooded well above capacity. Raymond Westerhouse was on I-15, just south of the El Cajon Pass, when traffic ground to a standstill. The air was sweltering, but Raymond feared opening the windows would risk exposure to fallout contamination. He also didn't want to run the air conditioning and risk running out of gas. Sarah was getting restless in the back seat. Her MP3 player's battery was dead, and they couldn't play the car's DVD player for risk of running the battery down. Raymond tried to entertain his daughter the best he could. "How many different license plates can you see, honey?" he asked.

Sarah craned her neck and looked around. "Eight. All California."

"Hey, here's a question…why do they call Rhode Island an island, if it isn't an island?"

Sarah sighed, too hot to care. "I don't know." She gazed outside as the sun continued to bake their car. They wouldn't be moving any time soon. The line of cars stretched for miles, all the way up the pass.

Half a mile north, a tanker truck carrying gasoline inched ahead, then screeched to a halt. Behind the truck, a driver in a sedan gazed at the red warning placard on the tank's surface. A bead of sweat ran down his temple as he looked at the flame illustration. He had been driving behind the truck for the last three miles, and in this creeping traffic, his mind was dulled with ennui. But something struck him oddly now—a feeling that he'd be better off somewhere else. *Nonsense*, he thought to himself. *There's nowhere to go.*

Inside the truck's cab, the driver knew his time had come. Like any foot soldier, his value lay in his expendability. Like any fanatic, he believed his reward lay in achieving his plan. That plan would bring his death and that of countless others. His brothers-in-arms had succeeded in doing their part this morning; now he and seven others still had their jobs to do. For most of his life, he had been a marginalized man. The world would not respect him, but they would soon fear him. That fear would live on long after his death. He looked to where the mountains met the azure sky and wondered what paradise would be like. Would dying hurt? No matter. It would only be a moment, and now the time had come. He reached next to his seat and pulled out a small box. Inside lay a device with a button. A wire ran from the box to the underside of the chassis, where a bundle of powerful explosives lay directly under the tank. The driver inhaled sharply and pressed the button.

The tanker exploded in a massive fireball, enveloping cars a hundred yards on either side of the truck. A few seconds passed before the fuel tanks of these cars ignited, setting off another massive explosion with a percussive wall of flame. Another tanker exploded on the other side of the freeway. Now the firestorm expanded and spread, catching more cars on fire like a destructive row of dominoes. Drivers began to flee in panic. The road was completely blocked by the inferno.

Westerhouse saw the smoke rising in the distance and heard the distant booms. Before long, an exodus of panicking people came running past them. Raymond saw the crowd was getting thicker. It wouldn't be long before he wouldn't be able to open his car door for the surging throng. "Honey, get your bag," he ordered.

Sarah grabbed her bag and stepped out of the car. A frantic man tried to dart past, but tripped over Sarah's bag and knocked her to the ground.

"Sarah!" Raymond wailed, seeing his daughter was about to be trampled by the mob. The man got up and ran on, not bothering to check the girl. Raymond was at his daughter's side in a second, helping her to her feet and pulling her and her bag out of the traffic. Taking her hand, Raymond led Sarah to the back of their Four Runner, where they were momentarily shielded from the crowd that squeezed by. He opened the hatch and removed what supplies he could carry. They would weigh him down, but he needed enough food, water, and blankets for both of them. When the load was too much for him to bear, Raymond turned over the lightest items to Sarah.

The mob now sprinted in panic through the narrow lanes between cars. Raymond didn't know why they were all headed south; it was away from the fireball, but fallout lay in their path. He looked to the mountains. They were steep, but a better sight than the burning road or the chaotic metropolis they had left behind. Raymond took Sarah's hand and lifted the duffel bag onto his left shoulder. Using it as a shield, he led her across the lanes of people and through the maze of cars toward the edge of the freeway. He kept himself and his daughter crouched low so they would be braced against the crowd. When they passed the second lane, someone hit his duffel bag and bounced off with a groan. Raymond absorbed the energy of the blow in his legs and feet, then moved on. At the third lane, he heard someone shout, "Hey!" from behind his bag, apparently frustrated with the momentary blockage in his path.

The man shoved the bag, but Raymond moved on, letting the duffel bounce off the hood of a car.

They were now at the edge of the road, free of the mob. Ahead lay a large field with long brown grass, and beyond it, the mountains. Raymond looked to Sarah, who had been terrified in their dash across the freeway. Now she was beginning to calm down. He reached into his bag, grabbed a water bottle, and handed it to his daughter. Sarah took a gulp. "Slowly," Raymond cautioned. They sat by a fence just beyond the road and rested until Sarah had caught her breath. Raymond wiped Sarah's long, sweaty hair from her eyes and wrapped his arm around her shoulders. "Ready?" he finally asked.

"Ready, Dad."

Raymond and Sarah threw their gear over the fence. He held the barbed wires apart so his daughter could slip through, then climbed over himself, making sure to not get snagged. They had a long way to walk before they would even reach the base of the mountains, but the heat and sound of the flames pushed them on. Raymond worried the dry grass might catch on fire and spread toward them, but none did. By now, firefighting helicopters were dumping water on the fire, and a large tanker plane had even dumped red slurry retardant to box in the flames. It was far more frightening to see this carnage than the bomb, which they had only witnessed on TV. Sarah kept turning back to watch, filled with fear, but Raymond urged her to keep going. When they had climbed the bench of the mountain, they stopped and looked back one last time. The sky was black with smoke from the fire. To the south, toward Los Angeles, the horizon glowed. Raymond stared in stunned silence. The apocalypse had come.

19

Out of the Ashes

Kyle had searched every room he could see in the ICU. There wasn't any sign of Joshua or his mother. He stood in front of a directional sign, wondering which wing he should head to next, when his phone started to ring. The chime was a startling but welcome sound; he had no service for some three hours. Better still, when Kyle picked up, he heard the voice of his mother.

"Kyle?" Lyla sounded strong but concerned.

"Mom? How are you and Josh?"

"We're okay."

Kyle sighed with relief.

"Are you safe?"

"I'm fine," Kyle said.

"We've been trying to get hold of you."

"Me too. I had no service. Where are you?"

"At the zoo."

Kyle's mind raced as he tried to process this information. The zoo was out of the range of the blast, not far from him now, so they must be truly all right—but why were they there? "Dad said you went to the Air & Space Museum."

"Joshua changed his mind on the way. He wanted to see the pandas."

Kyle shook his head and smiled. His boy's fickleness had saved their lives.

"Are you in the middle of all this?"

"I'm at Hospital Center."

"It's so terrible." Lyla's voice was shaking for the first time. She had clearly fretted as much about her son, even though he had left a note and voice message that said he had gone to Princeton that morning. The hours they had not been able to reach each other must have been just as long for her.

"I'll come to you," Kyle said.

"They're closing the zoo—we have to leave."

"I'll meet you by the Columbia Heights metro in half an hour."

"Okay." There was relief in her voice, but also a reluctance to hang up. "Bye."

A new set of faces appeared on the video screens in front of Barnes—the generals at the head of NORTHCOM, or United States Northern Command, and the Chairman of the Joint Chiefs of Staff. Secretary of Homeland Security Mike Tibbetts had finally gotten his feed fixed, and was coming through clearly. General Bump Foley also remained on the center screen. The general at the head of United States Northern Command was concurrently the head of NORAD, the North American Aerospace Defense Command, and stationed at Peterson Air Force Base in Colorado.

"So what's the initial assessment?" Barnes asked.

"All ground-burst nuclear detonations, sir," the general at the head of NORTHCOM answered. "The largest was in Los Angeles, about the size of the recent African bomb. The smallest was in Washington."

"Do y'all agree with that?" Barnes asked. As the day progressed, his polished and constricted tongue loosened, allowing his natural southern dialect to resurface. Formalities of speech were the last thing on his mind.

"We concur," Foley answered. The others nodded their heads.

"But if they were ground-based, how'd they get them in?"

"The bombs in Washington and the Hoover Dam were tactical nukes," Foley answered. "Possibly one or more modified suitcase bombs."

"Suitcase bombs?" Barnes raised his eyebrows. "Didn't they debunk that?"

"Well, 'suitcase' is a misnomer. They're the size of a large backpack, 50 to 100 pounds in weight. Still easy to hide."

"And our assessment is that they've hidden them for a very long time," Tibbetts said. "These, like the African bomb, seem to be Soviet-era manufacture. At least the Washington bomb—we haven't been able to get close enough to run tests in the other zones yet."

"There were rumors, decades ago, that the Soviets hid tactical nukes in the U.S. to use in case of war, but we couldn't confirm it," Foley said reluctantly.

"So you assumed they weren't there," Barnes snapped. "Anybody else got something to tell me we were wrong about today?"

There was an awkward silence. Then Tibbetts haltingly spoke. "Sir, to go back to your original question of how they got them in…one of our surveillance cameras showed a small submarine approaching Hoover Dam just before the detonation. We believe it was the delivery vehicle."

"Don't tell me it's that easy," Barnes shook his head in disappointment. "What else?"

"We're not sure about the other bombs," Foley said. "Most likely a shipping container in L.A., given the location of detonation at the port. Most likely a large vehicle in D.C.—maybe a delivery van. Both would have to have been lead-lined to avoid detection."

"Aren't our sensors more advanced than that?" Barnes was becoming more agitated by the moment. This was a colossal failure.

It fell to Tibbetts to answer once again. "Sir, our radiation sensors in D.C. and throughout the country are over a decade old. They badly need upgrading. Unfortunately, we didn't receive the funds necessary for that from the last administration."

Barnes zeroed in on Foley and Tibbetts. "But why didn't we at least have warning of these attacks?"

"Mr. President, Director Farrell told you we received a message from the Apocalypse Men yesterday."

"I recall," Barnes prompted Foley to continue.

"It came initially to reporters at a Middle Eastern TV network, then wound through various channels to us." Rule Number One in intelligence, as in journalism, is never reveal a source—but Foley knew Barnes needed an explanation. He was being vague enough to protect identities and networks. "The message, like those that have come before it, was not specific to targets; it only mentioned methods, and those in very symbolic language. We were deciphering it when the attacks came."

Barnes had just about enough of these slack explanations. Their failure was clear, but could they get things turned around fast enough to retaliate? "All right," he sighed with exhaustion, "anybody got some good news?"

"Sir, we've activated all troops," the Chairman of the Joint Chiefs of Staff said.

"And, sir, in conjunction with local and state police units, any areas that are considered prime targets, such as nuclear plants and other public utilities, are now being guarded," the general from NORTHCOM said. He didn't mention that major cities were also being extremely cautious. Just like on 9/11, Chicago's Willis Tower had been evacuated. New York City, still reeling from the smallpox attacks, was largely shut down. Most Americans outside the affected areas were either heading home or staying home. "The aerial cap is also in place," he added.

"All right," Barnes said. He sounded satisfied, but then something grabbed his attention. He pointed to the screen still showing the news, although the other men on the video conference couldn't see it. It indicated the situation in Los Angeles was deteriorating—aerial TV shots showed people smashing shop windows, looting stores, overturning cars, and setting random fires. "What are we doing about this rioting?"

"Sir, the governor called up the National Guard in Los Angeles," the NORTHCOM general said. "We've liaised with them and the mayor, and will send up Marines from Camp Pendleton if necessary. The National Guard has been called up in a dozen cities across the country, and curfews will be enforced. We expect things to calm down tonight."

Barnes appreciated the military's response. They were swift and professional, but like the rest of America's security agencies, they were playing catch-up. "What do we have on the Apocalypse Men? How are we going to fight them?"

"Mr. President, we're throwing the full force of all our agencies against this threat," General Foley said. "We'll track them."

"And when they find them, sir, we'll get the bastards," the Chairman of the Joint Chiefs of Staff concluded.

An adjutant officer entered and dutifully apologized for his intrusion. "Sirs, we've received another message."

"Where is it?" Barnes asked.

"On the news, sir."

Barnes changed the news screen to a national broadcast. The blood-red backdrop appeared once again, with the featureless but now familiar silhouetted man in front of it.

We know the destiny of the world, the man said, the hoarse whisper of his voice sending chills through Barnes. *Now you see. We are not just messengers. We are Death, the Destroyer of Worlds. And even those brave soldiers who fight against us—none of you will survive.*

Barnes set his jaw in anger, but quietly swallowed in fear. So far, the Apocalypse Men had always been right.

Kyle watched the message on TV in his Maryland home. He sat on the couch, cradling his sleeping son on his lap. After this long day, he was relieved to have Joshua safely back in his arms. But the message was deeply disturbing. This wasn't just a terrorist gloating over a successful attack—one that overshadowed 9/11—but a solemn promise that this was a fight to the death.

Kyle turned off the television, checked to see Joshua was sleeping soundly, and turned to his parents, who sat on the adjacent couch. Fearing their Chevy Chase home was too close to the chaos, they had come with him. Only Washington, D.C. itself had been evacuated, but since their home lay within the beltway, they feared they would become trapped if the mass exodus expanded. "Maybe you should take Josh and leave for a while," Kyle whispered.

"I was thinking the same thing," Jack said.

"Where will you go?"

"Canada, maybe Europe."

Kyle nodded. "Seems safe. For now." His mind started to race with the data he knew so far. Canada and Europe had been spared each wave of the attacks, but could that change? "You might have to go farther if—"

"We can't leave you," Lyla interrupted.

"You know I can't go," Kyle insisted. More than ever, he had a job to do. "But if the fallout winds change, or another attack occurs, you shouldn't be here."

Jack grunted as he got to his feet. "I'll head back to the house and pack us up."

"Good," Kyle said. "All civilian flights are grounded, so you'll have to drive—"

"To Canada?" Lyla asked doubtfully. "What if the highways get clogged?"

"That could happen. The sooner you leave, the better."

Clive Cordell sat in his rustic cabin and ate a humble meal out of a heated tin can. He didn't mind the simplicity of his new domicile; he had spent as much time here as in his old home on the grid. Cordell liked to hear the crickets at night and the hushing sound of the wind in the pines. Those were the only companions he needed. He scraped the last of the beans from the bottom of the tin, the spoon clanging off the container. As he downed the last morsel, he froze.

He didn't bother to pull the spoon from his mouth, but listened. The crickets, which usually provided a constant serenade, had stopped chirping. In a moment, their nightly song returned, but Clive was now on alert. Something had disrupted them. Cordell moved silently across the floor and grabbed his shotgun off the rack above the fireplace. He trimmed the Coleman lamp on the kitchen table and laid it on the floor, shading the beam from the window. The cabin had a propane tank which provided it with heat and limited electrical power, but he preferred the camping lamps.

Quietly, Cordell crept across the room to the cabin door and slipped outside. With the lamp trimmed, the open door betrayed no light. He kept one hand on the door as it shut behind him to keep it from slamming against the frame. Cordell stood and felt the night breeze against his face. He peered into the darkness but saw nothing. The moon was shaded tonight, and everything within the brush lay in deep shadow. Still, he sensed something. He waited, and then he heard it: an unnatural rustle, far clumsier than any bear, moose, or deer. Something was moving out there, and it was coming toward him. Cordell raised his shotgun and crooked his finger over the trigger. He wasn't afraid. He was ready.

Sarah and Raymond Westerhouse trudged through the forest, dirty and exhausted. The gear Raymond carried felt twice as heavy as when they started, and Sarah was frustrated with branches constantly slapping at her face in the darkness. Somewhere through the rustling branches they had seen a light ahead. Now the light was gone, but Sarah had definitely seen it. The night was getting colder. Raymond worried Sarah wouldn't be able to stand the exposure to the elements all night, even with several fleece blankets.

They had matches, but the wind was strong, and he feared it would either blow out a fire or set the forest ablaze. Shelter was now a priority.

Raymond stumbled as he made his way up the slippery slope behind his daughter. Sarah paused, trying to reorient herself. "I saw it up there. A light in a house. You think they'll let us stay for the night?"

Raymond set the large duffel bag down and tried to catch his breath. "I don't know."

"We could pay them. You've got money, right?"

"Right." The idea was sounding better by the minute.

"Let's go ask."

Raymond grunted as he heaved the gear onto his back. "Right after you, baby."

Sarah, now sure of the house's location, bounded through the brush. She slapped the tree branches away, driven by the excitement of finding refuge. Plenty of branches still scratched at her face, but she no longer cared. She wanted a hot meal and a cozy bed.

On the porch, Cordell heard the crunching in the underbrush and wheeled his shotgun toward the noise. This was no animal. Confident he had a bead on the intruder, he shouted into the darkness. "You're trespassing!"

A man's voice drifted toward him faintly. "Excuse us! We're lost!"

"Get lost somewhere else!" Cordell had never liked people, and he certainly didn't want anyone intruding on him now. This was the Apocalypse. God's judgment was on the world, and if he hadn't been raptured up to meet Him, Cordell wasn't about to share his fate with some sinner. He was going to meet God's judgment alone. Cordell cocked the shotgun loudly, hoping the sound would give enough warning for the intruder to back off.

Sarah kept pressing through the bush. She was confident they'd be able to convince the owner to shelter a young girl and her father once he saw them. Raymond, however, felt a sharp and imminent sense of danger. "Wait! Wait!" he called out.

A loud boom rang out into the night. Before its echo faded, the flapping of an owl's wings and several other creatures could be heard scampering away for fright. It was the loud, near-animal screech that pierced Cordell's ears. Urgent and plaintive, Cordell realized something was definitely not as he had reckoned. Lowering his shotgun, he ran into the brush toward the sound. Cordell pulled a flashlight from a clip on his belt and shone it into the thick underbrush. It wasn't long before he found it. A young girl, about ten years old, was hunched over on the ground. Cordell flinched, fearing he had shot the girl. When she reared up to meet the beam of his flashlight, he saw her hand covered in blood. Cordell drew back in horror, his worst fear confirmed—until he heard the raspy breathing on the ground in front of her. Lowering his flashlight, Cordell saw the blood had not been the girl's, but her father's. He lay with a large bloody wound covering his torso. Raymond weakly reached an arm to his daughter as he struggled to speak, but no words came. The girl tried frantically to stanch the blood with her hands, but in vain. She whimpered, then looked up at Cordell, her eyes pleading for some explanation why he had done this. To his shame, Cordell had no answer.

Mashiri was overjoyed. This day had been decades in planning, and it had gone off without a single hitch. Vasquez and Al-Salameh stayed after the meeting to watch news of the attacks on satellite television. Though Mashiri's island was incredibly remote, his dedicated satellite relay ensured the coverage would come in crystal-clear. Vasquez and Al-Salameh watched in stunned celebration. They had carefully planned each phase of their mission, but the success of detonating three nuclear bombs on American soil and killing both the President and Vice President left them speechless. Vasquez and Al-Salameh only stayed a couple hours before leaving to oversee the next phase of their mission. There was much work to be done. Still, Mashiri was able to sit alone in quiet satisfaction and reflect. There had been so many ways it could have gone wrong—the bombs might have fizzled, there could have been a decoy motorcade, the foot soldiers might have been caught or chickened out at the last minute. But Mashiri had been successful because his planning had been so precise.

The foot soldiers he recruited were zealots of many flavors—most were jihadists, but there were others in the mix, too. A third of them came from America, but the rest were foreigners. Getting visas for each of those men was surprisingly easy. He had strict rules for their recruitment—they must not have been on any terror watch list or have any associations that would bring them to the attention of law enforcement. This requirement was difficult enough to meet, but it was not the only one—Mashiri also needed to know they were men of fortitude and commitment. They had to fulfill their missions. It had taken infinite patience to find the eleven teams that would sacrifice themselves in these attacks. The two men in the armored truck were the most capable, so they won the honor of leading the Washington attack. The team at the Hoover Dam had two men, but the submarine could only hold one man and the bomb. The bomb on *Last Horizon* didn't need to be detonated in person, but two crewmen were sent along to ensure everything went as planned. Each of the eight tanker truck drivers was alone. There were also the spotters and other backup personnel who were prepared to sacrifice themselves if necessary. Altogether, over twenty men had taken part in the attacks. All did precisely as ordered. The suicide attacks killed thirteen agents. Three of the spotters also died in the Washington blast. The handful who survived were just as elated as their leaders. When darkness fell, the last two spotters slipped into a small boat and motored toward a yacht in the Chesapeake Bay. Once aboard, their comrades joined them in unrestrained celebration.

At Mashiri's island retreat, the time for celebration was over. It was time to look ahead. Four woes were past; three remained. Only when all seven had been achieved would Mashiri's plan be complete.

CIA Director Leslie Farrell met with Deputy Director Andrew Everton in the near-empty Headquarters building. Both of them were exhausted after a very long day, but there was still much to be done. To their surprise, Farrell's secretary announced a visitor: FBI Director Bill Taft.

"Bill…what are you doing here?" Farrell asked.

Taft looked as weary as Farrell, but was cordial. "I could say the same for you."

"Why should I go to Mount Weather?" Most high-level government officials, following protocol, had retreated to the emergency bunkers at Mount Weather, Virginia. The site is also the headquarters of FEMA, the Federal Emergency Management Agency. "My work, and the people I need to speak to, are here—or available at the touch of a button."

Taft shrugged. "Well, there you go." Taft and Farrell had a stronger professional rapport than most heads of the FBI and CIA. They were both absolute professionals, but they had risen to their positions against the grain. Farrell was the first female CIA Director; Taft was the first African-American FBI Director. Knowing the Bureau once persecuted Martin Luther King, Taft took great pride in his position at the head of a transformed agency. He ran a tight ship; the FBI was more efficient and just than it had ever been in its history. But tonight he felt a profound sense of failure.

He looked out the window at the eerie glow that colored the night sky over Washington. The fallout was blowing away from Langley, so CIA Headquarters lay in no particular danger. But Washington itself was nearly evacuated, and the roads leading to and around the Beltway were still jammed with traffic. "You hear about the tanker bombs?"

Farrell nodded toward the television in the corner, still playing news. "All four freeways out of Southern California. Poor people are trapped down there. 18 million in a cage."

"FEMA's trying to get people to shelter in place—"

"That didn't work from the beginning."

"At least the National Guard is assisting the Highway Patrol with traffic," Deputy Director Everton said. "That's keeping order, even if it will take weeks to get people out on small state roads."

"But that's just part of it. Hoover Dam, Washington, D.C., and New York before that." Taft sighed as he sat on the couch. His body seemed to lose all strength. "How did we get here? So blind that we can't clean up after one attack before the next one hits us."

Farrell leaned back in her chair, just as weary. "We've woken to some harsh truths today."

Taft balled his hands into fists so tightly that his fingernails drew blood. He should have seen this day coming. He knew Wallace's budget cuts had hamstrung the intelligence and defense agencies, but Taft's protests had fallen on deaf ears. Wallace was more concerned with social issues. "I tried to warn the President, but he just wouldn't listen." It was a delicate matter to speak ill of the dead, but Wallace had left them with this mess.

"Maybe that was his failing," Farrell said. "It wasn't Wallace's administration of national security matters, but his inattention to it."

Taft considered this, but it didn't ease his mind.

"Or perhaps he naïvely thought these threats were insubstantial," Farrell added. "We gave him our reports. The decisions were up to him."

Taft shook his head. "We should have convinced him."

"Well, that's the other problem," Deputy Director Everton chimed in. "We didn't know enough to make a convincing case."

As much as Farrell hated to admit it, Everton was right. "We didn't know enough." It was the most obvious of admissions, but the most painful she had made all day. All of them had to do their jobs better, hamstrung by a president's agenda or not. Thousands of Americans had lost their lives for their failure.

Taft was trying to make sense of it all, and he needed to pinpoint the biggest mistakes. "Maybe Wallace shouldn't have ended the NSA dragnet."

"No, none of the information prior to these attacks came through signals intelligence," Deputy Director Everton said. "Besides the videos, the Apocalypse Men have kept away from electronic communication as much as possible."

As desperate as he was for answers, Taft's mind was too tired to find them. He needed sleep, but he feared waking up to yet another attack. What more could they have done? The response had been admirable—every agent in the Bureau was now at work, poring over every bit of evidence they could find in the hope it would lead to arrests. The military, FEMA, and state and local authorities were bringing the chaotic sites of attack under a modicum of control. But what lay ahead? Their blindness had cost them, and they were still as blind as ever. Taft hesitated to ask the question, knowing how dangerous it was that he did not know the answer. "What do we do now?"

Barnes' first day as president had been one of the darkest in America's history. It was also one of the longest in his life. He was angry that the Apocalypse Men had broadcast a victory lap speech before he was able to address the nation himself, but the nature of the disaster and how he had been forced to answer it hadn't allowed any time for public relations. An hour after the Apocalypse Men broadcast, Barnes finally addressed the nation for the first time. His speechwriter, Peter Field, had been left this morning in South Carolina, and had to be flown in separately. It was by far the most difficult speech he had ever written, and the most difficult Barnes had ever delivered. How do you tell the nation they'll press on after they've been hit with three nuclear weapons and the President and Vice President have been killed? Chief of Staff Rask was impressed with his boss' composure during the speech. Barnes, in his opinion, had shown mournful sympathy and stoic resolve. It was just the right note, he thought.

The President of the United States is widely considered the most powerful man in the world, but Barnes was acutely aware of his limitations. It wasn't just the dire situation that was daunting, but the secret doubt he harbored concerning his abilities. How could he—how could anyone—be up to this task? Abraham Lincoln had faced such challenges, but Barnes knew he was no Lincoln. Future generations wouldn't be carving his face into a mountain, building a monument on the Mall in his honor, or putting his likeness on money. He was a forgettable man in an unforgettable time. He only had to make less mistakes than his predecessor, so that neither he, nor any other American, would suffer Wallace's fate.

By 11 o'clock that night, aides reported that the evacuation of Washington was complete. The fallout threatened parts of the lower Chesapeake Bay, but the radiation levels within the city were falling. Still, the Secret Service would not allow the new President to return to the capital. They offered transit to the presidential bunker at Mount Weather, but Barnes refused, seeing he could manage just as well with direct contact to the military officials whose response he deemed his highest priority. FEMA was doing its part in the three affected areas, and he had given orders as necessary, but here was where he needed to be. The Secret Service flew in Barnes' family, and he had spent ten minutes with them to reassure each other and have a quick bite to eat.

By 2 A.M., the tide had turned, and things were finally starting to go Barnes' way. The military and emergency response teams were starting to report with confidence from the disaster areas. Though marginal, they were beginning to establish control. The nation as a whole, though deeply shaken and entirely unsettled, was still holding together. Barnes only had twenty minutes' sleep after 4 A.M. But as he closed his eyes, he felt assured that he would awaken as president of a country in crisis, not a land of anarchy.

Kyle sent off his family shortly after dawn. The drive to Canada would be a long one, and the freeways were nearly clogged as he predicted, but at least traffic was still flowing. He called Sadiq to check on the situation at CIA Headquarters, but the area was still in lockdown. He wouldn't be able to return for at least another day. Shut out from work, his mind weighed down with the cataclysmic events of the past day. Most of all, his thoughts turned to Joshua. The boy was the most important person in his life. Though the boy had been in no physical danger at the zoo, the feelings that overcame Kyle as he searched the city and hospital were too raw, too close to how he lost Adam. Kyle swore he would protect Joshua at any cost. He had no way to guarantee that promise, but he swore he would not lose the boy.

At the same time, Kyle felt utterly hopeless about the state of the world. His family was safe, but he and the rest of the intelligence community had once again failed in their duty. The results of their failure were apparent at the hospital, where he had seen thousands of innocent children and families suffer. For Kyle, the failure was especially painful—he had dreamed about this disaster, as he had of others before it—and yet he was powerless to stop any of the attacks. Why did he have these dreams if they could not help him? What more could he do?

If there was a way he could do more to protect his son, Kyle was determined to find it. But that meant he'd have to stop the Apocalypse Men. Was there something about his dreams he had not yet realized? He had been reluctant to share his dreams with others for fear of being written off as crazy. In his work facts and evidence, also known as data, were paramount. But he needed to know why he was cursed with foreknowledge of these disasters and an inability to stop them. The more that weighed on him, the more he was sure of what he needed to do. He had to see Dr. Hightower.

20

A Prophet

"You saw the video last night?" Kyle asked Dr. Hightower as he sat across from him in his office.

Hightower nodded. "Clearly things have escalated."

"'*The Destroyer of Worlds*'...normally I'd call that crazy, but after yesterday..." Kyle shook his head, unable to finish the thought. It was unthinkable.

"That was a quote from the *Baghavad Gita*, Chapter 11, Verse 32. Fitting, really—Robert Oppenheimer quoted it after he invented the atomic bomb."

"So Hinduism is part of their syncretic belief."

"Maybe."

Kyle sat absorbed in thought for a long moment. Hightower waited, but he could see Kyle's agitation growing. "I guess it's not surprising. It's been going on for centuries. The Crusades, Inquisition, Jihads and ritual killings — probably more humans have been killed in the name of religion than for any other reason," Kyle said.

"But the secular ideologies of Communism and Nazism brought about 100 million deaths in the 20th century—a much faster rate than in any era of religious killing. So is the problem really with God, or man?"

Kyle mulled that over. He inhaled sharply, then paused for a moment. He finally breathed out when he spoke.

"Maybe they're cherry picking quotes to suit their purposes—make us believe they're syncretic."

"There's that possibility," Hightower conceded. "A risky strategy, if that's the case. Their messages reach a more diverse audience but the efficacy is diminished. If the quotes are chosen purely for effect, Revelation makes sense to a Western, Christian-based target. Throwing in a quote from the *Baghavad Gita*, as ominous as it sounds, loses some resonance."

"They obviously want their targets to believe what they say; it spreads fear," Kyle asserted. "But this isn't just about propaganda. Three of these messages have come as predictions, and they've been successful fulfilling them every time." He receded into thought again. After a moment, he stood and started to pace. Something was clearly bothering him.

Hightower, an unusually patient man, waited. Though their conversation was held in private, anyone who could have observed the two would have had the distinct impression Hightower was awaiting Kyle's confession.

"It sounds crazy, but what if they are fulfilling prophecy?" Kyle asked. "What if everything they say is inevitable?" He expected Hightower to mock him, but the professor didn't. He didn't say anything at all—just waited patiently for Kyle to continue. "I mean…" Now Kyle really was making a confession, even if it wasn't to a priest. He didn't believe in that sort of thing anyway, but he had never admitted what he was about to, and it was just as hard as confessing a sin. "I had dreams before every attack. I saw them."

"You dreamed about the attacks?" Again, there was

nothing accusatory in Hightower's tone, and he encouraged Kyle to continue.

"It was abstract, but I saw each one before they happened. We had the messages as warnings. We tracked all the data we had, but…" he broke off in frustration, then spat out the last words. "*None* of it helped."

Hightower waited for another moment, ensuring that Kyle was finished. When he spoke, it was softly but clearly: "What do you make of the dreams?"

Kyle sat down, nearly collapsing into the chair in exasperation. "I don't know. I haven't told anyone else because it seems crazy. You understand, in my line of work, you have to go on evidence. Premonition without evidence is no good." He shook his head again. "And I've heard of the Cassandra Complex, but this is…" he couldn't seem to find the right words. "…Something else." The Cassandra Complex is a psychological condition named for the character in Greek mythology. The daughter of King Priam of Troy, she predicted the great city's doom, but she was cursed by Apollo so that no one believed her. Thus, those suffering from the Cassandra Complex experience distressing perceptions, but are disbelieved when they share the cause of their suffering with others.

"Do you think God is telling you something?" Hightower asked.

Kyle chuckled at the question, but as he looked back at the professor, he saw it was asked in earnest. "If God exists, he hasn't said anything to me in a long time."

"Why is that?"

Kyle locked eyes with Hightower. "You remember the bombing five years ago at the Jefferson Memorial?"

Hightower nodded solemnly, inviting Kyle to go on. He could tell this was a sensitive topic for him.

"My son Adam was hit by shrapnel. I stayed by his bed for three days." His eyes started to well with tears as the emotion of the memory hit him. "Every moment I prayed for his life, but in the end, he died. I don't know if God answered the prayers of the jihadist who murdered my son, but he sure didn't answer my prayer for Adam's life."

Hightower paused respectfully before responding in a soft and even voice. Clearly he had a gift for discussing sensitive matters. "I don't know why God doesn't answer some of our most fervent prayers. Even Christ on the cross, at his greatest hour of need, felt abandoned. But I do know this—it shouldn't keep you from listening. God may still have something to say that you need to hear."

Kyle wasn't sure if he was more surprised by the content of Hightower's words or the fact that he had so easily shifted from the role of academic to something of a spiritual counselor. This wasn't at all what he expected from this consultation, and yet it reached the heart of his struggle. Kyle hadn't seen Dr. Hightower as exactly a man of faith—more a man of knowledge—but now his spiritual side was undeniable. Still, Kyle wasn't convinced Hightower was right. "*If* he's saying anything, it's not good. The message I'm getting is this is inevitable. I saw hundreds of people at that hospital yesterday who were just like my son. I couldn't help any of them." He clenched his teeth and breathed out in frustration. "I couldn't stop it."

Hightower, steady as always, answered softly but resolutely. "God wins in the end—that's the message of Revelation. So if it is the End of Days, there will ultimately be rejoicing, after much tribulation."

"But there are millions of innocent people suffering, dying—is that God's plan?"

"I don't discount the suffering of the innocent, and I don't have the answers for everything. For myself, I trust God has farther vision than I."

Kyle considered this as he looked over the book titles on Hightower's shelves. One caught his eye: *Reawakening and Revival: Christianity and Spiritualism in 19th Century America.* It led to a more academic thought, one that made Kyle more comfortable as it shifted the focus from his personal belief. "What about the Rapture? Isn't God supposed to take the good people to heaven?"

"I respectfully disagree with Evangelicals on that issue," Dr. Hightower said. "God's elect have always had to suffer through tribulation—why should now be any different?"

Kyle mulled on that. He liked the logic in the answer. But eventually, perhaps inevitably, his mind returned to the original question, and uncomfortable or not, he needed it answered. "So…it's useless to resist?"

"I didn't say that. We don't know this is the end. And even if it is, I don't think God would want anyone to surrender to evil."

"But what if it *is* inevitable?" Kyle asked, insistent for an answer.

Hightower took a breath and leaned back from his desk. "The media are calling this group the 'Apocalypse Men.' *Apocalypse* comes from ancient Greek, meaning 'to reveal.'" He leaned forward slightly. "You mentioned your dreams. If God wanted to stop this, he'd give foreknowledge to someone who was in a position to do something, don't you think?" Hightower now leveled his gazed at Kyle. "You—are an *Apocalypse* man."

Kyle chuckled. The idea sounded ridiculous. "No, I'm not."

"You're so sure?"

Kyle shook his head adamantly. "For one, I'm not in a position to do anything."

"Of course you are. In your job, you observe, you assess, and you report. That's something. Although, in this case, you'll also need to convince…"

"That's hard to do when your only evidence is a dream," Kyle countered.

Hightower smiled, undeterred. "Then it's a question of faith."

"In God?"

"And yourself."

Kyle was now looking at Dr. Hightower with new eyes. "You're not just a professor, are you?"

"I was once a priest," Hightower said. "I had to choose between living a life of service to God, and loving a good woman." He stood and walked to the window.

Kyle was somewhat stunned by this confession. It seemed to fit—just about everything he knew about the professor now made more sense—except for one thing. Hightower's faith didn't seem so much rooted in Catholic tradition as in a more ecumenical understanding. Perhaps it was just the professorial side of him on display, but Kyle wondered if that also played into Hightower's decision to leave the priesthood.

At any rate, Kyle was now looking at Dr. Hightower differently. It hadn't been easy to keep an open mind about religion. For years, Kyle held especially a certain skepticism for Catholicism. To him, the myriad of sins Catholics could commit—combined with the relative ease of absolution through confession—made for an economy that kept the priesthood thriving. But this was the simplification of an outsider's perspective that did not consider the lives of the faithful. The service to others, combined with a belief which gave hope and definition to life, was too easily dismissed by religious skeptics. Kyle tempered his skepticism when he began to see the benefits of devotion and discipline in the lives of religious colleagues such as Sadiq, but his experience at Adam's death kept him from renewing his own faith. Since Kyle did not understand the devotion required to become a priest, he could not understand the difficulty of Hightower's decision. However, he was willing to accept this had been a life-changing decision for the professor. Kyle only wondered why he had shared it with him.

Dr. Hightower continued to gaze out the window. From where Kyle sat, he looked like a figure in a religious painting, his face turned toward the light as if to seek inspiration from it. "Not every man is equal to his calling," Hightower said. "Let us hope that you are."

21

The Fifth Vial

Kyle didn't know what to make of Hightower's counsel. The professor had made one thing clear to him—his premonitions were not just haunting coincidences, but an ability. Had he recognized that earlier he might have been able to harness it to make clearer assessments. Only yesterday did he start to have an inkling that what he dreamed could be useful. If he thought it through he could determine where the attacks would occur. Yesterday he had been too late, and seeing the suffering of thousands, he had felt a powerful hopelessness. It was a feeling he experienced after each of these attacks, but the magnitude of this one was overwhelming. Hightower was right—Kyle needed to listen. But the source of this ability was another question.

Kyle wasn't sure if his premonitions were psychic or prophetic. He doubted God was speaking to him, as Hightower asserted, but without really knowing the source of his dreams he had to acknowledge the possibility. Still, it seemed unlikely. Kyle wasn't much of a believer in psychic powers, but they too could be the source of his dreams. He knew of *Stargate*, the highly controversial military-CIA psychic remote viewing program of the 1980s. The program had been shut down and written off as a complete failure, but Kyle knew one of the participants. An otherwise level-headed intelligence officer, the man told spectacular anecdotes of seeing hostages held captive half a world away and psychically viewing Pan Am 103 in the moments before it blew up. These would have sounded like tall tales and drinking stories, full of exaggeration, but the man was completely sober when he told them. Kyle always doubted the stories' veracity but never the man's earnestness. Now he was rethinking his position.

These questions had kept Kyle awake long into the night when another question presented itself. Since he could not ascertain the source of his dreams he could not control them. He could analyze them after they happened, but what if they stopped happening? Kyle knew he and the rest of the intelligence community had too little to go on to stop the Apocalypse Men. They had failed four times to stop major attacks and if something didn't change they could not stop another. Kyle prided himself on his intellect for his whole career. Now he needed something more. Each of the dreams had been distressing but now he needed another. He needed something that would give him the information to fight back. He promised himself if he received another dream he'd set his mind immediately to deciphering its message, and daunting or not, he would do what was necessary to convince his superiors to act upon it.

Kyle didn't know how long his eyes had been closed when he felt he was flying over a great expanse in the darkness. Ahead, the lights of a cityscape were fast approaching. As he drew closer he saw the lights were reflected on a river below. Kyle was transported to the edge of the city, where the smokestacks and transmission lines of a power plant stretched out into the darkness. An explosion rocked the power plant, sending a shower of sparks up like fireworks from a transmission tower. A fireball rose from the plant's core. In the distance further explosions flared in the night. As their flames faded the lights of the city blinked out, bathing the entire countryside in total darkness.

Kyle sat up with a start. His face was covered in sweat and his arms were shaking. Haunted by the immediacy of the dream, he fumbled through the darkness for his bedside lamp and breathed a sigh of relief when the light switched on. Kyle reviewed the vision in his mind, then grabbed his laptop. He knew what to search for.

Three hours later, Kyle was at CIA Headquarters. The drive had been cumbersome. Kyle had to show his ID at several police blockades before he was let through. Officers were just beginning to let CIA personnel return to work. Kyle met with Sadiq and Parks, who had both been in the building at the time of the blast and never went home. He briefly shared his thoughts with them before all three headed to Larsen's office.

Kyle remembered Hightower's counsel that he'd have to convince his superiors and went into his analysis with vigor. "We've been a step behind the Apocalypse Men every time, even though we know they're working on a set plan—the Seven Vials of Revelation."

"That's because the language of Revelation is vague," Larsen said. "Without further data, we can't know where to mount a defense."

"And we received the last message too late," Sadiq added.

"Right," Kyle agreed. "But this time we don't have to wait for a message. Look..." He handed his tablet over to Larsen. The screen showed a verse from Revelation:

And the fifth angel poured out his vial upon the seat of the beast; and his kingdom was full of darkness; and they gnawed their tongues for pain, And blasphemed the God of heaven because of their pains and their sores.

Kyle pointed to the screen. "*The seat of the beast*—the Apocalypse Men have focused their attacks on America, and particularly Washington. I think they believe that *seat* is here."

Larsen was skeptical. "That's conjecture."

"But this—*kingdom full of darkness*—I'd say it's pretty clear they'll hit the power grid," Kyle added quickly.

"I agree," Larsen nodded. "But how? An EMP?"

"The data doesn't support an electromagnetic pulse weapon, but rather attacks on individual plants and segments of the grid."

"But there's over 7,000 power plants across the country. Which ones do we concentrate on?"

"There's three main grids," Parks said. "East, West, and Texas. Hit eight or nine key points within those three and it will bring the entire country to its knees."

"But there's more potential targets than just eight or nine stations," Kyle said.

"Right," Parks acknowledged.

"Still, it's a manageable number."

"What kind of attack? Cyber or physical?" Larsen asked.

"Combination of both," Kyle answered. "A cyber attack hits the control systems while physical destruction takes out hardware. Our transformers aren't manufactured in America. Destroy any of those, and it will take weeks to replace them."

"You sure it would be both? The physical destruction

of Hoover Dam is already causing brownouts across the Southwest," Larsen said, picking up a brief. "It's also causing water shortages in Las Vegas, Southern California, and Arizona. Effective enough."

"And the Apocalypse Men have avoided using any computer technology to this point—it's one of the reasons we've been unable to track them," Sadiq said.

"True," Parks conceded, "but to hit the entire grid hard, there'd have to be a cyber component."

Larsen wasn't convinced. "Is a cyber attack even possible? We've been guarding against those since 9/11."

"All I know is they'll try."

"We've been wrong about our security before," Sadiq said. "Look where we are now."

That comment smarted, but Sadiq was right. Larsen was more open now. "So where do we mount a defense?"

Kyle brought up a power grid on his tablet. "First, we focus on the power lines feeding Washington. 'Seat of the beast', right? Then any major facilities along rivers."

"Why rivers?"

"The red tide attacks included poisoning the New York City water supply. An intrusion was detected at a utility plant along the Hudson River. Since we haven't located any of the culprits, they could also access power plants in similar locations," Kyle explained. It was a bit of a jump, but he pitched it convincingly. With so little to go on, it was as good a shot as any.

Larsen mulled it over. "Okay, we'll start with that."

The response from Homeland Security and other defense forces was swift. The increased security at power plants and other facilities was both visible and intensive. At the Capitol Power Plant in Washington, officers led bomb-sniffing dogs through the boiler rooms. Homeland Security officers also set up a checkpoint and examined each of the workers as they entered the plant. Various armed guards took positions around the plant and its perimeter. Washington was still largely empty, as most citizens and officials wouldn't be cleared for return until a week after the attacks, but leaving any power station in or around the capital unguarded would be unwise.

The security at some plants was especially visible. At the Niagara Hydroelectric Power Station, guards armed with M-16s and dressed in SWAT gear took positions around the plant. Armed guards were stationed at plants near Chicago, in Texas, and in California.

Not all security measures were visible. Olivia Parks and other technicians were hard at work at NSA headquarters in Fort Meade, Maryland. They liaised with Information Technology experts at various power plants, looking for any intrusions into their computer networks. A cyber attack would most likely entail the insertion of malicious code that would operate as a time bomb. The code would not go into effect until a precise time that was coordinated with physical attacks. Working through the various systems was a tedious chore, but if an intrusion was discovered, it would bring more reward. A cyber attack would leave digital traces—something the Apocalypse Men had not left until now.

It would take a week and a half before NSA computer experts located the intrusions. Within that time, Washington was back up and running, though a section of city three-quarters of a mile in radius was still off limits. The Secret Service recommended the new President Barnes stay at

Camp David, but when he learned the White House interior posed no significant radiation levels he refused. Returning the President to the White House, albeit with its scorched-black facade, was an important symbol to the American people that the country was soldiering on. Nevertheless, Barnes kept his family away from Washington for the time being.

Things had stabilized to some extent in California and Nevada. The exodus of over eight million people took ten days, but most of the citizens who had wanted to leave California were now gone. The National Guard had restored order in the streets. However, there was an uneasy tension in poorer neighborhoods where people did not have the means to leave. The draining of Lake Mead caused widespread water shortages in Las Vegas. Arizona residents who hadn't been hit with the flood from the Hoover's Dam destruction were also afraid of water and power shortages. But the greatest impact of the bombings would be long term. On 9/11, the world realized America was not impregnable. These attacks showed it was downright vulnerable. For a short time, America's allies mourned in sympathy. But soon there were murmurs of discontent. With America weakened, its allies now stood completely alone. Worst of all was the economic impact of the attacks. The combined Ports of Los Angeles and Long Beach were the largest in the U.S. Over 40% of America's containerized goods entered through those ports. Now they were completely demolished. Cargo from China and other large Asian exporters was now heading for ports at Oakland and Seattle, but with the additional security checks, trade had ground to a standstill. Dozens of cargo ships—a veritable fleet—now sat offshore, waiting to be processed. Life had been transformed in America, but for now, life went on.

Parks had spent ten days staring at computer screens until her eyes would no longer focus, but she was excited to share the NSA's findings with Kyle and Sadiq. "We've identified and eliminated 17 total intrusions at various control centers throughout the country. Just as I suspected, they were all time bombs."

"When would they activate?"

"All at the same time, six days from now."

"So we know their Zero Hour," Sadiq said.

"Will they know their code has been detected and eliminated?" Kyle asked.

Parks shook her head. "Not likely. Not unless they try to hack in again."

"Why would they do that, if the code they inserted was a time bomb?" Sadiq argued.

"Exactly," Parks said. "They won't, unless they somehow lose confidence and feel more steps are necessary."

"So they don't know we've stopped the hacks."

"Safe to say, they don't."

"Then they won't know we can anticipate their physical attacks too." Sadiq smiled. "We've beaten them."

Kyle wasn't ready to celebrate. "Not yet."

The third shift was just starting to file in at the power plant outside of Chicago. There were the usual security checks at the gate, but this time when the workers approached the building complex, armed guards stood outside with bomb-sniffing dogs. They were running further checks: each worker was asked to open his lunchbox or other personal belongings for inspection. The man with deep-set eyes had only worked at the station for three weeks, but he had never seen these security measures. He was a quiet man, and had not gotten to know his coworkers well. No one noticed when he stepped out of line and returned to his car. The security guard at the gate asked what was wrong, seeing the man had only just arrived, but the worker hastily explained he had been battling a severe case of stomach flu all day. He had tried to report for work but realized he couldn't tough it out. The security guard lifted the gate and waved him on with a wish to feel better.

That night in Pennsylvania, two men crept through the forest until they reached a clearing. Before them, the 180-foot tall transmission towers that stretched in a line to the horizon. The buzzing of the high-voltage wires was so loud that no crickets, tree frogs, or other creatures of the night could be heard. The men watched for several minutes to ensure they were alone before they ventured into the clearing. One of the men carried a small package that held powerful explosives. Just as they placed the package at the base of one of the towers, a spotlight came on in the darkness. Both men were blinded like deer.

"Freeze!" a harsh voice commanded from the black.

The two men hesitated as footfalls came crunching through the long grass toward them. The first man saw the barrel of a gun emerge out of the darkness, but the other flinched, reaching for the detonator on his belt. "No!" the first man shouted to his companion, but it was too late.

Crack! Crack! Crack!

A volley of gunfire sounded as the men went down. The package tumbled away into the grass. Now floodlights snapped on, bathing the scene in harsh light. The field was swarming with FBI agents. One agent rushed toward the second man and kicked the detonator out of his hand, fearing he might reflexively press it in death. A bomb squad technician ran to the package and gingerly picked it up, cradling it like a baby bird.

FBI Special Agent Ben Sherman took news of the shootings to Kyle the next morning. "Looks like we got two of those Apocalypse Men last night." He handed a brief to Kyle.

Kyle scanned the brief. "How'd you track them?"

"They were on our watch list. After the last attacks, we've been keeping a sharper lookout for men like them."

Kyle shook his head. "They're not members of the Apocalypse Men."

"How are you so sure?"

"Very few of the Apocalypse Men have been fingered. Postmortems identified two of the truckers, but none have been captured alive, and none were on any watch list or had known terrorist ties. Besides, we haven't even received word of the Fifth Vial yet."

"Isn't that what you said was coming next?"

"Sure, but all of the attacks have been preceded by the messages of each vial. Not a single attack came before."

"Maybe they jumped the gun on this one."

"I don't think so. Their Zero Hour isn't until tomorrow."

Sadiq entered with a thumb drive. "They just announced the Fifth Vial." He played the message for them. Again, the silhouetted man appeared against the blood-red background, and once again, he quoted Revelation. The words were just as Kyle predicted, from Chapter 16, Verses 10 and 11.

Sherman pointed to the screen. "Why don't you track these videos?"

"We've tried," Sadiq explained. "Neither we nor NSA can get anything useful from the videos themselves."

"And the way they were delivered?"

Kyle looked at Sadiq, wary if they should reveal any information about their source. Of course, others outside CIA knew about their contact, but only at the highest levels. Sadiq cleared his throat. "We have a consistent channel that feeds them to us, but we've tried tracking the source. With one exception, it's always been delivered by courier—from a different location and different company. No pattern so far."

"What was the exception?" Sherman asked.

"Uploaded directly to the internet. We tried to track that, but it didn't give us anything useful."

Sherman was baffled, but Sadiq was also stonewalling to an extent. "I see."

Kyle walked Agent Sherman to the door. "Thanks for the report. They're not the Apocalypse Men, but it's not surprising other groups are now coming out of the woodwork. I'm glad your guys got them before they did any damage." He exhaled deeply. "It's time we get ahead of these attacks."

An hour later, Olivia Parks returned from NSA Headquarters to report on their progress. "We tried to backtrack the source of the intrusions, but it's not that easy," she explained.

"Why?"

"We've identified the viruses at the 17 sites, but as time bombs, they were inserted months ago. In the meantime, they've erased their tracks."

"What chance do we have of catching the hackers, then?" Kyle asked.

"Not much."

"But if they've covered their tracks, closed off communications with the control programs, they definitely won't know we've resolved the threats," Kyle concluded.

"Right."

"What if they have someone in the control centers?" Sadiq asked.

"Slim possibility. Those personnel have been thoroughly screened since 9/11. But if there was a mole, the increased security around the facilities might tip him off."

"True," Kyle conceded, "so we may disrupt attacks on the hardware, too. But I'm sure these attackers will take whatever they can get."

"Sure," Parks nodded.

Kyle ran a hand over his chin. "So they're expecting the cyber attacks to go off like clockwork because they don't know we've stopped them. When they fail, there might be chatter. 'What happened?' 'Why didn't it go off as planned?' *That's* when we can track them."

Parks nodded in agreement.

"Stands to reason," Sadiq agreed, "but where do we look?"

That, as always, was the key question.

By that night, Kyle had spent another ten hours looking over the data from the four waves of attacks. He had reviewed it countless times in the last several weeks, but here he was again, trying to put fresh eyes on the data and tease something new out of the morass of information. Unfortunately, his eyes weren't fresh at all. His eyelids were heavy, and his head began to nod. He tried to support his chin under his fist, but gradually he nodded off.

At first he thought he was only daydreaming, but as Kyle felt transported over a dark and surreal landscape, he knew his subconscious had taken over. All of his previous attempts to experience lucid dreaming ended the moment he was aware of the dream, but this time he stayed asleep. Kyle did not try to control the dream; he let his subconscious carry him on, almost as if it was guiding him.

This dream, like the one before, was at night and over a great expanse of water. On the horizon, a large shape loomed out of the void. Kyle tried to focus on the shape and draw closer. Soon he recognized the white superstructure of a tanker ship and the black exhaust funnel just behind it. Kyle seemed to spiral down onto the funnel, where a raven landed on its edge. A burst of sparks and smoke belched from the funnel just as the raven stretched its wings, singeing them. Still, the raven launched out and soared over the water. The flames trailed from its wings as it glided toward shore. Before long the raven had reached a city. It flapped its wings as it soared over a harbor, then glided over a working-class neighborhood of brick homes and apartment buildings. Then the raven tucked its wings and dove toward a row house. As the raven plummeted down, it burst into fire, driving toward the house like a meteor. Then, just as the burning ball hit the house, Kyle awoke.

22

White Horse

The man with deep-set eyes stood in line at Chicago's O'Hare Airport, waiting to go through security. His eyes scanned the Transportation Security Agency personnel at the metal detectors and x-ray machine. They handled their job dutifully; not particularly watchful, nor lax, but as routine. Yet the man with deep-set eyes felt trapped. Beyond the checkpoint lay freedom. If he made it to a plane, he could leave and never turn back. But he'd have to make it beyond the checkpoint, and he knew he never would with what lay in his carry-on bag. He had brought it with purpose, but now the man's courage began to waver. He could go to the bathroom and leave its contents in the trash, but he was sure they would be found before he could ever board a plane. He could walk out of the airport and return later without the bag. But as all of these possibilities ran through his mind, the man knew none of them were viable. It was too late to do anything else. His destiny awaited at the checkpoint. It didn't seem fair, he thought. There was so much more he wanted to do. He also wanted to appreciate more of life—to see one last sunset, to hear the chirping of birds—not sight of glass and steel in an airport, not the smell of hundreds of people standing close in line and removing their shoes. But he never considered the fate of those around him.

By the time the man reached the conveyer belt, his forehead was covered with sweat. He lifted his bag onto the conveyer and placed his shoes next to it. The TSA agent at the metal detector waved him through. Though the man cleared the machine, the agent stopped him and looked at his sweat-covered face. "Are you all right?"

The man opened his mouth to answer, but the TSA agent at the x-ray machine interrupted. He was looking at the man's bag on the screen. "What is that?"

A *ding* chimed from the x-ray machine. The man closed his deep-set eyes; it was little more than a blink, but he would never open them again. The sharp sound of a phosphorus hot-white explosion ripped through the air. A fraction of a second later, the entire checkpoint was consumed in a roaring ball of flame.

Back at CIA Headquarters, Sadiq burst into the counterterrorism bullpen. Breathing fast, he turned on the television. "You need to see this."

The TV was already tuned to a news station. Kyle could see the caption under the shot—*Bombing at O'Hare Airport: 19 Dead, Dozens Injured*. The all-too familiar sight of flashing red emergency lights filled the image. Dozens of people were streaming out of the terminal as clouds of black smoke belched behind them.

"It's not a power plant," Kyle said with some bewilderment as he checked his watch. It was past Zero Hour, and so far, this was the only attack.

"Maybe we've got them on the run," Sadiq shrugged. "This is all they could manage."

"No blackouts yet."

"Nope," Parks confirmed. "But what concerns me is we haven't seen any recognizable chatter. We still sweep all communications outside the U.S., but that's a mass of information. We've set up dozens of keywords to flag any possible communication about the grid, but nothing yet. It's Zero Hour plus two, and no one's panicking." She started to pace. "Did we get this one wrong? Was it a decoy?"

"I don't think so," Kyle said. "The Fifth Vial clearly infers an attack on the grid." As Kyle tried to think, his eye caught sight of Sadiq's Baltimore Ravens coffee mug on the table. Images from his dream flashed back to him—the raven on fire, soaring over the water, a harbor, and a row house. Now it seemed clear to him—those images, albeit surreal and fragmented, were of Baltimore. "Try this," he said. "Monitor all ship-to shore contact between the Chesapeake Bay and Baltimore."

"Why there?" Sadiq asked. For a moment, he was afraid the strange look Kyle had given his mug meant someone had put something distasteful in it when he wasn't looking. One of the analysts in their section, Craig Bishop, had a habit of lightening the hours of long work with the occasional prank. Now he saw Kyle was serious, and his interest was piqued.

"The red tide attacks. That's the connection."

"World's End?" Larsen scoffed. "We looked into that. Doesn't check out. The dispersion of the red tide makes it difficult to pinpoint the location and time of release, and yes, they might have been dumping offshore. But no ship from the World's End line ever entered the Chesapeake."

"I know," Kyle admitted. The answer threw Larsen off. "The four sightings were of ghost ships—ones that never made shore and were never identified. They made no radio contact, had their identifying beacons off—just when the Coast Guard moved in, they all vanished. But four dumpings from any size tanker wouldn't be enough to generate the amount of red tide we've seen in the Chesapeake."

"What are you saying?"

"There had to be registered, identified ships that did make port, but also dumped red tide water along the way."

"How's that possible?" Sadiq asked. "If they were tankers, they would have arrived empty."

"We'll get to that," Kyle said. "First, the shipping lines."

Larsen didn't like where this was going. "Which lines?"

"You check on Mar Azul?"

Larsen fell silent. He hadn't, although he had promised to check them out. Larsen had always considered Kyle's links between Mar Azul and World's End too tenuous to authorize surveillance on Fernando Vasquez. The next wave of attacks diverted everyone's attention, and Larsen conveniently forgot his promise. In his mind, he was protecting Kyle. Larsen was sure surveilling Vasquez would get messy, and he wanted to prevent Kyle from committing career suicide. But now Larsen had a problem. Deputy Director Andrew Everton had quietly slipped into the room behind Kyle, and he was listening. Larsen didn't want to admit in front of the Deputy Director that he hadn't checked something out, even if Everton was well aware of the consequences. Larsen's mind raced to think of something to save face, some way he could play off Kyle's question, but under pressure his mind blanked.

Kyle pulled out a file and handed it to Larsen. "I did.

Mar Azul's ships have entered the Chesapeake 59 times in the last two years."

Larsen scanned over the document. "I don't see any tankers."

"Thirteen were tanker-container ship hybrids," Kyle pointed to a column. "Every time they docked in Baltimore, they offloaded plenty of containers, but their tanks were empty. They hid the dumps in plain sight."

Larsen seemed impatient. "What's it all add up to?"

"The Chesapeake is too narrow for a ship to go unnoticed on frequent trips. That's why there were only four sightings—and mind you, the most recent was months ago. World's End has to be responsible for the offshore dumps, but they turned over the ones in the Chesapeake to Mar Azul. Mar Azul's ships haven't had to hide their identities, because they've got regular cargo to offload as hybrid ships. No one cared that their tanks were empty when they docked in Baltimore. You look up the ships in the Chesapeake now, and I guarantee we'll find at least one from Mar Azul. Track their ship-to-shore communication, and you've got them."

Parks brought up a screen that mapped the ships in Chesapeake Bay. It was crowded with dots. Following the attack on Los Angeles Harbor, traffic had increased on the Atlantic seaboard to compensate as well as avoid the jam in West Coast ports. "Looks like rush hour on the Beltway," Larsen said. "You expect to pinpoint a specific ship-to-shore communication in that?" It was a weak excuse, but Larsen was still thrown off by Deputy Director Everton's presence. That Everton hadn't said anything but merely kept his arms folded as he listened only made things worse.

"Here," Kyle pointed to a tab on the screen. Parks

clicked it and a column of ship names and registries appeared. "These three are Vasquez's."

"Okay," Parks said, convinced, "but why Baltimore? They could be communicating to any number of places on shore, and with a satellite link, anywhere on earth."

"Trust me." Kyle remembered he'd have to convince his colleagues, and Larsen most of all. He still hadn't seen Deputy Director Everton listening quietly behind him, but he spoke with conviction.

Larsen wanted to say trust wasn't enough, but he held his tongue. Kyle knew he'd need some evidence fast so he sat at a computer station and pulled up a satellite image of Baltimore. He wanted to retrace the raven's flight in his dream. If he could locate the exact row house, they'd see he was right when transmissions came between it and one of the ships. He began to zoom in on the satellite image, but seeing a day view of the landscape, rather than the surreal abstractions of his night vision, made the task challenging. There were also limitations in the angle. The satellite image was taken overhead, while the bird's flight came across the land. Using the 3D aspects of the satellite image to show a side angle only resulted in a warped image. To Kyle, his search seemed to last forever. He was acutely aware of Larsen, Sadiq, and Parks watching over his shoulder. The task, however, only lasted longer than a minute. Deputy Director Everton watched Kyle work with purpose, zooming in until he located the exact row house.

"Here," Kyle said, pointing to the screen.

"Not the port?" Larsen was still skeptical.

"If we monitor transmissions, they'll be coming from here."

"How did you—" Larsen wanted to know how Kyle

came to choose this location, especially since he hadn't offered any files or other data, but Everton cut him off.

"Do it." The Deputy Director's voice wasn't just authoritative, but confident. He watched Kyle working for the past few minutes and knew to trust his gut. It was telling him to trust Kyle's.

Parks started a scan on her computer. It took twenty minutes before anything came up. "Hmm, that's weird," she said.

"What?" Larsen asked.

"Two signal bursts, 98 seconds apart. Both are encrypted."

"Let's see," Larsen crowded over the screen. He wanted to see where the transmissions had originated.

"Just a second," Parks said, bringing up a decoding program. "Encryption's good. This might take some time." She started to attack the coding, adjusting the parameters on the program as necessary.

Sadiq looked over Park's shoulder. "Can you break it?"

"That's what I'm here for, right?" she said with a smile.

Larsen slid over to another computer, where he tried to bring up the location of the transmissions. He wasn't nearly adept as Parks. After ten minutes, he gave up. "Where are the transmissions coming from?"

Sadiq sat at another computer and began keying in commands. Within minutes, he had the answer. "It's one of the three ships." He pointed to the dot on the screen.

"Which one is that?"

"The *Reina del Mar*."

"And the other transmission?"

"It's from shore." Sadiq zoomed in on the map. "Not in the port." He zoomed further, until he located the street.

It was a residential area, a far too unusual place for an encrypted signal burst to originate from. "It's a row house," Sadiq breathed out in a hushed voice. How did Kyle know?

"How long will it take to decode the messages?" Larsen asked.

"Not sure. Maybe an hour," Parks answered.

"That could be too long," Kyle said. "If the messages were calling everything off, they might scatter."

"We can't ask for raids on targets we can't verify as threats," Larsen said.

"All right. Then have the Coast Guard board the ship for inspection. Stake out the row house. Just don't let them go anywhere."

Larsen and the others turned to Deputy Director Everton, who nodded his assent.

The row house sat on a quiet street in Baltimore, but no one paid attention to the sedan that pulled up to the curb four houses away. The two undercover FBI agents in the sedan began their vigil. In the back alley behind the house, another agent crouched between a fence and some garbage cans. He could see the house clearly, but he was well out of sight.

Another FBI Agent sneaked along the wall toward the back of the house. As he stopped by the utilities meter, the spinning dials caught his eye. "These guys are sucking a lot of juice," he whispered into his radio.

In the mobile command unit six blocks away, Special Agent-in-Charge Lou Davis heard the transmission. He looked at a bank of monitors that showed video feeds from each of the agents stationed around the row house. Davis turned to a technician. "What would take that much electricity?"

The technician pointed to another monitor, where an infrared thermal image glowed on the screen. "Looks like they've got generators they're charging on the first floor."

Davis pointed to two large cylinders. "Are those fuel tanks?"

"Looks like it, sir. Likely backup for the generators."

"All teams, be aware there are fuel tanks on the first floor," Davis radioed.

"Copy that," a voice crackled over the radio. It was a SWAT team leader who sat in a truck with his team a block away from the row house. A second team was in another truck on the other side of the house, also a block away.

Davis studied the infrared image. There was no sign of life on the first floor. He turned his attention to another monitor. This one showed the second floor of the row house. The image glowed brightly with heat signatures. "Looks like four suspects," Davis said. "And a lot of computers."

The technician next to him whistled low. "Looks like a telecom hub."

The SWAT team leader's voice came over the radio. "Tell me it's my cable company's new offices. We'll love taking the place down."

Davis smiled. "Forget to pay your bill again, Cobb?"

"Been trying to cancel for months. They won't pick up the box. Maybe I'll return it with a flash bang attached."

On the monitors, one of the four men moved to another room. Davis was now all business. "Standby."

The Navy Black Hawk helicopter touched down at Coast

Guard Air Station Washington, D.C., located at Reagan National Airport. Colonel Nate Knox hopped out with a SEAL team and strode across the tarmac to the nearest Coast Guard helicopter. A petty officer watched in surprise as Knox and the SEAL team slid open the cabin door and climbed aboard. "Just coming along for a ship inspection," Knox explained. The Coast Guard helicopter, brightly decorated in white and orange trim and *U.S. Coast Guard* lettering, would make a good cover. No ship's crew would anticipate a SEAL team abseiling from a Coast Guard helicopter, even if it was relatively the same Black Hawk model as a Navy one. The Coast Guard pilot turned back to ensure his passengers were safely on board before powering up and taking off. Within minutes, they were headed east toward the Chesapeake.

Inside the cabin, one of the SEAL team members leaned over to Knox. "Bet it feels good to be out in the field again."

"You bet," Knox said as he stuck a piece of gum in his mouth. It was his long-time habit before any mission, when en route by helicopter or plane, to chew a piece of gum. It kept his nerves down and soothed the boredom of waiting. Knox had served on dozens of SEAL team missions, but not since moving into higher-level Naval Intelligence duties over eight months ago. Following old habits was easing him back into the routine. Knox had specifically requested to go on this mission. He had seen too much chaos caused by the Apocalypse Men, and he wasn't going to stand by and let someone else take the chance to strike back. Still, that didn't quite save him from his old SEAL teammates' ribbing.

"Sir, you forgot to pack your walker," one of the team members teased.

Knox looked out the window. They were just reaching the shore of the bay. "If you're so strong, bucko, we can drop you off here and let you swim to the ship."

Chastised, the team member receded into the wall. "No thank you, sir."

Back at CIA Headquarters, Parks was still working on breaking the encryption. Kyle watched over her shoulder. Kyle had no experience with decryption or this kind of signals intelligence, but he watched intently. Parks was an expert, yet she still ran into several corners. Every time, Kyle helped direct her by making quiet, instinctive suggestions. Every time his advice was dead-on. Parks began to wonder where and how Kyle gained his new-found skill, but she was too busy to question him. Every time she saw wisdom in his advice. Sadiq, who had no skill in decryption, was also reluctant to interrupt. He was even more astounded by Kyle's prowess. After a long hour of work, Parks sat back and exhaled. It was finished.

"What's it say?" Sadiq asked eagerly.

"It's a conversation. The first message, from the row house, says, *'Sunset no-go.'*"

"And the response?" Larsen asked.

"*'Acknowledged. Standby.'*"

"That's it?" Larsen scratched his head, expecting more. "That's no smoking gun."

"But it's enough," Deputy Director Everton said. He picked up the phone to call the FBI and Navy. Kyle watched, a strange mix of tension and satisfaction simultaneously flowing through him.

The first mate looked over the bridge of the *Reina del Mar* and saw a Coast Guard cutter coming towards them. The cutter was flying over the waves at great speed, leaving a large wake it its path. The signal light was blinking. The first mate looked over his shoulder. "Captain?"

The captain came over and both men read the blinking signal light together.

"Coast Guard's going to board us," the first mate said.

Above them, a sudden sound shook the roof. A helicopter was rapidly descending above them. Alarmed, the first mate went to a locker at the back of the bridge and retrieved a handgun. The captain caught the first mate's hand, holding the gun down. He shook his head, telling him to remain calm.

Knox and the SEAL team abseiled from the helicopter onto the deck of the tanker. Within seconds, the SEAL team divided into two groups and began to search the ship. The crew, stunned by the quick movement and firepower of the SEAL team, didn't resist. Most of the crew raised their hands and froze in place.

The first group of SEALs headed to the bridge. Knox approached the captain, recognizing him instantly as the oldest and most confident-looking crew member.

"Afternoon, captain," Knox said. "We're here for an inspection."

The crewman at the helm, astonished to see soldiers and not regular Coast Guard on board, was baffled. "Inspection?"

The captain shot a look of condemnation at the crewman, but said nothing.

In Baltimore, Special Agent-in-Charge Davis picked up the radio. "The order is to detain—*detain* suspects only."

"Copy that," the SWAT team leader responded.

"We are Go, go, go."

"Copy, we are GO." The team leader slapped his hand twice against the front wall of the truck, alerting the driver. The truck flew down the street, screeching to a halt in front of the row house. Before the tires had even stopped the doors flew open and the SWAT team charged out. They mounted the front steps and smashed open the door in one smooth motion. The SWAT team surged up the stairs in a black-clad wave and burst into the master bedroom. The room was filled with computers, networking equipment, and three startled men. The oldest, an Arab-looking man with a beard, froze but did not flinch. The other two men flinched at the sight of the SWAT team and raised their hands. A fourth man appeared with a bowl of soup in the doorway, oblivious to the SWAT team until he looked up. The man immediately dropped the bowl and ran.

"We've got a runner!" the SWAT team leader shouted into his radio.

Outside, the FBI agent hiding behind the garbage cans looked up and saw the fourth man sticking his head out a second-story window, looking to escape. The FBI agent aimed his sidearm at the fugitive. "Freeze!"

The man raised his hands, and then, as if sucked by some beast, was pulled back inside by the SWAT team.

While two of the SWAT team members grabbed the fourth man, two remained in the master bedroom with the other three. Wagering the failed escape had provided a distraction, the most intrepid of the three men raised his laptop in a foolish attempt to smash it. The SWAT team leader raised his gun to the man's temple, causing him to freeze mid-motion. "I wouldn't do that."

On board the *Reina del Mar*, the SEAL team moved down the passageway, clearing rooms quickly. Only the captain's cabin, at the end of the passageway, remained. The SEAL team knew this would be the largest cabin, and as they approached the closed door, they prepared to meet anything on the other side. Once in position, the lead SEAL gave the signal and the team kicked the door open in a flash.

On the bridge, Knox and his team had the crew under control. His radio came to life—it was the other SEAL members in the captain's cabin. "Colonel, you're going to want to take a look at this."

Knox excused himself from the bridge, leaving the next ranking officer in command. He slid down a flight of stairs and headed down the passageway to the captain's cabin. As Knox stood in the open door frame, he saw the figure sitting on the edge of the bed. Even in the captain's comfortable quarters, the figure was well out of place on a working ship—a well-dressed Latin businessman. The other SEALs had their weapons trained on the man. "Well, well, well," Knox said, smiling.

It was hours later when Kyle got the final word. "You were right," Larsen said. "They were running the cyber attacks out of the row house. The Coast Guard also confiscated the ship."

Sadiq shook his head in disbelief. How did Kyle know?

Larsen wasn't finished. "You're not going to believe this." He clicked a few keystrokes on a computer and brought up an image on the wall screen. It was an FBI mug shot of the bearded man from the row house. "You might not recognize him with the beard, but he led the cyber team in Baltimore. Amir Anwar Al-Salameh."

Parks' eyes widened. "The billionaire tech mogul?"

"That's him. And quite a team with him." It was the closest thing to a compliment Larsen could manage, but Parks saw the admiration for her work in tracking him down.

"Fitting about the team," Sadiq said. "Amir Anwar Al-Salameh means *ruler of the bright ones*."

"There was never any inkling he was involved with terror," Parks said, still astonished at Salameh's image.

"What about the tanker?" Kyle asked.

"Guess who Knox's team found in the captain's cabin?" Larsen pulled up another mug shot, this one of the well-dressed businessman. "Hector Serrano."

Kyle nodded in satisfaction. "Fernando Vasquez's right-hand man."

Larsen's pride had taken a hit, but given the astounding success they had achieved from Kyle's analysis, he could put that aside. The results were what mattered. They had survived the fifth attack without a single spot on the grid damaged. The bombing at O'Hare was tragic, but in Larsen's estimation, it was far better than the attack they expected. Within the next few days, they'd find links between the bomber and Al-Salameh's row house. The CIA concluded the bomber had deemed his target impregnable and set off the bomb at the airport in desperation. That would be no comfort to the families of the victims, but to an intelligence officer, it was a sign the tide had turned. But there was much to be done.

Sadiq asked the question that was on everyone's mind. "What about Vasquez?"

23

Black Horse

Fernando Vasquez left his office building in Caracas, passing a cadre of guards as he headed to his waiting limo. It was nearly eleven at night—far later than he usually stayed at the office, even though he had a reputation as a workaholic. Vasquez preferred to take his work home with him. Today he had plenty to do. But what weighed on his mind was what hadn't happened. He hadn't seen anything major on the news. He also hadn't received a call on the satellite phone he kept for an emergency. In the five years he had owned it, the phone had remained silent. But when nothing happened in the U.S. he expected it to ring now. Tired of waiting, Vasquez decided to go home.

Vasquez had just reached the pavement when the phone began to buzz in his pocket. Turning away from the building's entrance for privacy, Vasquez strode to the corner and answered the phone. It wasn't the person he expected to hear.

The voice on the other end of the line didn't bother with a greeting. "What happened?"

"It didn't go off," Vasquez said. "What now?"

"We move to the next."

Vasquez wasn't sure that was a good idea. "If they're on to us—"

The voice cut in confidently. "They won't know what's coming." The line clicked off.

Vasquez turned to see one of his guards holding his car door open for him at the corner. He nodded to him and slipped inside. "La Casa, Chago," Vasquez ordered his driver, speaking into the intercom. He stretched his legs and tried to relax as the limo pulled away from the curb. Vasquez was alone in the back of the limo. Usually, his head of security rode in the seat across from him, but when Vasquez was particularly tired or wanted space, he rode in the front next to the driver. Vasquez was happy he needn't ask for this favor tonight; his head of security had read his mood properly, and seen he needed his space.

Now the billionaire closed his eyes and tried to think. What had happened? Was his role really finished? He had invested so much with Mashiri, but his part had achieved so little. There was too much to be done to simply move onto the next phase of the plan. Mashiri had made promises. Surely he would let him finish what they had started. Even if Salameh had failed, there was more he could do. There was the embargo, and he could arrange another set of attacks. Somewhere in the grid were weaknesses to be exploited.

Vasquez idly opened his eyes and looked out to the street. They were not on the correct route. Suspecting his driver hadn't heard him clearly, Vasquez lowered the privacy divider. "Chago—" He stopped short. The man at the wheel was a stranger. "Who are you?"

The man did not answer. Vasquez looked toward the passenger seat, where another stranger turned with a gun in his hand. Vasquez raised his hands as a shield, but the man fired first. A dart hit the billionaire in the neck, instantly knocking him unconscious. Vasquez slumped back as the limo sped on. The two CIA agents whisked the sleeping billionaire onto a plane before his limo was even expected at home. Vasquez didn't awake until the next morning, when he found himself in a Miami cell, facing an FBI interrogation.

Barnes looked across the table in the White House Situation Room. DNI Foley, CIA Director Farrell, NSA Director Hudson, FBI Director Taft, and Secretary for Homeland Security Tibbetts were all seated there.

"So what's the day's tally?" Barnes asked.

Tibbetts checked his notes. "We had four minor intrusions that knocked out power for 20 minutes. The outages were isolated, localized, and resolved."

"And no physical attacks on the grid at large," DNI Foley added.

"What about O'Hare?"

"It's our assessment that was a bomber who chose a new target when he saw hitting a power plant wasn't feasible," Farrell said.

"How are we doing on tracking these people down?"

Foley couldn't help breaking a smile. "We nabbed two of the key planners, Amir Anwar Al-Salameh, and Fernando Vasquez."

Barnes knew the names of both men. He was surprised to hear them mentioned as sponsors and planners of terror, despite their known disregard for the U.S. "They're part of these Apocalypse Men?"

"At the top, we believe," Foley said. "Salameh was heading up the cyber attacks. We're still collecting data on Vasquez. Apparently he backed the red tide attacks, the planned hits on the power grid, and it looks like he was planning to orchestrate an embargo."

"Oil embargo?"

Foley shook his head. "All food products shipped to the U.S."

Barnes was aghast. "We never had a whiff of this."

"We didn't," Foley admitted, "until we captured him. He would have even involved Mexico. But that's all off now."

"Thank goodness," Barnes said. "And the other attacks?"

Taft fielded that one. "Regarding the planned hits on the grid, we've made 29 arrests so far, Mr. President. We engaged and killed two more."

Barnes held his breath. "So it's over?"

"I wouldn't let our guard down yet, Mr. President," General Foley said. "But I think we can score this one for our side."

Barnes exhaled in relief and closed his eyes. When he opened them, he was at peace. "This was a good day for us. We've needed one."

Mashiri had waited all day, watching television and anticipating news from America. By late afternoon Washington time, he knew something was wrong. The blackouts hadn't happened as planned, and though he might have expected a snag or two, the fact that *everything* was still up and running indicated a major failure. What puzzled Mashiri is how the American intelligence community could have learned enough to stop them. His security measures, as usual, had been impeccable. His men were dedicated. There was no logical reason for this colossal failure.

Mashiri knew something was seriously wrong by that night. Neither Salameh or Vasquez had checked in. He finally heard from Rasul, his trusted emergency contact, after 11 P.M. Washington time. Rasul had called Vasquez, who, stationed in Caracas, was in the same time zone as Washington. Vasquez had been similarly perplexed by the mission's failure, with no answers. Mashiri tried contacting Vasquez at home by his secure satellite link, but there was no answer. Vasquez would never ignore his call. Mashiri knew Salameh and Vasquez had been captured, and more than that, he knew he was now alone. He was the last of the Apocalypse Men. But Mashiri wasn't finished yet. Even now, the greatest phase of his plan was getting underway. Despite the blackout's failure, Mashiri knew this next phase would succeed. It was entirely independent of the energy operations and he had chosen the leader for this mission well. The first four attacks had fulfilled their purpose—they needed to lay the groundwork for what was to come. Now this next attack would usher in the age of the Apocalypse Men. After tomorrow night, the world would never be the same.

24

The Sixth Vial

Kyle didn't finish work until after nine that night; by that time, he was too tired to drive home, so he retreated to his office. He pulled out his phone and dialed his mother's cell.

Joshua answered. "Hello?"

"Hey buddy! It's Dad. How's it going?"

"Good."

Kyle checked his watch. "You're up late."

"I can't sleep."

"Why can't you sleep, buddy?"

Joshua, like young children are wont to do, abruptly changed the subject without answering the question. "We're in Canada."

"I know."

"I drew you a picture, Daddy."

Kyle smiled. "That's great. What'd you draw it of?" There was a rustle on the other end of the line. "Hello?" Kyle waited another moment. "Hello?"

"See, Daddy?"

Kyle suddenly realized his son was trying to hold up the picture to the phone. "Oh, Josh. The camera isn't on."

"Do you like it?"

"Just a second. Josh, have Grandma start a Skype session."

There was another rustle on the line, then Lyla's muffled voice. "How do I do that? Which button is it?"

"It's the one with—"

Josh's voice cut in, more insistent. "What do you think, Daddy?"

"Just a second, Josh." Kyle tried to sound patient and firm.

"The camera? Photos?" Lyla asked.

"Well, yeah, you could take a picture and send it."

"How do I do that?" Kyle's mother was not tech-savvy.

"Press the—oh, forget it." He addressed Josh, "It's great buddy. Really like it." Kyle leaned back and closed his eyes. It was good to hear his son's voice.

"Joshua's got to tuck in now," Lyla said.

"Just a second," Kyle said hurriedly. "I'd like to keep talking with him for a moment."

"Night, Daddy!" Joshua called, his voice farther away from the phone.

"Buddy? Hey, buddy?"

There was silence for a moment, then his mother's voice again on the line. "Kyle?"

"Hi, Mom."

"We're glad you're all right."

"Yeah, I'm fine."

"Did you see what happened in Chicago?"

"I did," Kyle said wearily.

"It's horrible. This just keeps happening." Lyla's voice was wrought with fear.

"I know. But we've made some real progress today," Kyle said confidently.

"Is it safe to fly?"

"From Canada? Sure."

"Then we'll head over to Europe. Just until this is all over," Lyla said. "We'll call you when we arrive."

"All right. Good night." Kyle hung up. As strange as it seemed, the silence now—just after speaking with his family—made his loneliness even more acute. Kyle ran a hand through his hair and rubbed his tired eyes. A soft knock at his door pulled him from his stupor. Kyle turned and told the visitor to enter. It was Sadiq. He sat across from Kyle and spoke quietly.

"You've got to tell me something. How did you do that today?"

Kyle turned away, reluctant to answer. "You'll think it's crazy."

"I already think it's crazy. I want to know how you did it."

Kyle stammered, unsure how to answer.

Sadiq leveled his gaze on Kyle. "I'd rather know for sure. Right now I think you're some kind of wizard."

"I…I can't explain it."

That wasn't good enough for Sadiq, whose eyes widened.

"Okay," Kyle said, finally grasping onto an analogy he thought fit, "it's…it's like when an artist creates a painting—you just see it."

"Like making a painting, huh?"

Kyle shrugged. "Just moments of inspiration, I guess."

"Inspiration. Hmm." Sadiq sat back. "You know, the ancients believed '*inspiration*' was 'the divine wind'."

"Dr. Hightower seems to think it's that, too."

"And you?"

"I don't know. I respect your beliefs, but…I'm not so sure about it myself."

"Have you thought about what it is?"

Kyle shook his head. "I don't know if it's God, or psychic ability, or what. I just know I should trust it."

Twenty minutes later, Kyle found a couch in a darkened lounge and tried to bed down. He closed his eyes and tried to relax, but he couldn't fall asleep. The couch was comfortable enough, but Kyle couldn't find a good sleeping position. The more he tried to adjust on the couch the more he became uncomfortable. After nearly two hours of tossing and turning Kyle retrieved some sleeping pills from a drawer in his office. The pills were no help. Four hours later Kyle was still wide awake, staring at the ceiling.

Somewhere in the middle of the night Kyle began to wonder why he was experiencing insomnia. He knew without sleep, he could not dream. That alone would not prevent him from finding inspiration. Today he had been able to pull together details he hadn't seen in dreams by instinct, if not intuition. But Kyle felt drained. Something was off and yet he could not say what it was. As the night dragged on, the feeling took the form of a fear that his predictive abilities were somehow at an end. He had no way to explain it; he hadn't been able to explain the ability in the first place. One thing was clear: the Apocalypse Men weren't finished. As talented and wealthy as Salameh and Vasquez were, they were not the type of men to mastermind all of the attacks or create an alliance with Zyuganov. They were also not religious. The person at the center of the Apocalypse Men was still out there.

Deciding sleep was a lost cause, Kyle returned to his office and turned on his computer. He was deep into research an hour later when Larsen came by.

"You're here early."

"I thought it was late," Kyle sighed as he rubbed his sore neck. His eyes were bloodshot from a lack of sleep. There was something behind them, a fear that Larsen sensed.

"What's the matter?"

Kyle shook his head. "The Sixth Vial." He pointed to the screen. It showed Revelation, Chapter 16, Verse 12:

And the sixth angel poured out his vial upon the great river Euphrates; and the water thereof was dried up, that the way of the kings of the east might be prepared.

"I don't think we're the next target," Kyle said.

"And?" Larsen raised his eyebrows.

"This might be worse."

It was eleven o'clock the next night, halfway around the world. The squadron of F-16 fighter jets skimmed over the open desert, hurtling towards their target. They were still hours away from their destination, but as their mission took them unauthorized into their neighbor's airspace, the pilots flew low. They had no intention of being detected. This mission was the most difficult and dangerous the Israelis had flown in almost forty years. It had a striking similarity to the 1981 raid on Iraq, for tonight's target was an Iranian nuclear facility.

The Israelis had long suspected Iran was breaking its 2015 international nuclear treaty. The conditions of the deal, allowing 24 days between requests for inspections and the inspections themselves, gave Iran plenty of time to move materiel around in a giant shell game. Iranian leaders had long chanted *Death to Israel*. Now Israeli intelligence feared the Iranians would make good on their threats.

New data showed a tactical nuclear attack was imminent. Two Israeli sources, codenamed *SAMPSON* and *JERICHO*, showed corroborating evidence that the Iranians would have a functional nuclear weapon in just over two months.

Mossad prompted the two sources for details. In time, *JERICHO* produced evidence that the bomb would be a ground-based tactical nuke; the Iranians knew the Israelis' missile defense system is one of the best in the world, and wouldn't risk a missile against it. The *Iron Dome*, *Iron Beam*, and *David's Sling* defense systems had already intercepted short-to-medium range missiles with tremendous precision. *JERICHO* claimed the Iranians would hand off the bomb to a member of Hezzbollah or Hamas for delivery in Israel. *SAMPSON* couldn't verify that information, but confirmed the bomb would be ground-based. More frightening, *SAMPSON* and *JERICHO* agreed on the target—either the Knesset in Jerusalem, or Tel Aviv.

The Iranians only had to finish the bomb before they could put it into play; Israel could not allow that. As they had done to the Iraqis before, the Israelis would destroy Iran's nuclear facilities. The pilots knew their actions would lead to war, but then they felt war was inevitable. And if they were successful, at least the Iranians would not be able to wage it with nuclear weapons.

Driven by the ticking clock of Iran's secret bomb development, the eight best pilots in the Israeli Air Force drilled night and day for the mission. Now the moment they had waited for had arrived. Each of the men flew willing to die for their country, but more willing to make the Iranian nuclear troops and scientists die for theirs.

In the lead plane was the commander, Captain Idan Ben Ami. He was a grim man, though barely 30 years old. Ben

Ami's motivations for taking the mission on were deeper and more personal than duty to his nation. His eyes narrowed over his oxygen mask as he thought of Maryam.

Idan Ben Ami first met Maryam nearly ten years ago. He had gone to visit a cousin in the West Bank on one of his leaves from the Air Force. Back then, Ben Ami was a new pilot, full of talent, but also a brashness that only gets worn down with age and maturity. Idan knew he was a great pilot; he just didn't have the humility to hold back from letting everyone else around him know. He had joined the Air Force with a sense of youthful idealism and the ethics of justice and honor that he had inherited from his parents. Perhaps it was these latter traits that made him intervene when he saw a group of teenage Israeli settlers throwing rocks at the two young Palestinian women.

Maryam and her friend were both 18. They had been walking along the street, minding their own business, when four Israeli youths began to taunt them. An Israeli settler had been killed by Palestinians the day before, raising the youths' jingoistic ire. Even as a brash young soldier, Ben Ami could see the boys had no appreciation of the complexity of the situation. They had simply heard of a killing they deemed unjust and taken out their anger on the first target they could find, no matter how inappropriate and unjustified it was. At first the boys made fun of the girls' hijabs, but soon the taunts escalated into calls of "whore!" Maryam and her friend started to run, but the boys pursued them and began to throw rocks. Maryam stumbled and fell. Although her friend tried to help her, the hail of rocks forced her to flee for her own safety. With Maryam left behind, the boys gleefully converged on their prey.

If Ben Ami hadn't rounded the corner at that moment, the youths would have likely killed Maryam. She was lying on the ground, balled into a fetal position—a feeble attempt to protect herself from the rocks.

"Hey! Stop!" Ben Ami called, running over to the boys.

"Shove off!" the largest youth spat in response, then raised a large rock above his head. Had he been able to bring it down on Maryam, that alone would have killed her. But Ben Ami was faster. Using a *krav maga* technique he had learned in the military, he quickly disarmed the youth and left him on the ground writhing in pain.

Ben Ami maneuvered himself between Maryam and the other boys, shielding her. The youths looked at Ben Ami in disgust, but seeing their ringleader on the ground, realized they wanted no part of this fight. They dropped their rocks and ran.

When he was a safe distance from Ben Ami, one of the boys turned back and shouted a cowardly retort, "Goat lover!"

The boy didn't realize Ben Ami could have thrown a rock from where he stood and still knock him out cold, but Idan knew it wasn't worth it. The boys were retreating; even their once-bold ringleader was slinking away on the ground, and Maryam was safe.

Ben Ami reached a hand out to the young Palestinian woman. "Are you all right?"

Maryam looked up, more than a bit frightened to see a man in an Israeli Defense Forces uniform offering his hand. Still, he helped her up gently, and Maryam was grateful for the rescue. Ben Ami would never forget the first time he looked into Maryam's face. He had never cared much for Palestinians, but at that moment, he instantly felt she was one of the most beautiful women he had ever seen. His flush of attraction was accompanied by one of anger. She was not unscathed from her encounter with the boys. Her dress was torn, her arms, legs, and hands bloodied, and her cheek scraped and bruised. Only her head, which she had shielded with her arms, was untouched. "I'm sorry," Ben Ami said. "They're animals."

Maryam's body wasn't the only thing bruised. Her pride had taken a hit, and she wasn't about to let an Israeli condescend to her, especially after what she'd been through. She pulled back from him. "It's fine."

"No, it's not," Ben Ami said softly. He wanted to condemn their behavior, especially seeing how she was linking his uniform to the boys' actions. He needed her to know they were nowhere near the same. But it wasn't all he wanted. Ben Ami found himself drawn to Maryam, though he noticed how cool she was to him. He had to play this right. "Let me walk you home."

"I'm fine," Maryam said, her voice gaining strength. She was starting to calm her nerves.

"Just to your street, then. I don't want you to run into any more of them."

Maryam looked at Ben Ami, her eyes fiery with temper. "Can an animal protect me from other animals?"

Ben Ami smiled. "Yes. As long as he's not a jackass."

Against her will, Maryam cracked a smile, then quickly caught herself. She liked that this Israeli soldier didn't take himself too seriously, and he had come to her aid. She quickly drew her face back into steel, but Ben Ami had already seen how he cracked her defenses. He enjoyed the walk with her.

Three blocks from Maryam's home, the couple passed a

snack shop. Ben Ami bought a cold soft drink and handed it to Maryam, motioning for her to press it against her check. Caught off guard by this soldier's unpretentious gallantry, Maryam placed the soft drink against her face as an ersatz icepack. "Thank you," she said quietly.

Before long, they reached Maryam's door. She was surprised that she let him accompany her the entire way. She was even more surprised to find herself attracted to him. Ben Ami gently brushed his hand over Maryam's bruised cheek, wishing he had the power to heal with his touch. The Air Force had trained his hands to kill. No one would teach them to heal, but Ben Ami would have embraced such training with purpose.

Ben Ami had waited for Maryam outside her house the next morning. When she saw him, she suppressed a smile. "You again?" She tried to sound annoyed, but found it hard to disguise her delight.

"Me again," Ben Ami said. He felt like a sad puppy that wanders after the first person it attaches itself to, but at least he was owning up to it.

"What do you want this time? You can't convince me that Superman wears an IDF uniform." She was teasing him now.

"No, but I thought you could still use some protection."

"Protection?" Maryam frowned.

"Yes. It's a jungle out there."

Maryam laughed and nudged his side as she fell into step with him. "You're so corny."

Ben Ami came back to himself in his cockpit. He stretched his fingers and wrapped them back onto the stick. His eyes caught sight of his bomb release, and soon he was back in his memory. This time it was to his wedding night, some eight years ago. Ben Ami and Maryam had been forced to retreat to a bomb shelter. Above, a rocket attack pelted the earth and destroyed half a dozen buildings. The cramped shelter shook with each impact. Over a dozen other people had crowded into the quarters, but Idan and Maryam found a corner for themselves. As they looked into each other's eyes, the rest of the world, even the ear-shattering *boom* of each explosion, faded away.

Ben Ami pulled himself from the memory. His eyes were burning, and the cockpit suddenly felt terribly claustrophobic. He breathed sharply into the mask, nearly hyperventilating, until he couldn't take it any longer and tore it from his face. It was too painful to remember Maryam, but Ben Ami could not help thinking of her. He had gone through so much to marry her; convincing her family that an Israeli was an acceptable mate was toughest of all, but he also had to win over his own family and friends. Even his commanding officer was skeptical and ordered him to go through a series of loyalty questions before he could continue with his military career. Ben Ami couldn't understand the flak he received. If any example proved the divide between Israelis and Palestinians could be bridged, wasn't this it?

Ben Ami had been away on duty the day of the raid. Maryam used the time to visit her family in the West Bank. She had been playing with her older sister's children in the living room when one of the boys pointed out the window. "Army men!" the boy cried in fascination.

Maryam went to the window and looked out. A squad of Israeli commandos was mounting a raid on the house across the street. Maryam saw the troops with their guns drawn and tried to hustle the children to an inner bedroom. They were too late. A hail of gunfire sounded as the rebels in the house and the soldiers outside exchanged bullets. Maryam's sister hustled the children out of the room, keeping their heads ducked. Maryam brought up the rear, pushing the children in front of her. One of the girls suddenly screeched in pain and fell to the ground. A stray bullet had grazed her arm. Maryam scooped up the girl and hunched as she ran to the door.

Just then, another stray bullet whizzed into the room, hitting Maryam with a dull thud. Maryam spun and dropped to the ground. Maryam's sister ran to her and shook her, but it was too late. Maryam was dead.

Ben Ami's eyes welled with tears. *Bastards*, he thought as he gritted his teeth. *I was a peacemaker, and they gave me war. They will suffer as I have suffered. Earth is for burying, and I have done my share. Now they will do theirs.* For nearly a year after Maryam's death, Ben Ami had contemplated suicide. He didn't know if he could join his wife after death, but death seemed the only way to escape his pain. Then a new idea dawned on Ben Ami—one that gave his life purpose. He could exact revenge.

Only Ben Ami knew the real reason they were now over Iranian airspace. The data was false. The Iranians might well be planning a nuclear attack, but not in the manner *SAMPSON* and *JERICHO* had reported. That was because their reports weren't evidence drawn separately and corroborated—they were from the *same* source—and that source was Mashiri.

Mashiri knew the raid on the Iranian nuclear plant

would start a war. Ben Ami had also known this well before he ventured into Pakistan to meet Mashiri face-to-face. But this no longer satisfied Ben Ami. The Israelis might win a war against Iran. The commandos who killed his wife, the aggressive fighters of both the Israelis and the Muslims—they all had to pay. A war between two countries was not enough. There had to be a firestorm. It had taken Ben Ami years to find the perfect target. He had it now. He hadn't told anyone, including Mashiri, but the pilot figured Mashiri would be pleased when he saw the results.

Ben Ami throttled back his engine and dipped below the formation. Another pilot, seeing his commander's plane drop, radioed over to him. "Captain?"

The men had been ordered to maintain radio silence, but Ben Ami knew he had to respond. "There's a problem with my fuel line." He paused, pretending to work the problem. "I can't go on."

The other pilots held their breath. This was devastating news. "Do we abort?"

"No. Proceed to the target. Good luck, men."

The other pilots watched as Ben Ami's plane banked to the left, then headed back, a lone black shape skimming over the shadowy landscape. None of them expected to see him again. They didn't know how right they were.

25

Igniting an Inferno

Ben Ami reached his target in a few hours. Looking down, he could see the golden and lead domes lit up in the night. Hitting them couldn't be easier. Both of the structures had stood for over 1,300 years. Both were well fought over. At one time, one of the structures had been a palace for Crusaders. They only reverted to their original purpose, one extremely important to the Muslims, when Saladin conquered Jerusalem in 1187. Ben Ami circled once around the target, then came in on a bombing run. His bunker-busting bombs leveled the stone buildings within seconds, turning the structures which had been venerated for centuries into dust.

Ben Ami pulled his F-16 into a sharp climb, then circled around the site once more. As he surveyed the damage, he could see the broken and hollow shell of one of the domes remained. Ben Ami had dropped his entire bomb load, but he still had weapons. Banking sharply, he dove low over the wreckage and strafed it with his 20mm Vulcan cannon. It was late at night, and though the pilot hadn't seen any people at the target, onlookers were now pouring out in the city to see the cause of the explosions and smoke. Ben Ami could see crowds gathering, looking on in bewilderment. He strafed the site a second time, riddling the wreckage with bullet holes, but causing little structural damage. He pulled back on the stick and flew into a steep climb once again. As he broke free of the smoke, he could see the stars glowing brilliantly in the night sky. Since Maryam's death, Ben Ami had looked at them as cold and unfeeling. Whether the distant stars coldly dictated man's fate or operated completely independent of it he didn't know. But now, strangely, they seemed to beckon him home. Ben Ami closed his eyes and thought of his dead wife. "Maryam," he breathed, wishing to be reunited with her. Then he pushed the stick forward, forcing the F-16 into a steep dive. The sharp pull back into his seat would only last a moment.

At CIA Headquarters, Kyle had spent most of the day trying to figure his theory out. Now he was sharing it with Larsen and Sadiq.

"You think this Sixth Vial attack will target Israel?" Larsen asked, trying to clarify.

Sadiq shook his head. To him, Kyle's theory didn't wash. "Why the change in target?"

"Maybe Israel has been the long-term goal all along," Kyle explained. "Weaken the U.S. so we're unable to defend them. Then their enemies can move in."

Sadiq and Larsen frowned, unsure about this theory.

"Are we not weakened?" Kyle asked.

Sadiq didn't say anything, but inwardly he had to admit Kyle was right.

"How will this attack occur?" Larsen prompted. None of them knew it was already underway.

Kyle spread his hands flat over his eyes and rubbed them. It was the key question he had asked himself since this morning, but he hadn't found a satisfactory answer. "I don't know," he admitted, annoyed he hadn't gotten farther.

Sadiq was alarmed by this answer. Kyle had been downright prophetic in recent days. Why didn't he know now? "Who's behind it?" Sadiq asked. "Vasquez and Salameh are powerful, but I can't imagine they formed the alliance with Zyuganov, or planned this entire campaign."

"I agree," Kyle said.

"So far we haven't gotten anything out of Vasquez, Serrano, or Salameh," Larsen said. "But we will."

"Could the Apocalypse Men be state-sponsored?" Sadiq floated the theory as a question. "By Iran, for instance?"

"If the Iranians were behind this, wouldn't they have gotten the bombs from Zyuganov and used them to another end? Why deploy them in the U.S., and especially Africa?" Kyle reasoned. "Wouldn't they attack Israel directly? The Iranians want to see Israel wiped off the map."

"You've got a point," Larsen acknowledged, "but Sadiq isn't the only one to suspect a connection between Iran and the Apocalypse Men. It's a theory that has legs around here. If you're convinced it's something else, put a brief together so I can send it up."

"Yes sir," Kyle said.

Larsen left the room. Kyle leaned forward and exhaled a long breath.

Sadiq watched Kyle, concern growing on his visage. "You don't look so good."

"Thanks," Kyle said sarcastically.

"Have you slept?"

"Not much."

"Why don't you try to catch some now? I'll get working on this."

Kyle didn't respond. Sadiq watched Kyle's face turn ashen. He turned to follow Kyle's gaze to the television screen behind him. The image was dark and largely obscured by smoke, but rising flames illuminated the night sky just enough to discern the silhouette of a Middle Eastern cityscape. Sadiq turned up the volume to hear the reporter's voice.

"The attack has brought immediate outrage throughout the Muslim world. Deemed the third holiest site in Islam, the Al-Aqsa Mosque is where the prophet Muhammad is said to have ascended to heaven. But Jewish leaders also quickly denounced the action, citing this is the holiest site in Judaism, where Solomon's Temple was built. Though some Jews and Christians believe these Muslim structures must be destroyed to make way for a prophesied rebuilding of the Temple, the Chief Rabbinate strongly condemned the attack."

The image changed to a closer angle of the smoldering debris. The reporter continued. "Here, where a giant crater is all that remains of the Al-Aqsa Mosque and Dome of the Rock, the violent divisions of culture and religion are clearly drawn. Jerusalem, this holiest of cities, now faces an uncertain future, marred by a reawakening of the violent struggles of the past." The reporter wasn't quite right—there was more than a mere crater remaining. The half-broken shell of the Dome of the Rock stood, its interior ripped open like the ruined apse of the Temple of Venus and Roma in the Roman Forum. What had destroyed the 1,300 year-old building was not the wear of time or even force of nature, but a sudden, violent act of human aggression.

Parks burst through the door. "You see it?" she exclaimed, her words coming so fast they were almost indistinguishable.

Kyle was stunned by the images. "What happened?"

"An Israeli fighter jet dropped its entire bomb load on the Al-Aqsa Mosque and the Dome of the Rock, then crashed into what remained."

The TV now cut to another angle—this one showing a piece of wing from the fighter jet sticking out of the wreckage, the insignia of the Israeli Star of David clearly marked. Kyle groaned at the sight as his shoulders slumped. That image alone would inflame the entire Islamic world.

"That's insane!" Sadiq shouted at the screen. "What Israeli would want to be a kamikaze?"

Kyle shook his head in disbelief and closed his eyes. He had feared this attack, but he hadn't been able to stop it. Once again, the all-too familiar feeling of being right but helpless overpowered him.

"That's not all," Parks said. When Kyle opened his eyes, he could see she was pointing to the television. A new graphic showed a map of Iran. A jagged explosion-like star marked the point of a conflict. The reporter's voice continued:

"The attack in Jerusalem coincided with an Israeli strike against Iranian nuclear facilities. A major processing plant was destroyed, but Iranian officials claim to have shot down two of the attacking jets."

"This will unite the world against Israel," Kyle said grimly. The attack on Iran would have a political cost, but the destruction of the Muslim holy sites would spark rage.

"No kidding," Parks agreed. "There are already protests and riots stretching from Morocco to Indonesia."

Idan Ben Ami, dead now for twenty minutes, had set the world on fire.

President Barnes stood in the White House Situation Room and watched the TV screens in shock. He turned to General Bump Foley next to him. "Is this really how it looks? This mosque thing doesn't make a lick of sense."

"I hate to say so, sir, but it looks like it. They confirmed it was an Israeli fighter jet."

Barnes shook his head vigorously. "Why would an Israeli pilot do it?"

Foley shifted a file in his hand and opened it in front of Barnes. "This is extremely sensitive, sir, but preliminary reports identify the pilot as Idan Ben Ami. He was a captain in their Air Force, clean record. But three years ago, his Palestinian wife was killed by Israeli gunfire in the West Bank."

Barnes groaned. "You got to be kidding me."

"No sir." Foley swallowed, then continued: "Ben Ami was away on active duty at the time. Took it pretty hard, but was checked out thoroughly, and kept on flight status."

Barnes still couldn't believe it. Foley wouldn't have, either, except that the hard data was right in his hands.

"What about the Iranian raid?" the President prompted. "Israel has the right to defend itself, but they had to know this would inflame the region. Did our data show a threat was imminent?"

"No sir. And there's been ripples through the IDF. Apparently some of their top brass weren't informed of the operation."

As Barnes watched the images from Jerusalem, he felt nearly as helpless as the day he took office. What could he do now to control this blaze? And as strained as America had been under its own spate of attacks, how could he lend Israel any aid? How could a handful of zealots change the world, while the President of the United States felt powerless? Barnes was disgusted with how surreal it had all become. "So a squadron of pilots goes rogue and starts World War III."

An aide approached Foley and whispered in his ear. Foley nodded. "Mr. President, there's another message from the Apocalypse Men."

The video had somehow bypassed the normal contact at Voice of the World and hadn't gotten to the CIA—this time it was broadcast right on the air when Kyle, Sadiq, and the rest of CIA first saw it. As before, it featured the same silhouetted man against the blood-red backdrop. Kyle had always viewed the production values of the Apocalypse Men's propaganda as fairly rudimentary; ISIS had far better videos, including soaring aerial shots, albeit from stock or stolen footage. The basic setup of the Apocalypse Men messages had never looked amateurish; just plain. They knew their words and actions were far more effective than appearances. The cumulative effect of the videos preceding or immediately following devastating attacks had taken its toll. Kyle, Sadiq, Larsen, and Parks watched as the silhouetted man's voice sent a paralyzing chill through their veins.

"*And the sixth angel poured out his vial upon the great river Euphrates; and the water thereof was dried up, that the way of the kings of the east might be prepared.*"

Larsen nodded grimly. He had just received a report

from Jerusalem. "They might not be draining any rivers, but they have started a war. Israeli forces are already engaged from nearly every direction but the Mediterranean."

Sadiq, like everyone else, had expected this—just not so quickly. "Who's attacking them?"

"*Everybody*. Jihadists and Palestinian rebels are there now, but regular troops will follow. The Iranian, Lebanese, and even Syrian armies are on the move. There's also guerrilla fighters coming out of Egypt, Jordan, and Saudi Arabia. Blow up the third holiest site in Islam and you've got instant war."

Kyle's throat tightened. "Where's the thickest fighting so far?"

"Ramat David Air Force Base," Larsen said. "Iranians started firing missiles at it as soon as word of the attack on their nuclear facility got out. Clearly in retaliation. The crazies are joining in." *Crazies* meant short-range rockets fired by guerrilla fighters. The Ramat David Air Force Base is the only airbase in northern Israel, and the second-largest unit in the Israeli Defense Forces. That made it an immediate target of the attacking forces.

The video wasn't finished. "*And he gathered them together into a place called in the Hebrew tongue… Armageddon*." The last word hung in the air as the entire bullpen fell silent. Indeed, with the speed the conflict had been accelerating, the build-up to Armageddon might just have begun. Kyle's pulse throbbed in his ears. He knew the Ramat David Air Force Base lay in the Jezreel Valley, not far from Mount Megiddo, the predicted site of Armageddon. John the Revelator's 1st Century vision of the great battle at that location is not surprising—even in his day, it was one of the most blood-drenched sites in history. Thirty-five battles have raged in the valley stretching from the ancient Egyptian era to the Lebanon War of 2006. In that conflict and the one immediately preceding it, the 1973 Yom Kippur War, the fighting was restricted to rocket attacks. Kyle suspected that wouldn't be the case this time. Ground forces were moving southward from Lebanon, Syria, and Jordan. If the Ramat David Air Force Base were captured or destroyed, these forces would continue moving south, along Highway 66 toward Jerusalem.

Kyle turned to Larsen. "What are we doing about this?"

The longer Barnes watched the video, the angrier he got. "I knew it," he spat. "Those Apocalypse bastards got to those pilots." It was a strange vindication of his belief that the Israeli leaders would not have acted so recklessly, but it didn't improve the situation. There was still a war raging.

General Foley cleared his throat. "Sir, the Apocalypse Men can take credit for the attacks, but it's highly unlikely they were capable of—"

Barnes cut him off. "Don't you see their objective? They wanted to weaken us so they can pull this off. They drew blood so this pack of dogs will come running!" He stood, now fuming. Barnes knew he didn't have the makings of a great president, but he was tired of losing. The Apocalypse Men had put him against the wall, and all that was left was his resolve. He wasn't going to let them win. "Terrorists may have started this thing, but we are not going to let them finish it!"

There was silence as Foley and the rest of the President's key advisors considered this pledge. Of course, they all agreed. It was just a matter of strategy and cost. Foley was first to speak. "So you're suggesting, Mr. President...?"

"There should be no question about what we're going to do," Barnes said forcefully. "We are going to take out the Apocalypse Men, and we are going to defend Israel."

Standish hadn't gotten to know the new President well, although he, like most of Wallace's surviving staff, had been kept on. He knew he was treading into dangerous territory to question Barnes, but he felt it was his job. "Mr. President, how exactly will we defend Israel?"

Barnes sat and looked at each of his advisors. "I want to know all our options."

Barnes knew diplomacy would be a key element in the path forward, so he looked first to Secretary of State Marsh Adamson. He had little faith in Marsh; he had seen how foolish the Secretary's comments were following the African bombing, and in Barnes' mind, that was just par for the course with Adamson. But he also hadn't any time to restock the administration—the crises that faced them with Barnes' sudden inauguration didn't allow for new staff; besides, they could all be out of their jobs in a few months. The election was still officially on, although Barnes was from Huntington's party and a replacement candidate for Wallace hadn't been found. Barnes had no desire to run—he had a job to do that took his full attention. The election would work itself out, but Barnes wondered who would really want the job now.

Adamson didn't notice Barnes' gaze until an awkwardly long silence had passed. When Adamson noticed the new President was looking at him, he knuckled under the pressure, and suddenly found himself mute. Most people would have found it ironic that a diplomat, a man whose career hinged on his ability to speak, now had nothing to say. But Barnes wouldn't be found in the category of 'most people'—he found Adamson completely living up to his expectations.

The President shifted his gaze around the table. The Chairman of the Joint Chiefs of Staff met his eyes and spoke up first. "Sir, the military is stretched incredibly thin. Our troop strength is depleted, due to the attacks here—"

"Our might doesn't lie only in our troop strength, does it?" Barnes fired back.

The Chairman feared Barnes was talking about the Bomb. He sensed the new President was acting out of fear and anger, and those are the worst motivations for any military action, let alone a nuclear strike. It didn't matter how committed Barnes was to our allies, the Chairman needed to nip this one in the bud and calm the President down. "No sir, but if you're talking about our weapons capabilities, you should carefully consider—"

Barnes saw the general's thinking and broke in. He needed to show everyone he wasn't being emotional—just resolute. It was time to lay out the ground rules. "I want the world to know we will not let Israel be wiped off the map. I want peace, ladies and gentlemen. Even if we have to use threat of force to get it."

Barnes knew if the Apocalypse Men intended to wipe out Israel all along, then they had miscalculated in thinking they had crippled the United States to the point it could not lend aid. Whether or not all his advisors agreed with him, Barnes was sure he could show the world the U.S. still had power and influence. That power would make others think twice about wiping out Israel. If there was any purpose in his rise to the presidency, whether by fate or Providence, Barnes felt it was this: to defend Israel. From his earliest days as a politician, and even before that, he had never wavered in his support for the country. Now his conviction seemed to flow right to his fingertips.

"So we back Israel," Foley conceded the point to the President. "Then what?"

Barnes leaned forward, and unaware of himself, scratched at his collar. It was a nervous tick that betrayed a fear he hadn't wanted to show, but what he was about to propose did seem daunting. He had no practical means of going forward, but he was determined to figure that out, too. "Then we all sit at the table and work this out. I don't want just the Israelis and Iranians—I want the Saudis, the Jordanians, the Palestinians…even the Russians. I want every country that has any interest or influence in the region to sit down and work this thing out."

Adamson's mouth dropped open as he let out a strangled cry. All eyes turned to the Secretary of State, who had visibly turned white. "What you're asking is like trying to win a dance competition with both legs broken."

"I know," Barnes said, regaining his determined posture, "but we can't accept the alternative."

Adamson started to shake his head rapidly. "You're not hearing me. It's impossible." He lowered his head in a quick bob for emphasis, but the gesture appeared awkward. The Chairman of the Joint Chiefs nearly laughed, given Adamson's 'forceful' gesture looked like something between a chicken and a bobblehead.

Barnes straightened. "Don't worry about it then," he said with a grimace. "You're fired." That got the attention of the room. "The rest of us are going to find the answers." Barnes had made a few missteps in this meeting, but he was satisfied with this close. Another president might have scared up the troops with the firing, then laid on expectations by declaring *you are going to figure this out* to the rest of the staff. That had been Barnes' inclination, but he caught himself, and decided this was a moment to build unity with his team. *Us* was such a small word, but words mattered. Attitude mattered. A team mattered. He'd need them to figure this out.

Israel is no stranger to war. The country has fought for its existence at its founding in 1948, two subsequent major wars in 1967 and 1973, and several minor ones since. Motivated by the memory of the Holocaust in World War II, the Israelis have lived every breath by the motto, *Never Forget, Never Again.* That determination has resulted in some tremendous victories—especially the Six-Day War of 1967. Israel was attacked by five nations—Egypt, Syria, Jordan, Iraq, and Lebanon—which were supported by a further nine Muslim nations. Israel fought alone, against an army more than twice its size. But the Israelis fought so tenaciously that they not only won, but massively increased their land—capturing the Golan Heights, West Bank, Gaza Strip, and the entire Sinai Peninsula. Israel returned the Sinai to Egypt after the Camp David Accords, and subsequent agreements have changed Israel's status with the other conquered territories as well. But despite relative post-war conciliation with Jordan, Egypt, and other once-opposing governments, the Israelis have struggled with their status in the world. A country that lives every day with the fear of annihilation is bound to act out, and Israel has borne its share of criticism for its actions towards its neighbors and especially the displaced Palestinian population within its borders.

Many nations still consider Israel a nation of interlopers. So it came as no surprise when a large contingent of the United Nations asked for immediate sanctions against Israel following the dual attacks. It didn't matter that Iran has sworn to wipe Israel off the map; Israel had committed an unprovoked act of war against Iran. The destruction of the Al Aqsa mosque and the Dome of the Rock was considered beyond the pale, and though both Israeli political and military leaders immediately condemned the actions of the crazed pilot, it didn't matter. By dawn, Israel was engaged in another full-scale war.

Iran began firing medium-range missiles overnight, while insurgent rocket attacks pelted the nation just before dawn. Israel's new *David's Sling* missile defense system worked extremely well against the Iranian missiles, while the well-tested *Iron Dome* and *Iron Beam* defense systems continued to block most of the short-range rockets.

The Iranians were the first to send fighter jets over Israel, and while most of the rockets failed to damage the Ramat David Air Force Base, an Iranian sortie managed to bomb one of the runways and destroy several jets on the ground before all of their own planes were shot down.

On the ground, insurgents began both a civil war in Israeli-held Palestinian territories and attacks along the border. Lebanese forces converged on Israel's northern border at dawn, while a brigade of Syrian troops managed to pull itself from its own civil war and attack the northeastern Israeli border. Guerrilla fighters from the south were largely pushed back by Israeli Defense Forces, but the guerrillas kept coming in wave after wave. In many cities around Israel, especially border towns, the morning was marked by smoke, fire, and the concussive sound of explosions.

Yet for all of the chaos surrounding Israel on the military front, a diplomatic miracle was working behind the scenes. Barnes hustled more than he had ever done in his political life to create the framework of a diplomatic solution. He enlisted the help of dozens of diplomats from America and allied countries to solicit a peace conference. Saudi Arabia was one of the key elements to fall into place; Barnes called on Senator Walter Merrick, the former ambassador to Saudi Arabia, to address them with his plan. The Saudis agreed; the sudden conflagration throughout the region had taken them by surprise and threatened the overall stability of the Middle East. Many countries followed suit. Although several Muslim countries wondered if this might be a chance to end the Israeli conflict once and for all, the fact that they could not guarantee an ending favorable to their side was enough to prompt them to sue others for peace. Barnes pressed hard and astoundingly assembled a conference within an 24-hour period. Amazingly the Iranians, Israelis, Saudis, Jordanians, Russians, Egyptians, and half a dozen other countries agreed. Germany would host, with Berlin being the site of the conference. Ultra conservatives in Israel said the location was a sign that the conference would end once again in the slaughter of Jews, but the Germans saw it as a symbolic opportunity to mend the past while safeguarding the future. There was also a practical reason for the location—Berlin was relatively close, but out of the region. Germany was also considered a relatively safe country since it had not suffered the recent terror attacks. Some argued Geneva would have been a better location, but Barnes knew Germany was an economic player with many Middle Eastern countries and could help lean on them to agree to a peaceful resolution.

Kyle was watching the war footage from Israel in the bullpen when Larsen strode in. "Listen up, gang, you've heard about the conference in Berlin? Well, the Director wants us there too."

Kyle raised his eyebrows. "All of us?"

"That's right. We need you to liaise with other agencies, and if necessary, make the case that the Apocalypse Men are behind these attacks."

"Other than the video, we haven't found a connection yet," Kyle responded.

"We better. It might be the only thing that pulls us out of this mess."

26

The Seventh Angel

Three hours later, Kyle was flying over the Atlantic. He looked out the window and as the setting light tinted the waves below, much as he had seen on his last transatlantic trip.

Sadiq slid into the empty seat next to Kyle. "You look exhausted. You get any sleep?"

Kyle shook his head. "Not much." Even with heavy eyelids, he hadn't slept well for days.

"Try," Sadiq said. "We're going to need it." He slipped back to his own seat across the aisle.

It was good advice, so Kyle figured he might as well try to sleep. He closed the shade and leaned back against the headrest. Closing his eyes, Kyle tried to relax. He had almost reached a point of stillness and embrace of the blackness before his eyes when a jolt shook him awake. Kyle opened his eyes and looked around. The plane was vibrating slightly. They had hit turbulence. The plane bumped along through the air for the next twenty minutes. Kyle tried to sleep two more times during brief lulls in the shaking, but these both lasted less than a minute. He gave up after the third time and opened his laptop. Something had been gnawing at the back of his mind. If this war was the objective of the Sixth Vial, what was the Seventh? What was the overall objective of the Apocalypse Men? Kyle wasn't sure it was just to destroy America and Israel. That was what a growing number of his colleagues believed, but to him, there seemed to be something missing in that goal.

Kyle brought up Revelation Chapter 16 in his browser. He scanned over the chapter until he reached the 17th verse.

And the seventh angel poured out his vial into the air; and there came a great voice out of the temple of heaven, from the throne, saying, It is done.

Kyle frowned as he read. The verse didn't answer anything—in fact, it left him with more questions than he had before. He read on.

And there were voices, and thunders, and lightnings; and there was a great earthquake, such as was not since men were upon the earth, so mighty an earthquake, and so great.

And the great city was divided into three parts, and the cities of the nations fell: and great Babylon came in remembrance before God, to give unto her the cup of the wine of the fierceness of his wrath.

And every island fled away, and the mountains were not found.

And there fell upon men a great hail out of heaven, every stone about the weight of a talent: and men blasphemed God because of the plague of the hail; for the plague thereof was exceeding great.

Again, none of what Kyle read made sense. For the first time, the events sounded far beyond the capability of any human. Were the Apocalypse Men trying to trigger these natural events? Did they believe God would make them happen if they had done all that was required beforehand? Kyle couldn't find the answers, but the more he contemplated these events, the more uneasy he became. Suddenly, he felt extremely claustrophobic, flying in an aluminum tube at 30,000 feet. He scrambled to open the window shade, hoping to find natural light, but they had already flown into night. Still, the scene calmed him. Moonlight glittered off the waves below, and the stars were visible in the clear night sky. It was a serene picture. Kyle breathed slowly until he could close his eyes once again. He didn't sleep, but his mind was clear. Kyle laid his head back and closed his eyes for the remainder of the flight. He thought of Joshua and wondered how he was enjoying the time with his grandparents.

Kyle arrived in Berlin at 8:30 in the morning. A taxi took him to the Hotel Adlon Kampinski. Looking around the familiar surroundings, Kyle thought back to when he received the phone call concerning the African bombing. It had only been a couple of months since this had all started, but it seemed a lifetime ago. Larsen gave Kyle the morning off and told him to get some sleep; he, Sadiq, and Parks had gotten enough on the plane to be ready to go to work. Kyle checked into his room and collapsed on his bed, not bothering to even remove his shoes. Finally, for the first time in days, he slept.

Sleep wasn't a welcome companion. Once again, Kyle had a bizarre dream. Flames rose as if from a giant cauldron. Above the flames was a golden angel. Kyle couldn't tell if the angel was rising from the flames or being consumed by them, but it spread its wings as the flames seemed to rise and cover his vision. Eventually the flames died away in darkness. As the light faded, he saw the glimpse of a man's face. He was lit dimly, as if by the dying embers of a fire. In the reddish glow, Kyle could see the man was a distinguished older gentleman he did not recognize. Kyle tried to study the man's features before the image quickly faded into darkness. Aware he was still asleep, Kyle tried to recall the man's face or bring it back, but he could do little other than stare into blackness.

The sound of his cell phone ringing pulled Kyle from slumber. His face was buried deep in his pillow, and he struggled against the drugged feeling in his body to will his arms to move. Eventually he pushed himself up from the bed and answered the phone on the seventh ring. "Hello?" Kyle said groggily into the phone.

"Dad!" Joshua's voice pulled him from sleep.

"Hey Josh."

"Guess what!" Joshua said excitedly. "We're in Europe!"

Kyle scrubbed his sleep-tousled hair. "Yeah, me too."

"Where are you in Europe?"

"I'm in Berlin. Where are you, buddy?"

There was a slight rustle as Joshua turned to his grandfather to confirm. Kyle could hear Joshua ask, "Grandpa, where are we?" but he didn't hear the answer. Joshua was back on the phone soon enough. "That's where we are, too."

Kyle sat up, wide awake now. "Wait…you're in Berlin? What are you guys doing in Berlin?"

Joshua didn't answer. Instead, Kyle heard another rustle on the phone.

"Josh? Josh?"

Kyle's dad picked up. "Kyle?"

"Dad, why are you in Berlin?"

"An old army buddy of mine married a girl from Germany. They have a house here and invited us to come visit."

Kyle was surprised to hear his father talk of his army days. That was forty years ago, before he went to law school, and he served only a few years in the reserves. But Kyle and his father didn't talk about many things, so it didn't surprise him that he didn't know much about it. He was concerned that his family was in Berlin. The Washington bombing had left him with a gnawing anxiety about his family, and he didn't like the idea of them being in the same place. "There's a lot of people here for the peace conference, Dad. Just watch yourselves, okay?"

"So you're the dad, now?"

Kyle exhaled, trying to mask his frustration with humor. "Just be careful."

Half an hour, later, washed up and changed, Kyle stepped into the Operations Center at the U.S. embassy. Station chief Connors, Larsen, Sadiq, and Parks were already there.

"This might be it," Larsen said, turning to Kyle. "We monitored Vasquez just before we nabbed him—and NSA intercepted a call he received from southern Oman."

Larsen nodded to Parks, who played the audio of the call for Kyle to listen to. It was the call Vasquez had answered just before his fateful trip in his limo.

"The phone was only used once—for this call," Parks explained. "It was probably an emergency line. We tracked the number, but the name was a dead end. So we analyzed the voice, and got a hit." She brought up the latest video from the Apocalypse Men and pointed to the silhouetted man, then a readout from a voice comparison program. "Ninety percent probability. All the videos have the same rate. There's some distortion in the video, but we're sure it's the same guy."

Kyle was elated at the news. This was a major break. "We got a name?"

"Not yet, but we're typing it against other calls."

"We've also sent agents to the neighborhood in Oman where the call was placed," Larsen said. "If he's still around, we'll identify him."

Kyle didn't know how successful that search would be, but a voice match at least gave them something to work with.

Larsen had the same idea. "Quietly, I want you to make our case at the conference. You can show the voice comparison to anyone necessary. You'll be working under our new acting Secretary of State, Tony Hobbs."

"Shouldn't we ID this guy first?" Sadiq asked.

Larsen shook his head. "We may not have time to wait."

The conference was being held in the Hotel Adlon Kampinski, one building down from the embassy. Police armed with submachine guns surrounded the perimeter, but security was much tighter near the conference rooms where the peace talks were taking place. Kyle entered the lobby and caught sight of Knox by the far wall. Before Kyle could walk over to him, Tony Hobbs approached, extending his hand. "Mr. Ferguson. I understand you're my surprise witness."

"Are we going to trial?"

"More than you know. I've arranged for a private meeting between the Israelis and Iranians. We're just waiting for them to get out of a session." He leaned in and spoke in a low voice. "I sure hope your evidence is convincing."

"Honestly, sir, I can't say. The Iranians may think it's manufactured." It wasn't what Hobbs wanted to hear, but without a name, Kyle doubted the Iranians would believe the voice evidence alone. They would already consider the video a tenuous connection to the attack.

An entourage across the lobby caught Kyle's attention. At the center was a wealthy older man. Kyle didn't know who he was, but he watched in stunned silence—it was the same man he had seen in his dream. When Kyle finally came to his senses, the man was almost out of the lobby. Kyle grabbed his cell phone and quickly snapped a picture just before the man disappeared down a corridor into the depths of the hotel. The picture was slightly blurred by the distance of the shot and the man's movement, but the image was clear enough to see his distinct features.

"Did you hear me?"

Kyle suddenly realized Hobbs had been talking to him while his attention was diverted. "Uh, excuse me, sir. This will just take a minute." Kyle strode quickly across the lobby toward the corridor where the man had gone. As he moved, he looked toward Knox, who followed him. Kyle emailed the photo on his phone to Sadiq, then called him. "Sadiq, I just sent you a photo on email. I need an ID on the subject right away." Kyle caught a glimpse of the entourage at the end of the corridor before they disappeared around another corner. He ran down the corridor and rounded the corner, but this time the entourage was gone. There was however an elevator. Kyle watched the numbers go up to the fifth floor, then ran up a stairwell in pursuit.

At the embassy, Larsen hung up the phone and went over to Parks. "We've got an ID on the voice. Agents in Oman recorded a conversation on the street. Langley typed it with the phone call and video." He brought up an image from the secure link to Langley on the computer. It was the photo of an Arab man in his late 30s. Parks and Connors watched over Larsen's shoulder, but Sadiq was still working on Kyle's picture. "Rasul Hakim Al-Hamra," Larsen identified the man. "Also known to associates as Al-Nasrani—'the Christian.' Get this—he's a cousin of—"

"Aaban Assad Al-Mashiri."

Larsen, Parks, and Connors turned to Sadiq. The match on Sadiq's computer was Mashiri.

"We need to pick him up now," Kyle said upon hearing the news from Sadiq. "He's the leader of the Apocalypse Men."

"Larsen will send in our agents," Sadiq said. "There's also a strike team on standby."

"Call them." Kyle hung up and looked down the fifth floor hallway. He wasn't sure which door led to Mashiri's suite. Kyle called Knox.

"I lost you," Knox said.

"Yeah. I almost lost them, too. It's Aaban Assad Al-Mashiri. He's the leader of the Apocalypse Men, and he's in the hotel," Kyle whispered into the phone.

"He's here?"

"Yeah. Staying somewhere on the fifth floor. I need you to get the suite number and bring your unit up here."

"I'm on it. Hold tight."

Mashiri retrieved the briefcase from the closet and placed it on the edge of the bed. Carefully, he opened the briefcase and began connecting the wires of the bomb inside. One of his guards had covertly brought the briefcase into the hotel, dressed as a worker, and had left it in Mashiri's room, bypassing security. Now Mashiri needed only a minute before the bomb would be ready.

In the adjacent sitting room, three bodyguards stood watch. A knock sounded at the door. One of the bodyguards went to answer. A man from hotel security stood in the hall.

"Yes?" the bodyguard inquired.

"There's an urgent matter for Mr. Mashiri," the hotel security man said.

"He's busy," the bodyguard said dismissively.

"It's very urgent, and won't take a moment," the security man insisted.

Mashiri was about to slide a detonator into the bomb when one of his bodyguards knocked on the bedroom door.

"Excuse me, sir. Hotel security would like to speak with you."

Mashiri sighed and put the detonator in his suit jacket's inner pocket. He closed the briefcase gently, then slid it under the bed. Before leaving the bedroom, Mashiri shot his cuffs and slid a small tube up his sleeve.

Mashiri closed the bedroom door behind him as he entered the sitting room. The hotel security man was still standing by the doorway.

"Mr. Mashiri, may I speak with you for a moment?" the security man gestured toward the hall.

"You can speak with him here," the stoutest bodyguard said gruffly.

"It's all right," Mashiri said casually. He followed the man into the hall. The bodyguard followed, but Mashiri raised his hand for him to stay. He was playing it cool. Although Mashiri didn't know what the security man wanted, he didn't sense danger.

"How can I help you?" Mashiri asked. He now noticed a second security man in his peripheral vision, standing behind him to his left.

"Mr. Mashiri—" the first security man began, just as the second moved swiftly to grab the billionaire. Mashiri side-stepped the charging man and whipped the tube out of his sleeve. He sprayed mace in the man's face, then swerved and sprayed the first security man too. Both men fell to the ground, screaming in pain. Mashiri wanted to go back into the room but the spray of mace hung in the air. He fled down the hall. He knew the security men were blinded, but that wouldn't stop other guards from coming.

Mashiri reached the door to the stairwell, his own eyes now watering heavily. His vision made him flee clumsily down the stairs, gripping onto the rail just enough to keep from tumbling headfirst. When he reached the second landing down, he pulled out his cell phone and dialed his driver Abdul.

In the hallway, Kyle reached the two agents. One was still writhing on the floor while the other was on his knees and reaching for his eyes. A mist hung in the air, making Kyle's own eyes water. Why hadn't the agents waited for the strike team to be set in place? Kyle dialed Knox on his cell phone.

"He slipped the agents. Do you have eyes on him?"

One of the bodyguards stepped into the hall. Kyle took one look at the brutish guard and ran. The man chased after him, hot on his tail.

Two bodyguards remained in the suite. One of their cell phones chirped with a shrill tone.

"Yes," the guard picked up.

It was Mashiri, nearly breathless. "The briefcase. It's under the bed. Do it!"

"Insha'Allah, sir." *If Allah wills it.* The bodyguard charged to the bedroom and pulled the briefcase from under the bed.

Kyle rushed down the stairs. He could hear a set of frantic steps far below him. He figured that was Mashiri. But what concerned Kyle was the loud stamping of feet close behind him. He began to take the stairs two and three at a time, but the bodyguard kept closing on him. Kyle gripped the rail tightly as he swung himself around a landing, but he couldn't get away. Two steps later, he felt the bodyguard's hot breath on the back of his neck. Kyle leaped toward the landing eight feet below, but his legs buckled to cushion him, slowing him down. Just as he sprung back up, the bodyguard flung him against the wall and pressed his muscled forearm into Kyle's neck.

The bodyguard in the bedroom opened the briefcase and looked at the bomb. Seeing the detonator was missing, he pulled another from his own suit jacket and carefully slipped it into the bomb. He wrapped his fingers around the switch and closed his eyes. Taking a sharp breath, the bodyguard gave an urgent whisper. "Allahu' Ackbar!"

Thap! Thap!

The bodyguard fell forward, his spine severed by Knox's carefully aimed shot at the base of his head. Knox and the strike force, all dressed in suits to maintain their cover, had already dispatched the remaining bodyguard in the other room. Knox took one hand off his silenced handgun and carefully removed the detonator from the dead man's hands. He turned to another member of the strike force. "Watch the case."

"Yes sir."

Knox headed out of the suite into the hall.

Fighting against the bodyguard's punishing hold, Kyle began to choke and flail his arms. The brute's forearm was almost crushing his larynx. Kyle knew he had to fight back or he would die. He struck his fist against the bodyguard's head, but the man was unfazed. Kyle clawed at the man's eyes, but the bodyguard pressed harder. Fighting off the bodyguard's free arm, Kyle managed to wrap his hands around the bodyguard's head. He tried to locate the man's eye sockets with his thumbs and press in, but the bodyguard delivered a dizzying blow to his temple. The bodyguard took advantage of Kyle's daze and clamped his hand over his opponent's nose and mouth in a talon-like grip. Suffocating, Kyle's vision started to fade to blackness when he saw a splatter of something like paint fly in front of his eyes. Suddenly, the crushing grip loosened, and the bodyguard slumped to the ground.

Knox marched down the steps, his gun barrel still smoking. "You all right?"

Kyle doubled over, then straightened, his hands instinctively going to his tender throat. "Thanks," he said hoarsely. He could barely utter one word.

"Where's Mashiri?"

Kyle struggled to speak, but the pain was too great. He pointed down the stairwell.

Mashiri's sexagenarian legs felt rubbery when he reached the bottom of the stairwell, but he still ran to the exit.

Once outside, he found himself on the Wilhelmstrasse side of the hotel. Mashiri slowed to a brisk walk and straightened the front of his jacket with his flat palms to look presentable. There were policemen stationed on either side of him, some thirty yards away, but neither of them took notice of Mashiri. He couldn't see the American agents who had reached the roof of the hotel and were frantically scanning the streets to find him. Abdul drove up in a black Rolls Royce Phantom and stopped to let Mashiri in. Normally, Abdul would have gotten out to open the door for his boss, but Mashiri opened the back door as soon as the vehicle was stopped. He climbed in but left the door open. "Abdul, the other briefcase," Mashiri ordered.

To Mashiri's surprise, Abdul gunned the engine and pulled away from the curb. Mashiri reached for the door, but Abdul turned with enough torque to cause the door to shut. Abdul swiftly locked the doors with a touch of a button. "Abdul!" Mashiri shouted, but his driver did not respond.

On top of the hotel, one of the agents spotted Mashiri as he climbed into the car. "I've got eyes on target," he radioed. "He's in a black Rolls Royce Phantom, heading towards Behrenstrasse."

Mashiri was livid. His bodyguards had failed to detonate the first bomb, and now, for the first time in over twenty years' of service, Abdul was insubordinate. "Give me the other briefcase!"

Abdul answered calmly. "Sir, I have served you for many years, but I cannot do this. It is not Allah's will."

Kyle and Knox reached the Wilhelmstrasse exit when they heard the report over the radio. Looking toward the end of the street, they saw Mashiri's car round the corner. Knox and Kyle ran after it. "Have the police lock down Behrenstrasse!" Knox shouted into his radio.

Mashiri opened the console next to his seat and drew out a 9mm automatic handgun. Leaning across the divider, he held the gun to Abdul's temple. "You will return to the hotel *now*."

Kyle and Knox ran past the British Embassy and watched as Mashiri's car turned north onto Ebertstrasse. Kyle was having a hard time keeping up. Knox radioed the other agents. "Ebertstrasse, headed towards the Gate!"

Mashiri pressed the gun harder against Abdul's skull, but it didn't dissuade his driver. Abdul reached Strasse 17. Juni, turned left, and accelerated. There was an assured serenity in his actions. In the last few months, he had seen the true face of his boss. Now he had the courage to stand up to him. "I have feared you would kill me since Peshawar. I do not fear that now."

"You think I'm joking?"

"If you kill me now, the car will crash, and we'll both die."

That was a risk Mashiri was willing to take. He squeezed the trigger—but the gun clicked. The chamber was empty. Shocked, Mashiri pulled the trigger again and again, each time hearing the hollow click. Abdul had emptied the clip. Just as this realization hit Mashiri, Abdul swiftly raised the privacy divider, trapping Mashiri's arm.

Mashiri screamed and swung at his driver with the gun, but Abdul leaned out of the way.

Mashiri pulled out the small tube of mace with his free hand and aimed it through the gap in the screen. He sprayed Abdul's face, causing him to scream and jerk on the wheel in shock. Suddenly blinded, Abdul reached for his face as his feet wildly shot out, pressing on the accelerator. The Rolls Royce swerved right, bounced over the curb, and collided with a streetlamp. The front of the car crumpled completely while the force of the impact carried through the rest of the vehicle, folding creases into the body like an accordion.

Despite the tremendous velocity of the crash, Abdul was restrained by his seat belt and cushioned by the driver's side airbag. Mashiri, however, was thrown against the divider screen, cracking his head against the pane and nearly snapping his arm off.

Dazed and bleeding from his head, Mashiri tried to collect himself. He saw the opaque divider glass had spiderwebbed with the impact of his body. Mashiri's right arm, still trapped over the divider, was badly broken, but he punched at the glass with his left fist until it shattered completely. Mashiri slid over the seat into the front of the car, where he found the other briefcase on the passenger side of the floor.

Abdul was also dazed by the collision, and blinded by the mace, he could not undo his seat belt. He fumbled blindly for the briefcase, but his arms could not reach it, and Mashiri pulled it away first. Mashiri opened the case and found a complete bomb, sans detonator, inside. He reached into the inner pocket of his suit jacket—a difficult task with his left hand—and drew out the detonator. Then he inserted the detonator in the bomb with the same hand. This, too, was not easy, and by now onlookers were starting to gather around the car, but Mashiri did it as quickly as he could. Mashiri closed the briefcase and laid it on his stomach, then unlatched the passenger side door. Seeing he could only push it a little way with his broken arm, Mashiri kicked it wide open.

Abdul could hear his boss climb clumsily out of the car. His eyes swollen red and shut by the mace, Abdul turned toward Mashiri and spoke like a blind seer. "May Allah judge you, brother."

Mashiri sneered at Abdul and kicked the door shut with a slam. Then he turned to take in his surroundings. He was a hundred yards from the *Grosser Stern* circle, where the large columned *Siegessäule* stood. It was topped by the golden angel-like statue of the Goddess of Victory. Onlookers stared at Mashiri in wonder but kept their distance. Mashiri looked down the avenue toward the Brandenburg Gate, where the blue flashing lights of police cars were approaching. There was no hope of going back to the hotel now. Mashiri grit his teeth and began walking toward the *Siegessäule*.

Kyle and Knox passed the Brandenburg Gate and began running down the Strasse 17. Juni. Kyle was winded from his bruised trachea, but pressed on. Knox raced ahead of him, his pace urgent but almost robotic in its smoothness. He wasn't winded and he wouldn't quit. A mid-sized sedan pulled over. The strike force agent in the front passenger seat called to them. "Sirs?"

The sedan stopped long enough for Knox and Kyle to hop in the back seat, then raced off after Mashiri. The men could see smoke rising from the edge of the avenue. The driver floored the accelerator as he weaved through traffic.

Kyle had barely caught his breath when his cell phone rang. Answering, he croaked into the phone, "I can't talk now."

Joshua's voice came excitedly over the line. "Dad! Guess where we are?"

Kyle held his sore throat as he tried to answer, but he was too slow for the boy.

"We're at the angel!"

Kyle's eyes tracked past the smoke from Mashiri's accident to the *Siegessäule*. His eyes followed the column up to the statue of Victory. He now recognized it as the golden angel from his dream. *Oh, no.*

"Josh, put grandma on the phone." Kyle's command came as a strained hiss. Still, it was stern enough for his boy to understand.

"What?" the boy was confused. What had he done wrong?

"Just put her on *now*."

Lyla's voice came over the line. "Kyle?"

"Get out of there now!"

Mashiri climbed out of the underground pedestrian passage, his right arm hanging limp at his side, his left holding the briefcase. He moved across the plaza at the center of *Grosser Stern* toward the pedestal entrance of the *Siegessäule*. At the entrance he passed Jack, Lyla, and Joshua as they were leaving. Lyla was frightened, Jack confused, and Joshua frustrated, but they were following Kyle's advice. The family was too wrapped up in their own emotions to notice the billionaire with a bloody head and limp arm, but the man selling tickets at the door reared back. Mashiri took one last look down the avenue, where the police lights were drawing closer, and headed inside.

"There he is!" Knox shouted, pointing at the entrance to the *Siegessäule*. The agents' car had just reached the large traffic circle at *Grosser Stern*. The driver swerved left, screeching tires as he cut across lanes to reach the center island where the *Siegessäule* stood. This caused a cacophony of horns to blare in protest, but the agent didn't care. The driver braked to a sharp halt. Knox and the two agents ran toward the *Siegessäule* with their guns drawn.

Kyle climbed out of the car and gazed up at the column. There was something imposing and ominous about the statue from this angle below. As he looked down, he saw his parents and Joshua. Kyle ran toward them and pointed to the nearest entrance to the underground pedestrian tunnel. "Over here!"

Joshua smiled to see his dad, but Kyle's parents saw the urgency in his face. They grabbed Joshua's hand and ran toward their son.

Inside the *Siegessäule*, Mashiri made his way up the narrow spiral steps. He rudely pushed his way past tourists. One woman was shoved aside and fell down face-first, scraping along each of the stone steps until friction stopped her just before the wall. Hearing the woman's screams, her husband turned toward Mashiri, ready to take him on. Mashiri glared at him, a cold and hard look that sent the man shrinking back. Mashiri moved past the man and continued upward.

Knox and the two agents began climbing the stairs. Seeing their guns, tourists fled down the stairs screaming.

Kyle took Joshua in his arms as he and his parents quickly descended the stairs into the pedestrian tunnel. When they reached the long, flat floor, they began to run. Despite his throat injury and previous run, Kyle sprinted down the tunnel. His parents, both near 70 in age, had a hard time keeping up. Kyle clutched his son tightly as he ran. He would not lose him. Not Joshua.

When they reached the other side of the tunnel, Kyle slowed to a stop. Lyla began to climb the stairs but Kyle caught her arm. "Stay here." The family huddled together in the tunnel as the sound of police sirens grew ever nearer.

Mashiri reached a group of older tourists that were moving slowly up the staircase and effectively blocking it. Mashiri began to elbow his way past the group, drawing their ire. He soon found himself face-to-face with the tour leader. "Excuse me, sir," she exclaimed, "but you are very rude!"

Frustrated, Mashiri shoved her aside with an angry, guttural roar. The tour leader tumbled down the steps, her head barely catching the leg of one of the tourists, saving it from hitting stone. Many of the group fell backwards like dominoes. Mashiri didn't bother to look back, but a loud voice made him freeze.

"Mashiri!"

The billionaire turned to see Knox and the two agents, their guns aimed dead at him.

"Drop the briefcase!" Knox ordered.

Mashiri knew this was the end. Resigned, he raised his good arm, still holding the briefcase. He tried to raise his broken right arm, but it wouldn't move far. Still, with his arms outstretched, Mashiri made a sacrilegious gesture of the cross.

Knox watched the billionaire for one false move. Mashiri hadn't dropped the case and that worried him. The other two agents aimed at Mashiri's head and heart. They were ready to fire, but they wanted the billionaire alive.

Mashiri sniffed as a bead of sweat dripped down his forehead to his cheek. He gripped the handle of the briefcase tightly in his left hand. Then he spoke, his voice gravelly but quiet. "It is done."

Mashiri pressed a button on the handle with his left thumb.

The *Siegessäule* exploded, a shower of pulverized concrete ripping out from the middle of the column. The shock wave shot up the monument in a hundredth of a second, expanding the burst of pulverized concrete along the length of the column. The sturdier marble pedestal below fractured, then crumbled. Above, the golden statue of Victory broke into pieces and rained down on the street. A large section of arm sheared off above the elbow. It hit the pavement just before it was driven over by a car. The arm wedged itself under the front axle and forced the car up until its tires were lifted off the ground. Sparks flew as the golden arm ground into the asphalt, eventually skewering the car to a halt. A thousand-pound leg fell onto the hood of another car. One of the golden wings clattered to the pavement, narrowly missing a sedan carrying a family of four. Others weren't so lucky. The head of the statue fell and crushed an Opel. Concrete chunks pelted cars and semi trucks as a shower of deadly shrapnel rained down on the traffic circle.

In the pedestrian tunnel below, Kyle and his family held each other tightly. The explosion shook the walls and floor violently, and the loud boom rang in their ears. Kyle kept

Joshua huddled in front of him, his head down. Jack and Lyla wrapped themselves around their son and followed suit. Kyle looked up and saw shrapnel and dust rain down at the far end of the tunnel near the *Siegessäule*. The thick gray cloud of dust entered the tunnel and moved towards them, but by the time it reached them it had dissipated to little more than mist. Hundreds of pieces of shrapnel thudded as they hit the ground above them, but the tunnel remained intact.

The destruction seemed to last an eternity, but when it ended, there was silence. Their ears still ringing from the explosion, Kyle turned to his family and examined each of them. They were safe and unharmed. Kyle prevailed on his family to stay in the tunnel while he ventured out to look. Jack and Lyla held Joshua tightly, afraid the boy might go into shock.

Kyle ascended out of the tunnel into a different world. Smoke and haze hung over the entire circle, obscuring most of it. There was a sharp acrid smell in the air. Thousands of pieces of the column, some no larger than a fist, others the size of a boulder, littered the ground in front of him. Through the haze, Kyle caught sight of the jagged remains of the pedestal. The *Siegessäule*, over 200 feet tall just seconds ago, was now no more than ten feet at the rubble's tallest point. Kyle looked down at his feet and saw shattered fragments of the mosaic that once covered the pedestal. Each fragment was no more than an inch in diameter. Had he been above ground when the explosion occurred, even these could have proven deadly.

The shrill noise of sirens broke the silence. Police cars and fire engines were approaching, their blue lights tinting the gray haze. Kyle coughed at the smoke, then went back down the stairs to his family.

27

Armageddon

The quiet hum of the embassy lounge was a far cry from the recent carnage Kyle's family had heard and witnessed. Here there was only the low murmur of office work down the hall and the hush of central air flowing through the ceiling vents. Still, Kyle's ears were ringing. Joshua dozed on his lap while Jack and Lyla comforted each other on another couch.

Larsen entered, and seeing Joshua sleeping calmly, whispered to Kyle. "Everyone all right?"

"Yeah, we're okay." Kyle handed his sleeping boy off to his father and followed Larsen down the hall. When they were out of earshot of Kyle's family, Larsen spoke again.

"We've got Mashiri's driver. He's banged up, but he's cooperating with us."

"Okay…" Kyle wasn't sure what this news meant.

"He confirmed Ben Ami and Mashiri met in Pakistan."

Kyle exhaled in relief. This was confirmation that the Apocalypse Men were indeed behind the attacks in Jerusalem and Iran.

"How'd we get the driver to cooperate with us?"

"He was only too happy. He's a devout Muslim. When he saw Mashiri ordered the attack on the Al Aqsa mosque, he knew he couldn't trust his boss anymore."

This wasn't entirely accurate. Abdul mistrusted Mashiri ever since his boss ordered the killings of the policemen in Peshawar. Then Ben Ami's attack was of his own volition, not at Mashiri's orders, although he carried it out while his squadron was bombing the Iranian nuclear facility as Mashiri had planned all along. But the conversation at the house in Peshawar had been vague enough that Abdul figured Mashiri had also ordered the attack on the mosque. He recognized the young man's face on the news and remembered that fateful night in Pakistan when his boss had been revealed as Satan. With the full breadth of Mashiri's evil realized, Abdul knew he had to thwart his boss.

Kyle almost felt like smiling. The evidence was now too compelling. They could make their case to anyone—the Iranians, the Israelis, and all Muslim nations—that this awful series of events, the Apocalypse Men attacks, had all been the machinations of one Aaban Assad al-Mashiri, recently deceased.

Larsen sensed Kyle's elation and brought him back to ground with a dour expression. "Knox is gone."

"I know," Kyle said soberly. "But we stopped them."

"I'm not so sure."

Larsen led Kyle into the embassy's Operations Center. Kyle immediately sensed the buzz in the room. As he glanced at the faces around him, he also saw fear.

"The Iranian delegation broke off talks after the bombing and left Berlin," Larsen explained.

"But the driver...didn't we let them know about Mashiri?"

Larsen shook his head. "They didn't give us a chance. They said it wasn't safe here."

"Bastards," Kyle said bitterly. "That's exactly what they wanted. An excuse to leave."

"You're more right than you know. In the last hour, half a dozen armies and Muslim guerrillas overran the Israeli border defenses. Now they're pushing deeper into the country, mostly in the north. Looks like even the Russians are involved."

They watched the screens which showed a combination of satellite footage, news feeds, and a battle map with markings indicating troop movements over Israel.

Kyle had thought Mashiri's death would end the threat. Now he saw just how wrong he was. "I can't believe this."

"Then you won't believe where they're headed."

"Where's that?"

Larsen pointed toward the map. "Towards Megiddo. Israeli troops are coming up to meet them, and it seems they'll be massing there."

Kyle shook his head. "What can we do now?"

"Now? We pray."

Kyle watched the screens for another half hour before he couldn't take it anymore. In spite of all his efforts he found the situation had spiraled out of his hands. There was nothing more he could do. He felt a real fear that this was the build up to the prophesied Armageddon. It didn't matter that the Apocalypse Men were dead if this was the end of the world.

Kyle retreated to the hotel where his family had gone while he was in the Operations Center. Joshua was still fast asleep. He watched his son's peaceful slumber and hoped Joshua would be able to grow up. For all Kyle had done to protect the boy, the future seemed more precarious than ever. In the course of his work he had seen so many horrible things in this world. But watching his son, he knew the love he had for him—and the desire to see Joshua grow up and have a bright future—were feelings shared by parents around the world. If that was a common desire—something worth fighting for—wasn't it also worth making peace? He could only hope enough leaders would see that before it was too late.

Kyle stared at the ceiling until his weary eyes closed. As he slept, he dreamed. It would be the last time he dreamed of future events. Kyle felt himself rapidly moving through a black void until he saw a window of light. As he moved closer, he saw this window looked into the White House Situation Room. Kyle knew this was impossible since the Situation Room, lying in the basement of the White House's West Wing, has no windows. Still, Kyle drew closer until he could see President Barnes sitting with his top military advisors. They were discussing the crisis in the Middle East.

"Mr. President, our troop strength is far too low to engage in Israel," the Chairman of the Joint Chiefs of Staff said.

"But we have our weapons ready, yes?" Barnes asked.

"Sir, I urge you to consider this our very last option," the Chairman of the Joint Chiefs implored. "They're not—"

Barnes cut in. "They're tactical, aren't they?"

The Chairman of the Joint Chiefs nodded. "Yes, sir, they're small yield. But this isn't like a smart bomb. It's much more messy, and the aftermath strategically is far more complicated. That is why I urge you to consider this our *very* last option."

"Relax," Barnes said. "I'm not going to start World War

III. I just want to know we can finish it. And more importantly," Barnes paused for effect, "I want them to know it. Just because the option is on the table doesn't mean it's the one I want to use first. I agree with you. It *is* our last option. But I will use it if necessary."

"So what do you intend to do first?" Standish asked.

"This thing has spiraled beyond the control of everyone. Now we have to see who can get it back. That means who has power. Who has leverage. I'm not talking about the Israelis, the Iranians, or the Muslims, but who can lean on them to settle this thing without an all-out bloodbath."

"And we're one of those countries?" Standish asked doubtfully.

"You bet. We still have muscle. That's why I want everyone to know we have our nukes ready. That way we might not need them."

"Who else has leverage?" General Foley asked.

Barnes turned to the Naval Yeoman manning communications for the room. "Get me the Russian President on video conference."

"Mr. President, the hotline has always been by written communication to avoid any misunderstandings," the Chairman of the Joint Chiefs protested.

Barnes stared intently at the general. "I want him to see my face so he knows I mean what I say."

In a few moments they saw an image on the wall screen. The Russian President was settling into his chair. "This is an unusual request, especially since we have never met before," the Russian began.

"I know," Barnes said. "But the urgency of the situation requires—"

"Requires?" the Russian objected.

Barnes continued, undeterred. "Mr. President, our two countries may not exactly be superpowers anymore, but we *can* stop this war, and it needs to be stopped."

"It's too late for diplomacy now. Besides, given both our countries' history of war in the Middle East, we best not get involved."

Barnes stared directly at the web camera so the Russian could feel he was looking at him. "Mr. President, there may be no other country that will stand by Israel, but we are committed to defending them. This situation has arisen only because of the actions of a terrorist organization. That same organization used your stocks of biological and nuclear weapons against us."

"Are you saying we're responsible for those attacks?" the Russian scoffed.

"If you had secured those stocks we wouldn't be in this situation. But you've used it to your advantage. Your troops have joined the invasion of Israel."

The Russian President's face flushed at being called out. Clearly he expected the Americans wouldn't know Russia was directly involved with the siege on Israel. He reached for the switch to turn off his camera and end the conference. "I have no wish to be lectured—"

Barnes exploded. "What I'm saying is you are *involved!*" The Russian President froze. Barnes thought he might have seen the slightest flinch.

"And where did you get this information? Perhaps from your Ukrainian friends?"

Barnes, unaware of the deal that led to the raid on Zyuganov, had no idea what the Russian was talking about. That threw him off long enough for the Russian to regain his composure and reach again to end the transmission.

"Wait," Barnes said. He could see the concern on his advisors' faces. The Russian President waited, this time more annoyed. Barnes adopted a more conciliatory approach. "We've gotten off on the wrong foot."

The Russian President looked perplexed—though it wasn't clear whether it was from Barnes' use of an American colloquialism or from his sudden change in tone. "Wrong foot?"

"We should hear each other out. Our predecessors had the wisdom to do so when the fate of the world was on the line, as I believe it is now. We should follow their lead."

The Russian sat back and exhaled, calming himself. "All right. Since you contacted me, what do you have to say?"

Barnes spoke with an earnest gravity. "We may be wounded, but we are committed to defending Israel, and will use extreme measures to do so if necessary. You know what that means."

The Russian blanched. He had expected something different. "Then there is no use talking."

"If you would call on the invading forces to pull back—"

"Out of the question."

Barnes paused, wondering which tact to take now.

The Russian had no patience for this. "I see you are unmoved. Goodbye—"

"Wait!" Barnes pleaded. "This thing is bigger than both of us, bigger than both our nations. So let's just talk as men, shall we, not as presidents..."

The Russian President shook his head. "That is even more wasted talk."

Barnes raised his hand. "Bear with me, just bear with

me." He paused for effect, giving more weight to his next words, but not so long this time that the Russian could take control again. "Tell me, what is it you strive for most as a man? As one man. What is it you get up for every day? And what do you think of when you ask yourself in bed each night, did I do right?"

The Russian paused for a long time. He considered Barnes' face, first evaluating the earnestness in it, and then the question itself. It surprised him to find this American President was being wholly honest with him. The Russian let out a long breath before he answered. "My family. My children. I want a better life for them than what I was given."

Barnes almost broke into a grin, but kept his lips pursed tight enough for a small smile. "Me too."

The Russian sat back, surprised by this guileless reply.

"So on that basis," Barnes continued, "can we agree to a cease-fire, and a pull back of all forces to the defensive positions prior to this conflict? I don't know where we will go from there—no doubt it will be difficult—but for the sake of our children, I prefer it to the alternative. And we must help our respective allies see it the same way."

The Russian President evaluated this proposal. Barnes' advisors waited with baited breath, but the pause was not as long as it felt to them. "Yes," the Russian said. "Agreed."

Kyle awoke with early morning light filtering through the curtains. He pondered on the dream. This one was far more detailed than any he had had before. It was also his first dream that did not see disaster looming on the horizon. Did that mean it was a vision of the future, or merely his own wishful fantasy? Kyle rolled over in bed and stared at the ceiling. As he contemplated the question, he realized what he had seen in his dream might be the only hope for the future. Then he considered the fragile negotiation and what might become of it. Things had to happen in precisely the right way for this to work out. The American and Russian presidents would have to come to an agreement. That agreement would have to lead to a cease-fire and a withdrawal of troops. Following the withdrawal, the split between the Israelis, Iranians, and Muslims would have to be mended—at least insofar as it could be to restore peace. That was a tall order, given the destruction of the Iranian nuclear plant, and even more so, the 3rd holiest site in Islam. But as unlikely as those events seemed, Kyle believed they needed to come true. They were the only way to bring the world back from the precipice of self-destruction. However, the world Kyle had known did not provide such a precise sequence of fortuitous events. Hadn't that also been what his dreams had shown? Man was violent and disagreeable. He had lost a son to such turmoil. But for the sake of his other son he needed this truce to happen.

Realizing man's limitations, Kyle stood at the beginning of belief. And for the first time since Adam's death, he prayed. It was a simple, two-word expression—one commonly used by Muslims today, as it has been at various times by Christians. Some have used the expression in the belief that God directs man's fate. To Kyle, that was too much to accept. For him, it was the simple, earnest hope that God would intervene in man's affairs when needed, or perhaps when called upon. And so, Kyle prayed.

"God willing."

Acknowledgements

This book is a work of fiction; all characters and events depicted therein are the work of the author's imagination, and no similarity to real persons is intended. However, several sources were used for background information. The Center for Nonproliferation Studies' report on the 1971 Voz Island smallpox outbreak provided research and historical information. Response to a weapon of mass destruction was inspired by the Edgewood Chemical Biological Center's report Guidelines for Mass Casualty Decontamination During a Hazmat/Weapon of Mass Destruction Incident. Operation World's statistics on the Evangelical population throughout the world were used. Eric H. Cline's *The Battles of Armageddon* provided the history of conflict in the Jezreel Valley. All research, including information on the structure and operation of military and intelligence agencies, was drawn from publicly available sources, and any errors or alterations in fact are the responsibility of the author.

ALSO BY JOHN CHENEY

"Infused with a deftly plotted story of unexpected twists and dramatic turns, *City of Spies* is a non-stop thriller that is pure entertainment from beginning to end."

–Midwest Book Review

Available from Amazon

READERS' PRAISE FOR

CITY OF SPIES

"I bought this as I was boarding a flight and wanted something to read. 8 hours later in the wee morning hours I was still ravenously turning pages. I could not put it down"

"Very cinematic, I was having grand pictures of the events in my head as I read. Would definitely recommend this read to anyone"

"The suspense, intrigue and plot twists balanced by a compelling love story, rich setting, artistry, and masterful depictions of human psychology make this book a page-turner…I felt like I was really there watching this all unfold. I had to force myself to go to work instead of reading"

"A good historical tale set at the height of the Cold War. Very accurate and scary, considering how many aspects are true"

"The highlight for me was Stasi Colonel Scharf—a well conceived, competent and credible villain. He ties the story together. His Machiavellian moves and counter-moves make the tension palpable throughout the story..If you like cold war spy thrillers, this will be a great read."

*Excerpts from reader reviews on Amazon.com

About the Author

It's no coincidence that dreams play a large role in *The Apocalypse Men*—the opening passage and general idea for the book came to author John Cheney in a dream. It took years of research and outlining, however, before the story became a reality. Most important was finding the core of the story—that of a man who, when the world appears to be hopelessly collapsing, finds something to hope and fight for. John earned an MFA in film at Chapman University. He has written and directed several short films that have played at festivals across the U.S. and in Europe. His first novel, *City of Spies*, was published in 2014. *The Apocalypse Men* is his second novel.

Follow John Cheney on Twitter: @JCheneywrites